Suddenly the door crashed open.

Without looking up, Blossom knelt on the floor and placed her forehead down, her arms outstretched, kowtowing as she had been taught to do.

"What the devil is this?" Darcy exclaimed.

"If you please, honorable lord," Blossom said, her words coming slowly, "I, worthless woman though I am, am sent by Honorable Wu to pay debt."

"English? You speak English? What's your name?"

"Fragrant Blossom, honored lord."

"Get up. And stop calling me honored lord."

Blossom obeyed, but kept her eyes lowered to show she understood her position.

"Look at me," Darcy ordered.

Slowly Blossom raised her eyes. He was taller than any man she had ever seen, and everything about him filled her with awe.

"You're not Chinese!"

"No, honored lord. I was born barbarian, like you."

Dear Reader,

As the holidays approach (at much too fast a pace for most of us) we, at Harlequin Historicals would like to take the time to wish our readers well.

This month, *Christmas Miracle* by Ruth Langan tells the story of a Southern family displaced by the Civil War. Though their lives would never be the same, Lizzie Spooner was determined to show them all that life was still worth living.

Impetuous Julia Masonet had always chafed under her guardian Richard's watchful eye, until she was faced with losing him. With *Tender Journey,* Sally Cheney has written a delightfully different story of a free spirit and the proper gentleman who has captured her heart.

China Blossom, Margaret Moore's second historical for Harlequin, offers the reader a glimpse of 19th-century England's elite society, and a young woman who dares to defy its strictest rules.

When a handsome drifter saves the life of an Irish-Mexican beauty, their love threatens to destroy them, in Elizabeth Lane's tale of the old West, *Moonfire.*

Also this month, keep an eye out for the HARLEQUIN HISTORICAL CHRISTMAS STORIES 1992 collection, wherever Harlequin Books are sold.

Thanks again for your continued support.

Sincerely,

Tracy Farrell
Senior Editor

China Blossom

Margaret Moore

Harlequin Books

TORONTO • NEW YORK • LONDON
AMSTERDAM • PARIS • SYDNEY • HAMBURG
STOCKHOLM • ATHENS • TOKYO • MILAN
MADRID • WARSAW • BUDAPEST • AUCKLAND

Harlequin Historicals first edition November 1992

ISBN 0-373-28749-6

CHINA BLOSSOM

Books by Margaret Moore

Harlequin Historicals

A Warrior's Heart #118
China Blossom #149

MARGARET MOORE

says that the first great love of her life was Errol Flynn. "Naturally I was devastated to learn that he died when I was three years old," she admits, but adds that her interest in historical romance writing developed from that early fascination. Margaret lives in Scarborough, Ontario, with her husband and two school-age children. When not in her basement at the computer, she enjoys reading and sewing.

With thanks to
Una O'Connor, Alan Hale, Edna Mae Oliver,
Barry Fitzgerald and all the other great
supporting players who made movies
so special for me,
and with love to Bill, Steven and Amy.

Chapter One

"If you please, sir, a note came for you. Important, the boy said, sir."

Having to strain to hear the barely audible voice of the maid on the other side of the heavy oak door annoyed Darcy Fitzroy almost as much as the unwanted interruption.

"What boy?" he called out, trying to get his necktie in a proper bow. Damn stupid thing. Maybe he'd have to get a valet, but he detested the idea of having somebody hovering around as he dressed. One of the most important things about being wealthy was the privacy money could provide.

"The ship's boy, from *China Lady*," he said, sir."

"Why didn't you say so?" Darcy demanded, his excitement not evident in his voice as he strode to the door. *China Lady* had been due to dock in September, and it was now nearly the beginning of April. Even he had begun to fear that the ship had gone down with all hands somewhere between Canton and England, despite his faith in Captain Driscoll and his outward calm when the investors came calling.

He threw open the door. The timid maid, who stood trembling on the threshold as if she expected him to gobble her up like an ogre in a fairy tale, held out a note. He took it, recognizing Captain Driscoll's round, large letters on the outside. Without another word, he slammed the door shut and walked toward the lamp.

He opened the letter, glad Captain Driscoll wrote as clearly as he issued orders aboard ship. Darcy's early years had been spent on sailing ships, which didn't leave much time for reading and writing. Even yet, he could read latitude and longitude more easily than many people's written words.

"Fitzroy," the note said, "God-awful bad weather this voyage. Now come at once and take this cargo off my ship or I won't be responsible."

Darcy felt relief and joy as he stared at the note. No doubt the voyage had been perilous, which would explain the extreme terseness of Driscoll's note, although the captain was not a man given to loquaciousness. Darcy could guess why Driscoll was so anxious to unload the cargo. Mitchell, his business agent in Canton, must have followed orders and compelled that rascal Wu Wing Toi to pay his debt of almost one thousand pounds—in silver, not trade goods. A cargo of small, portable silver ingots would be risky to keep safe, even from a usually trustworthy crew.

As Darcy took a moment to enjoy his pleasure at this good news, he caught a glimpse of himself in the huge gilt-framed mirror over the fireplace. In formal dress, he looked like someone only playing the part of a rich merchant. The sun-darkened skin of his face, the premature wrinkles around his eyes from hours on watch at sea and the permanent calluses on his large hands were evidence that he was not born into wealth.

The son of a wainwright and seamstress, Darcy had gone to sea at the age of ten. With a combination of guts and luck and shrewdness, he was now a rich man. With the safe, if late, arrival of *China Lady,* a very rich man.

It was about time he had some good fortune, he thought. His last two rotten turns of luck—the loss of one ship and the near wreck of another, which had arrived when the markets were already flooded with tea and silk—had caused many of his investors to think of abandoning him. Only Darcy's personal assurances and his partner's facility for soothing panicking upper-class fools had prevented financial disaster.

But now stock in Fitzroy Shipping would rise, he could pay off his most pressing debts and his damned faint-hearted investors would smile and say they knew they'd make a profit all along.

Deciding to change and head straight for the ship, he began to tear off his coat. He tossed the note onto his dressing table, then caught sight of the invitation there.

There was still the matter of Emmaline, who expected him at her party.

Lady Emmaline Whitmore was famous for redecorating one of the main rooms in her London mansion every year just before the start of the season. She made it a point to personally supervise the workmen. To be invited to one of her dinner parties before the first of May added tremendously to one's social status.

Darcy felt his pulse begin to quicken. Emmaline was surely the most accomplished woman he had ever had, in bed or out, and the fact that she was married to a nobleman made the game that much more enjoyable. However, the thought of seeing *China Lady*, the finest vessel of his fleet, stirred his blood even more than Emmaline.

He would go to the ship. Perhaps there would be time to get to Emmaline's later, after everyone else had left. Her footman knew enough to let him in no matter what hour. Emmaline always found it more exciting knowing that her idiotic husband slumbered in the next room while she and

Darcy made love, and Emmaline excited was something to experience.

He decided not to change and marched out of his room and down the stairs to the entrance hall. Powlett, by some second sense known only to butlers, stood holding Darcy's cloak at the ready.

"Don't wait up. I'm going to the docks first, then to Lady Whitmore's. I'll let myself in."

"Very good, sir."

Darcy knew that Powlett had probably guessed the nature of his employer's relationship with Lady Whitmore, but the middle-aged manservant was much too well trained to comment.

Blossom watched Ah Tup's trembling fingers as the maid put the finishing touches to her mistress's elaborate coiffure. She sighed and pushed aside Ah Tup's hand. "It is enough," she said softly, smiling up at her servant as she tried to control the terror building inside her.

Soon she would be taken by the Englishman.

She closed her eyes and tried to draw strength from the knowledge that she was here on this stinking *fan kow* ship to save the House of Wu Wing Toi.

It was her duty, as slave of his house, to do whatever he commanded. Yet it had not been his idea to give her to the Englishman to pay the vast debt. It had been hers.

She remembered only dimly the other ship and the man who was her father. What she could recall as plainly as the cut of a knife in wax was the terror of that day when her father had pushed her into the cupboard on the ship. The terror in his eyes. The awful sounds of the fighting. The overwhelming horror of being discovered by the pirates and seeing her father's lifeless body lying in a puddle of blood. Even now she could not blot out those stark images.

Her thoughts were interrupted by the small sounds of Ah Tup bustling about the tiny, smelly cabin. They would both be pleased to be off this ship. The one called *captain* had insisted they stay inside for most of the voyage, only allowing them on the upper deck at night. Even when the ship was in port, they hadn't been allowed to leave. That had not troubled them at first, but soon the idea of a fresh, cool breeze had come to mean heaven.

"It will not be long now, I think, Mother," Ah Tup said brightly, using the traditional form of address from servant to mistress.

Blossom forced herself to smile, and as always marveled at Ah Tup's ability to see the best of every situation. Silently she blessed Honorable Wu for giving her Ah Tup as a final gift so that she would not be totally alone in a strange land. He had known that Ah Tup was her only other friend.

The girl's clever resourcefulness had proved a boon. She had devised a way to cook proper meals using the oil lamp, a small wok and the store of supplies they had smuggled on board, so that they didn't have to eat the terrible food provided for them by the ship's cook.

Blossom sighed softly. Honorable Wu had been kind and gentle to her from the first moment he had seen her in the marketplace, with its strange babble of Chinese voices and the new, exotic smells. He stood out from the other men staring at her, the men with wondering looks in their eyes—and something else, something that filled her with nameless fear. He had smiled with pity and gentleness, and their friendship had been sealed in that first instant.

Her relief was indescribable when she realized she was to go with him, and it lasted until until she arrived at his house. One look at the women there, and she knew she was no more wanted than a plague of locusts.

But Honorable Wu liked her and because of their friendship, he had defied his *tai tai,* or wife, and kept her long past the age when most girl slaves were sold to brothels or other men.

Honorable Wu's simplicity made him seem foolish in the eyes of other men and his shrewish wife, who had never forgiven him for failing the Imperial examinations that would have insured him a position in the government.

Blossom hated Precious Jade. It had been she who had forced her husband to borrow more and more money until he was so in debt that the venerable House of Wu was threatened with destruction.

By then Blossom could understand Chinese well enough to know exactly what Precious Jade was saying that day in the courtyard. She was determined to force Honorable Wu to sell Blossom. Honorable Wu told Precious Jade why he had bought the foreign devil girl: you could never trust foreigners. If he had the girl, she might be useful as a tool with which to bargain. Precious Jade, understanding bargaining more than anything else, believed him. Blossom, understanding Honorable Wu, did not. Yet the memory of that quarrel stayed with her, until the terrible moment when she learned that the House of Wu was about to be ruined because there was no more money.

If she could help Honorable Wu, she would. She did.

She had asked him to sell her to one of the foreigners. They would pay more for her than anyone else. She was a house servant, not trained in the arts of pleasing a man, but surely they would never know that. It was common knowledge that in intimate matters between men and women, foreigners were astoundingly ignorant.

Tears came to Blossom's eyes at the memory of that conversation. He had only looked at her, but she had seen that he understood her sacrifice.

Precious Jade, delighted at finally getting rid of Blossom, sent for Water Lily, a famous concubine who owned many floating pleasure boats. After hours of subtle bargaining, Water Lily agreed to instruct Blossom in some of the arts of pleasing a man, thereby increasing her value. She bemoaned the fact that Blossom's feet were much too big to be beautiful, but wisely didn't mention the ugly scars on Blossom's back from the many beatings.

Water Lily was a remorseless teacher. She taught Blossom to serve food and to sing, as well as instructing her in several ways to arouse a man and how to treat him when the moment of passion was past.

One day a barbarian in a long black hat and ugly black clothes that made him look like a beetle arrived. Honorable Wu, a terrible bargainer with Chinese merchants, was easily able to match wits with the foreigner, and so Blossom had been accepted.

Blossom stood up, suddenly restless. She would give much to be back with Honorable Wu even if she was only a slave, and one with too-large feet at that. Surely he missed her, too, for she alone truly liked the thin, kind man whose weakness was a too-generous heart.

Suddenly Ah Tup froze and they both heard the harsh sound of male voices in the corridor outside their cabin. Ah Tup, trying to smile and not quite succeeding, spoke quietly. "You are lovely, Mother," she said. "He will surely find you pleasing."

Blossom couldn't return the smile. She was desperately trying to think in English, going over and over the words Water Lily had told her. Still, she remembered with some faint hope, she was trained to speak to a man in many different ways.

Suddenly the door crashed open. Hurriedly, without looking up, Blossom knelt on the floor and placed her forehead down, her arms outstretched, kowtowing as she had been taught to do. Behind her she could hear Ah Tup do the same.

"What the devil is this?"

To her surprise, she realized that the man was shocked, as well as very angry, his anger spilling into his words like thunder in a storm.

"If you please, honorable lord," Blossom said, the words coming slowly but coming nonetheless, "I, worthless woman though I am, am sent by Honorable Wu to pay debt."

"English? You speak English?"

Still without looking up, Blossom answered, "Yes, honored lord." She could see his boots now, big black shiny boots planted wide apart. The stance of a proud man.

"Get up."

She obeyed but kept her eyes lowered to show that she understood her position as a lowly, good-for-nothing female as Water Lily had commanded her in so many lessons.

"What's your name?"

"Fragrant Blossom, honored lord."

"Stop calling me 'honored lord' and look at me."

Slowly Blossom raised her eyes.

He was like one of the gods, taller than any man she had ever seen. Everything about him, from the furrowed brow to the broad shoulders swathed in a black cloak to the powerful legs encased in tight-fitted coverings filled her with awe.

"You're not Chinese!" The man walked around her, his heavy boots slamming the boards of the floor like the drums of the temple.

"No, honored lord." The brief spasm of shame quickly passed.

"Where *are* you from?"

To her surprise, she was actually understanding him. Somewhere, deep in the bottom of her mind, the language of her childhood stirred and rose to the top like mud from the bottom of a storm-tossed lake. "I was born barbarian. Then . . . bad men take me. Honorable Wu buy me. That is all I know, honored lord."

"Stop calling me 'honored lord,' for God's sake."

"Yes, master."

"God give me strength!" He stopped walking and now stood in front of her, staring. He reached out and took her chin in his hand. Instinctively she recoiled at the terrible impropriety of touching another's person.

But now you belong to this man, she reminded herself.

"I hope Mitchell has an explanation for this," the man muttered as he let go of her and opened the paper he had clutched in his fist.

As he read silently, Blossom studied his face. He was not young, but not old, either. He lived well but had known sorrow, to judge by the lines in his face. Power and strength seemed to burn in him, flashing out from his deep brown eyes.

She remembered what Water Lily had told her of strong men: they despise weakness, seeing all too much of it in others. Blossom smiled secretly. Without meaning to help, Precious Jade had made her strong, beating and berating her until she had learned to retreat inside herself and become deaf to the harsh words if not insensible to the pain.

Besides, now she was more of the Middle Kingdom than a foreign devil, and so was surely a match for any barbarian, even this one.

But her task would not be as simple as Water Lily had told her. The older concubine, who had met many foreigners, had claimed all Englishmen were weak and as liable to cry tears as cry out when they reached the zenith, and that even a third-class whore could easily please such a man. This man would not be so easy.

"Damn Wu! How the hell am I supposed to accept a *whore* instead of a thousand pounds?"

She heard the contempt in his tone and straightened indignantly. "I virgin," she said the word carefully, having repeated it many times until Water Lily had found her pronunciation acceptable, "and worth much silver."

The man's mouth twisted slightly in an expression Blossom could not quite comprehend. "So my agent tells me," he said. "He says that if he had not accepted you as the payment, Wu threatened to sell you to a brothel to get the money he owes me."

The man believed it. Blossom kept the pleased smile from her face. Such had been the story she and Honorable Wu had concocted, and that would make the barbarians take Blossom.

The man's eyes narrowed, and Blossom feared her face had revealed too much.

"You're *proud* of being sold like a slab of meat or a piece of cloth?" He sounded disgusted.

Blossom began to wish Water Lily was here to help her. "Yes, master. Men pay much for me, who taught many ways to bring men to the zenith."

He stared at her for a long moment.

"I'll be damned," he said at last, surveying her slowly. For the first time Blossom thought she saw what Water Lily called "the bloom of lustful thoughts." "Who's that?" He gestured toward Ah Tup, who still kowtowed on the floor, as unmoving as a frog awaiting a fly.

"She is Ah Tup, master. My slave."

"We don't have slaves in England," the man said harshly, glaring at her until she felt the tinge of a blush that she could not stop. Why should she feel shame, she wondered, when it was he who didn't understand the ways of civilized people?

He looked around. "Well, you can't stay here and that's for certain. Pack up and come with me."

Blossom nodded and turned to Ah Tup. "Gather our things. We are to go," she said quickly in a strange amalgamation of English and Cantonese that only they could understand.

"*Ayee,* of course, Little Mother," Ah Tup said, a relieved smile lighting her round, smooth face. Ah Tup was most unattractive, as Precious Jade was forever pointing out, but her perpetual joy at simply being alive made up for any shortcomings she might have had in beauty. "I shall be happy to get off this stinking hulk of rotten wood. He is quite a man, isn't he? Perhaps it will take us both to satisfy him, *heya?*"

Blossom would have smiled, but she couldn't be sure that Ah Tup's joke might not turn out to be the truth. She stood still as Ah Tup hurried about making a fine show of working. In truth, they had never unpacked most of their goods, not trusting the crew of the ship.

Darcy watched the little slip of a Chinese girl hurry about the cabin tucking in silks and crockery as the taller, older girl remained motionless. From her imperious stance, he could well believe this girl-woman was used to ordering slaves about.

He glanced at his "payment" covertly. If he had to hazard a guess at her age, he would reckon about twenty. Old for a concubine in the Orient, so the story about being a virgin was probably a lie. If anything, she was no doubt being given to him because she was getting too old to earn much money.

Who were the "bad men" who had taken her and taken her from where? From whom? She didn't seem to recall, and her English was so stilted it had probably happened many years ago. A small seed of pity sprouted to life in his heart. What kind of life had she led, a slave in a foreign land?

He looked away. He still didn't know what he was supposed to do with the wench and her servant. Driscoll had bluntly refused to have them another minute on the ship, even after Darcy had heatedly pointed out that *he* owned the ship, not Driscoll.

He supposed he could put them up in a hotel, but he couldn't risk being seen with two such females. It would severely damage his reputation. And only that morning he had read a letter to the editor of *The Times* complaining that the forthcoming opening of the Crystal Palace was leading to a dearth of rooms in hotels and boarding houses, so it might not even be a simple matter to find a lodging for them.

It would be even worse to take them to his house. Although he held the upper class in general contempt, he did plan to marry well one day, and if the girls were discovered there people might assume that he had the effrontery to establish a love nest without following proper form.

Unfortunately, he couldn't think of anyplace else to take them. Mrs. MacTavish, his housekeeper, could be trusted to keep quiet, as could Powlett. He would keep his charges secluded in a bedroom until he figured out what to do next.

At least it was night. Perhaps he could get them inside his house without being seen from the street.

They were standing there watching him. "Come."

He watched the taller girl as she moved toward the door, her gait in the narrow red silk gown swaying and unusual. Only once before had he seen a Chinese woman. She had been put on exhibition over twenty years ago. He was young and on leave, but even now he recalled the horrified fascination he had felt staring at the poor woman's incredibly tiny bound feet.

What if they had done this to *her?* He couldn't wait another second to find out, but quickly reached out and lifted her skirt.

Normal. Small but normal. He almost sighed with relief, until he caught the scandalized expression on the girl's face. He didn't quite know what to say, so he didn't say anything.

He turned away and saw the smaller girl valiantly try to hoist a huge trunk onto her slender back.

He went over and took the trunk, lifting it onto his broad shoulders. Ah Tup was too stunned to speak . . . for a minute.

"*Ayee,* Mother," she whispered as they followed him out the narrow door, "this is a good sign. Such strength! In bed he will no doubt perform with much vigor."

Blossom was thinking the same thing, but she signaled Ah Tup to be silent. She wasn't sure if the man would like to hear them talking or not, so it was best to be careful and speak little.

As they stepped onto the gently rocking deck, Blossom and Ah Tup took in deep gulps of air and then looked at each other in alarm. How it stunk! Worse than the ship.

The murky air, thick with a yellow fog, smelled like the farmers' fields outside Canton, which were manured with human as well as animal droppings. The air was damp and chill, and Blossom gathered her thin cloak more tightly. She had worn her best silk brocaded garment to impress her new master. She would have done better to wear something less fine and more warm. Voices, harsh and angry, drifted to them like ghosts.

Ah Tup grabbed Blossom's arm. "So many restless spirits! This is surely a terrible place."

Blossom swallowed hard. She told herself she didn't believe in ghosts, the perpetually angry spirits who could make a person's life miserable with their tricks and wiles.

They followed the man down the narrow plank to the dock. A group of boisterous men passed by with their arms around women who could only be the lowest class of whore possible, since they didn't even belong to a house.

Waiting on the wet, slippery street was a large black conveyance drawn by two horses. The man opened a door and motioned them inside. Blossom looked at Ah Tup but decided there was nothing else to be done but enter.

It was a stuffy, tiny little room with seats on the sides. As Ah Tup joined her, it shifted like a boat. When the man came in, it jostled as if the boat had encountered a high wind. He barked something, then the vehicle began to move. Ah Tup stifled a little scream, and they both held on tightly.

The man stared out the window, his face scowling.

"Where are we going?" Ah Tup whispered.

"To his house, I suppose," Blossom whispered back. The man turned and glared at her, his gaze running over her from head to foot. Acutely conscious of her huge feet, Blossom tried to tuck them in a little more. When he went back to staring out the window, she murmured, "My feet."

Ah Tup nodded sadly. It was a fact that Blossom's feet were much too big for a lady of beauty, since they had never been bound. Several times Precious Jade had tried to wrap Blossom's feet in the long, narrow bandages and several times Blossom had torn them off, despite the beatings and lack of food that inevitably followed.

Finally, however, Precious Jade had given up. Blossom had triumphed ... until she had learned how ugly her feet rendered her. By then Ah Tup had come to have great respect for the *fan kow* girl. Something inside the skinny, pale barbarian was stronger than the hardest iron and more durable than the mountains, whereas Ah Tup was simply glad to be alive.

There were many unhappy fates that lay in store for a female child. For Ah Tup, however, being a peasant girl from Szechwan, foot binding was not one of them. Secretly she had always been pleased to have ugly feet, since it kept away unwanted masculine attention. Nevertheless she understood why Blossom was trying to put her feet as far under her gown as she could.

While Ah Tup thought about feet, Blossom covertly watched their new master, trying to guess what he was like from his features. She noticed the calluses on his hands. Honorable Wu had told her she was going to a wealthy man, but clearly he had not always been so.

This knowledge made her a little happier. She had no liking for the smooth-skinned, pale hands of the rich men who had come to see Honorable Wu. They always reminded her of the bellies of the fish waiting to be cooked.

Then Blossom noticed that the air didn't smell quite so bad. As the strange cart rolled along, the air began to get better with each passing moment. She took a deep breath and realized Ah Tup was doing the same.

"What is it?" the man asked, looking at them.

Blossom felt rather embarrassed but knew she had to answer him. "The ship . . . too stinky." She held her nose.

Suddenly the man grinned. Only for an instant, but she felt strangely pleased. "I suppose it is, when you're below decks all the time."

The cart came to a sudden stop, and Blossom fell forward, almost landing on the man's lap. "Careful, there," he said, pushing her back. His big hands cupped her shoulders, then let go. "Wait here a minute."

She nodded, feeling rather giddy. It must be the fresher air, she thought.

"You have made a conquest, Mother!" Ah Tup cried. "I am sure of it. His face when he touched you! If I had not been here, who knows...?"

Before Ah Tup could continue, the man returned. "Come," he said, opening the door and helping Blossom down. Ah Tup, wearing loose-fitting trousers and blouse, jumped down with no assistance.

The girls stared at the building before them, then turned to each other, horrified.

"*Ayee!*" Ah Tup whispered, "the secret arrow!"

Blossom nodded, looking in dismay at the angle of the street, which seemed to point directly at the front door of the house before them. Evil influences, which always travel in a straight line, would surely flow directly at the entrance, which, to make matters even worse, was on the same level as the street.

"There should be a wall to turn back the *sha*," Ah Tup whispered fervently.

"What's the matter now?" the man demanded.

"Perhaps it is better inside," Blossom answered quietly.

Once again Ah Tup began to lift the trunk, but again the man took it on his shoulders and led them inside.

What they saw inside made their hearts sink. The house had the worst possible design, one that would encourage evil *sha* to enter and that would also prevent the beneficial *ch'i* from lingering. There was a long hall with wooden panels on the bottom of the walls and ugly patterned painting on the other half, a hall that seemed to lead directly through the house. A staircase ran directly up on one side, with no turning point. *Ch'i* would pass all too quickly through such a house.

Other rooms opened off the corridor. The man led them into the first one, set down their trunk and told them to wait once again.

Blossom looked at Ah Tup in dismay. This place was incredible. Although the room they were in was large, it was much too crowded with furniture, including something like a strange table with its top tilted up.

A fire burned in the wall, kept in its place by an ornate screen. There was no mirror over the opening to keep the *ch'i* in the room, and although the area seemed cluttered, it was with plants and other objects that she doubted had any special meaning. The *ch'i* would have no cause to linger, but would flow away. The paper on the walls, representing flowers, was the same everywhere she looked, making a terrible monotony. Heavy curtains were shut over what she assumed would be tall, narrow windows. Probably they faced north, the least favorable direction. Beyond the room they were in, she could see another.

"It is like a tomb," she said softly to Ah Tup, who wasn't smiling.

"It is the very strangest place I have ever been in and has the worst *feng shui*," she said solemnly, "but at least I think it is clean."

"Who could tell, with all the furnishings and rugs and ugly plants? And what do you suppose this is?" Blossom went over to the strange table. Little white and black tiles sat on a part like a shelf. Gently she touched one of the tiles, then jumped back when the table made a noise. Ah Tup came over and also touched it, making a sound. They looked at each other incredulously.

"That's a piano," the man's voice interrupted.

Moving away from the thing guiltily, they watched him come in. This time he wasn't alone. He was followed by a tall, white-haired woman who appeared to have the biggest hips they had ever seen.

Quickly Blossom and Ah Tup kowtowed, certain this was either the man's *tai tai* or his honorable mother.

Blossom risked a glance at the woman's feet but couldn't see anything under the gigantic skirt.

"Mercy on us, Mr. Fitzroy!" Mrs. MacTavish cried, her Scottish accent broadened by surprise. "They're heathens!"

"I haven't had a chance to question our guests on their religious beliefs."

As his housekeeper continued to stare, Darcy suddenly felt the corners of his mouth begin to twitch with an almost uncontrollable urge to laugh. Mrs. MacTavish was the widow of a former shipmate, sixty years old, and Presbyterian to the marrow of her bones. She had a back as rigid as a spar, a mouth as tight as a taut line and a sincere belief that cleanliness was indeed next to godliness. No matter what time Darcy summoned her, day or night, she always looked the same: black bombazine dress, watch pinned to a chest that looked so smooth and hard it could have been ebony, every iron-gray hair in the proper place, and her large skirt as unwrinkled as a full sail in a stiff breeze. He sometimes wondered if she slept upright and fully clothed.

He subdued the urge to laugh, and when he spoke, his voice was calm.

"Guests?" Mrs. MacTavish repeated, looking at him.

"For now. They arrived on *China Lady.* There's no place else for them to go, and it wouldn't be proper Christian charity to turn them out on the street."

His words hit their mark. "I suppose we could put them in one of the spare bedrooms."

Mrs. MacTavish's gaze returned to the prostrate figures. "Must they kneel down like that, Mr. Fitzroy?"

"Get up," he ordered, and the one called Fragrant Blossom obeyed instantly. Her maid followed her example.

"Mr. Fitzroy!" Mrs. MacTavish exclaimed when she saw Blossom's round blue eyes. "What's all this about?"

"It's a long story." He hoisted the trunk again. "Come."

He had decided the set of rooms intended to be a nursery, with a governess's bedroom, a classroom and a smaller child's bedroom, would be the best place to put them. Mrs. MacTavish and Powlett slept on the third floor, and the maids and the footman didn't sleep in the house.

He led the way upstairs and past the master bedroom, followed by the girls and Mrs. MacTavish, who was probably more rattled than she'd been in the past forty years.

Upon entering the small, feminine bedroom, he set the trunk down with a thud and began to leave as Mrs. MacTavish spoke to Ah Tup. "Now, if you'll come with me, I'll take you upstairs."

Clearly Mrs. MacTavish had guessed, from the younger girl's demeanor and dress, that she was a servant.

"No!"

Darcy turned around. The servant girl looked terrified, and the older girl was making a show of defiance, but underneath, in the depths of her blue, blue eyes, he saw fear. "Ah Tup stay with me."

"There's quite a nice maid's room just at the top of the stairs," Mrs. MacTavish said soothingly. "She'll come back to help you undress."

"Ah Tup stay."

Blossom felt a growing sense of panic that she might be separated from her friend. If she were, who knew what might happen in this barbaric place? Maybe she would never see Ah Tup's cheerful smile again.

Ah Tup sidled a little closer to her mistress's side and Blossom knew she was frightened, too. She glanced at the man, who was watching from the doorway. Blossom spoke to him, ignoring the black and gray woman. "I want Ah Tup stay."

The man nodded. "Very well. It's too late to stand here arguing about it."

"But where will the poor girl sleep?" the older woman asked.

Blossom couldn't believe the woman's stupidity. "On floor," she replied, as if instructing a child.

The man shrugged his shoulders and left the room.

"Heathens!" the woman exclaimed, going out and banging the door closed.

Blossom and Ah Tup smiled at each other, each feeling vastly relieved. Then they looked around the room.

It, too, was strange beyond belief. It had paper on the walls with lines running from floor to ceiling, like the bars of a cell. There was a white cupboard with doors, a table with a mirror over it and a stool. But the single most astonishing piece of furniture was the narrow iron bed.

"How are a man and a woman supposed to lie in comfort on such a thing as this?" Ah Tup asked incredulously. She went over and pushed down on it. "Well, it is soft, at least."

Blossom, too, couldn't quite see how she was to be sufficiently entertaining on such a bed. "Ah," she said after a moment's reflection, "undoubtedly I am to go to the master's bed, *heya?*"

Chapter Two

The smoke from Darcy's cheroot spiraled slowly around the bust of some dead Roman on the mantelpiece, then curled upward toward the ornate ceiling of his study. Around him were mahogany shelves of leather-bound books, not one of which he had read. His large desk, covered by papers, stood nearby.

He sat in his favorite wing chair, holding a glass of whiskey he hadn't tasted in the past ten minutes. Usually he enjoyed being here surrounded by costly but old furnishings, especially when the only light was the flickering glow from the coal fire in the grate at his feet. It was easy to think in this room, with its air of comfort and wealth, like the rest of the house, which Darcy had chosen more for its fashionable address than its actual design. It seemed the embodiment of his long-held dream of money and permanence.

Unlike many men who went to sea at a young age, the sea had never got into Darcy's blood. He was quite content to let other men captain his vessels, perhaps because he could never forget that the sea was ultimately stronger and more powerful than he would ever be.

Darcy took a sip of his whiskey. If someone had told him this morning he would have some whore and her maid in his house tonight, he would have roared with laughter, or taken a swing at the jester. However, such was indeed his current situation. He set down his glass, then absently ran his finger over the long, thin scar on his right hand, the reminder of the last time he had been with a whore.

That had been many years ago in Curaçao. The woman had given him something to drink that made him pass out, but he had come to in time to grab on to the man trying to rob him. The man had a knife and had almost killed him, but at least Darcy had got a good look at the pimp's face. Darcy's ship had left the port before he could find the man again, but the next time his ship docked there, Darcy went searching.

By then the woman was dead. But the thieving pimp was not—although he had wished he was by the time Darcy had finished with him.

He had never gone with a whore again. Instead he had devoted all his energy to the accumulation of wealth and made a rather interesting discovery. As he had begun to amass a fortune, he found that several married women were more than willing to satisfy his carnal desires. For free.

Darcy finished his drink in one gulp, then inhaled deeply on his cheroot. In the morning he'd write to Mitchell. That damn Wu couldn't get away with this, sending a girl who must have been kidnapped in payment for his debt.

How had she come to be in that predicament? Obviously she wasn't Oriental, and her English had a British accent. It was well-known that the Chinese lacked the intelligence to learn English, although there were some who claimed that the Chinese didn't learn English because they didn't think it was worth the effort.

He'd get his partner to find out what he could about English families in China. Charles might even know how to go about finding information about a girl who must have gone missing several years ago.

Of course he would have to come up with some reason for wanting to know about such things. The Honorable Charles Horton-Smythe had a marvelous head for business and the best of connections, but also a tendency to be curious. It would be difficult to try to keep Fragrant Blossom's presence a secret, but for now Darcy couldn't see any alternative.

Feeling as if he'd solved at least part of the problem of Fragrant Blossom, Darcy stubbed out his cheroot, tiredness beginning to creep into every muscle. He got up and went to the stairs. It was about time he went to bed.

Bed. Emmaline! He stopped abruptly. Oh, God, she'd be angry with him. He frowned for a moment, then resumed going up the steps. Well, he'd have to apologize for missing her party and take her something, a ring or a brooch, to show how sorry he was.

Not that he had any illusions that Emmaline would sigh over it and keep it in some secret spot. He had no doubt that she sold every jewel he gave her.

He had recognized her hunger for wealth the first time he'd seen her, perhaps because it was something they had in common. Already married to that idiot Whitmore, she'd come to his shipping office with her husband like a well-rigged clipper towing a barge. He was, she said, thinking of investing in one of Darcy's ships. It hadn't take long to realize just who was in charge of Whitmore's money.

He stopped again. Emmaline might have some small house somewhere that he could rent until he settled this business. He would ask her, although he wouldn't dare say exactly what he needed to "store." If Emmaline ever got terribly angry, she could make his social life extremely uncomfortable since she wielded enormous power in that regard.

He paused outside his bedroom. All seemed quiet. Then he went in—and halted confusedly.

Fragrant Blossom, wearing a white robe of silk so thin it was almost transparent, waited at the foot of his bed. As he stood there staring, she kowtowed, but so slowly and gracefully that he had a long, lingering view of her almost naked beauty.

She was exquisite. His hands could probably circle her waist. One of her white breasts would probably fit snugly in his palm.

"What are you doing in here?" he asked coldly but not unkindly. She must have been told to do this, to offer herself to him, by that old villain Wu.

She didn't say a word, but lifted her face and looked at him. He knew she would do anything—*anything*—he wanted.

He took one step forward, then caught sight of the crisscross of scars on her back. It looked as if someone had gone at her with a cat-o'-nine-tails.

He looked into her eyes. She was afraid. Did she think he would beat her, too?

"Get dressed," he said, "and go."

She stared at him, looking more terrified than ever.

"Go, I said."

As she got slowly to her feet, he thought he saw the glimmer of tears in her eyes. "I ... am ... not ... pleasing?" she whispered.

Not pleasing? By God, in another instant he wouldn't have given a damn who she was or how she got there. He would have thrown her onto the bed and made love to her.

He heard a small sound behind him and turned around to see her servant standing in the doorway. The girl looked horrified. She began to speak, not bothering to keep her voice lowered. It didn't seem to matter to them that Fragrant Blossom would be discovered virtually undressed in a man's bedroom.

Fragrant Blossom answered mournfully. Then she straightened, the action making him all too aware of her breasts beneath the thin fabric. "Why I not please you?" she demanded.

"Mr. Fitzroy!"

Darcy spun around. A shocked Mrs. MacTavish stood where the maid had been moments ago, looking like an artist's depiction of Moses before he threw down the tablets. Fragrant Blossom and Ah Tup hurriedly knelt on the floor.

"She was here when I came in," Darcy said defensively.

"Well, I don't know what those heathens teach their girls, but here in England . . ." Mrs. MacTavish gasped when she saw Blossom's back. Quickly she grabbed the satin coverlet from Darcy's bed and wrapped it gently around Blossom's shoulders.

"Ach, the poor wee thing!" she murmured, shooting a look at Darcy as if he were somehow responsible. "Beaten like that. Oh, the poor bairn!"

"May I be of any assistance, Mr. Fitzroy?"

Darcy scowled at the appearance of Powlett in the door. The butler wore a brilliant scarlet robe, an equally brilliant nightcap and an expression of complete calm.

Blossom, holding the coverlet around her, said, "My master's wife, I come to pay debt of Honorable Wu."

"Wife?" Mrs. MacTavish went beet red.

"Mrs. MacTavish is the *housekeeper,*" Darcy said.

"She is *servant?*" Blossom glanced at Ah Tup with something like triumph.

"In a manner of speaking. Now go to bed."

Blossom turned to a puzzled Ah Tup and fired off a spate of Chinese. Then she began heading toward Darcy's bed, a smile of satisfaction on her face.

"Not *my* bed," he said, trying to ignore the scandalized expression on Mrs. MacTavish's face.

"If you please, miss, I shall escort you to your room," the ever-unflappable Powlett intoned.

"What he say?" Blossom asked.

Mrs. MacTavish recovered. "That won't be necessary, Mr. Powlett," she told him. She turned to Blossom. "Come along, deary. You're in England now, thank the Lord, so you can forget whatever you've been told to do by those idolatrous pagans."

Ah Tup started to speak loudly, obviously chastising Mrs. MacTavish. Blossom joined in, refusing to budge from her place in the room.

"If nothing more is required of me . . ." Powlett began.

"You *can't* stay in here . . ." Mrs. MacTavish protested.

Darcy couldn't stand the noise and confusion for another moment. *"Get out!"* he roared. "Everybody—out!"

Blossom and Ah Tup scurried away like two mice in the pantry, Mrs. MacTavish swept out with her skirts swishing indignantly, and Powlett calmly and quietly closed the door.

The whole episode reminded Darcy of the time he'd been caught in a gale off Tortuga. What had happened to all his hard-won peace and quiet? How was he going to avoid a scandal?

Something was going to have to be done. That was obvious. The question was, what?

Slowly he undressed and climbed into bed, minus the coverlet. He would try to forget about all this business for now and get some much-needed rest.

Unfortunately, whenever he closed his eyes, he saw Fragrant Blossom, naked and perfect.

He lay awake until almost dawn.

* * *

"You do not think I have lost face?" Blossom asked Ah Tup worriedly the next morning.

"*Ayee-ah,* surely not," Ah Tup replied as she slipped Blossom's shoes onto her feet. "You did the proper thing, but that awful Crow Woman, who clearly does not know her duty, prevented you from fulfilling *your* duty. If anyone has lost *lian,* it is her. What a terrible creature! And as for that other servant in the blood robe, *huh!* I think he must be a eunuch."

"It is true I tried to do my duty," Blossom said, her brow still knit with worry, "but perhaps I did a thing I ought not to have done. Perhaps I should have waited to be summoned, or perhaps the master expected to come here, although—" she frowned at the narrow bed "—his bed seems much more suitable."

"Who can possibly understand these barbarians?" Ah Tup said with a sigh. "You remember nothing of these things?"

Blossom shook her head sadly. "I was too little. All I can remember is a big room with long seats and my father at the front in a white robe. Then his death."

"Ah, well." Ah Tup shrugged her shoulders. "We will have to learn. Until we do, I do not see how *you* can lose face. These are not civilized people."

Ah Tup went to the grate and stirred the rice in the wok. A delicious spicy aroma filled the small room.

"We shall have to try to find out the ways here," Blossom said thoughtfully. "Watch and listen until we know what is expected of us."

Ah Tup nodded and took the wok from the fire.

There was a brief knock and the Crow Woman entered, carrying a large tray filled with dishes.

"Merciful heavens, what's all this? I've brought you some breakfast. There's no need to cook in here. You'll be setting the house on fire."

Blossom looked at her coolly. Since this woman was merely a servant, she didn't have to talk to her.

Mrs. MacTavish set down the tray on the small table and left the room. Curious, Blossom and Ah Tup examined the meal the woman had left.

"Do you suppose this is for all the servants?" Ah Tup asked in wonderment.

"That must be so," Blossom said, for there was enough food on the tray to feed ten hungry people. "We must get to choose first, and then the others afterward."

"But," Ah Tup said with a dismayed look, "who can be expected to eat this?"

They stared down at the porridge, crisp bacon, toast, fried eggs, pots of jam and honey and tea, with cream and sugar beside it. Blossom glanced up at Ah Tup. Ah Tup looked back. Together they turned away from the unpalatable food.

Darcy set down his knife and fork and reached for his cup of tea. He felt absolutely wretched, as if he'd been on double watch at sea.

The doors to the breakfast room opened, and in came Mrs. MacTavish, the keys on her chatelaine jingling with irritation. Powlett, impassive, followed close behind. Together they stood at the opposite end of the table like soldiers on parade.

"Mr. Fitzroy," Mrs. MacTavish said, "Mr. Powlett and I would like to know what is going on here."

Darcy stretched out his long legs under the table. He couldn't say he was surprised by their question. After all, it wasn't every day a man brought home two young girls.

"A Chinese merchant owed me some money. This is his way of paying."

The full import of the payment—all too clear from the episode the previous night—didn't escape either one of the two people standing before him. Mrs. MacTavish's eyes grew wide. Even Powlett twitched an eyebrow.

Darcy nodded.

"But where did they come from?"

"Mitchell sent them on *China Lady*. I think you'll agree that the one girl, the one who obviously *isn't* Chinese, couldn't be left in Canton. Who knows what might have happened to her?"

Darcy didn't say what he suspected had already happened to her, or what Wu had threatened to do if Darcy didn't accept her as payment.

"It's...it's *monstrous!*" Mrs. MacTavish cried. "The poor thing! How did she come to be among those heathens?"

"Kidnapped, I gather. She doesn't seem to remember exactly."

Powlett cleared his throat. "Is it your intention that they remain in the house, sir?"

Darcy steepled his fingers. "For now, until I can find someplace else. But I want them to stay in their room."

"She'll have to have some decent clothes, Mr. Fitzroy," Mrs. MacTavish said.

His housekeeper was right. It would be impossible to move Fragrant Blossom anywhere without attracting attention if she was still wearing those Oriental robes.

Darcy reached for his wallet, then hesitated over the amount Mrs. MacTavish would need to get Blossom suitably attired. Like many self-made men, Darcy was leery of spending extravagantly, and despite the Scots' reputation for frugality, he had seen the presents Mrs. MacTavish sent to her family at Christmas. After due consideration, he pulled out two bills. "That should do," he said in a tone that didn't brook any protest, ignoring the displeased expression on Mrs. MacTavish's face.

The maid scratched at the door and sidled inside, bearing a silver tray with a card on it. Powlett took it from her and held the tray out to Darcy.

"It's Mr. Horton-Smythe," Darcy said after reading the card. "Show him into the study—and tell those girls to stay upstairs."

He pushed away from the table after his servants had departed and walked slowly to his study. Wu wanted this girl to repay the debt and, instead, she was costing him even more.

When he opened the door to the study, Charles Horton-Smythe turned quickly to greet him. "By Jove, Fitzroy, wonderful news, what? *China Lady* back when we'd feared the worst, eh?"

As always, Darcy was struck by the air of subdued excitement that emanated from Charles. It was as if the man were compressed in a body too small to contain his life force and might explode any minute. Even when Darcy had first met him and Charles had been as drunk as a sailor on a one-day leave, Darcy had been struck by the man's sense of vitality.

That, and his flamboyant manner of dressing. For someone from one of the oldest families in the south of England, Charles seemed to have a touch of the carnival barker about him. To be sure he wore black frock coats and black trousers, but his waistcoats, like the bright red-and-yellow one he now sported, could be glaring.

However, they made excellent partners. Darcy handled the shipping and Charles took care of the contracts, the money and the cultivation of investors. The man knew his way around a contract or a promissory note the way Darcy knew his way around a clipper ship, and Charles also knew the kind of people who had the money to invest in shipping. He had been to Eton and Oxford before the family fortune was too seriously depleted by his drunken father and equally debauched older brother.

Charles had proved his worth as a partner many times and had made his own fortune. It had always amused Darcy that the clever, amusing and well-bred Honorable Charles Horton-Smythe had survived without some woman managing to marry him, but perhaps he, too, was holding out for the most advantageous match.

"Driscoll didn't say much about the voyage," Darcy said, sitting at his desk. He gestured for Charles to sit down, too.

"Wish I'd known it'd arrived last night. Creditors getting rather nervous. That ass Whitmore even asked me about it after dinner.

"'I say,' he says, taking a pinch of snuff, as if he needed any—nose perpetually running, even when we were at Eton together—'Hearing disturbing news about your company, eh, what?'"

Darcy's lips turned up slightly at the accuracy of his partner's imitation.

Charles shook his head rapidly. "The man was born a hundred years too late. Would have made an excellent country squire, you know. Hunting and justice of the peace and all that. Anyway, I didn't reply, and thank heavens we joined the ladies directly."

He gave Darcy a sidelong glance. "You were conspicuously absent last night, old man. Lady Whitmore asked me especially where you were. Put me in a bit of stew, eh? But we all assumed it had to be business, you being quite the proper gentleman, what?"

Darcy smiled slightly. It was, he knew, common enough knowledge that he didn't frequent houses of pleasure or indulge in the more public vices of drinking and gambling.

Charles shook his head. "It's a mystery to me how Twitty Whitty managed to capture a beauty like her, but I suppose having an income of a hundred thousand pounds a year helps, eh?"

Darcy didn't respond. Charles's words were close to the truth, but he didn't like hearing Emmaline's situation put in such an unflattering way. Emmaline's family were country gentry, but her marriage had placed her in the upper echelons of society. She wasn't the only one who gained, however, because without her shrewd guidance, her poor fool of a husband would have been impoverished years ago by his spendthrift ways. With Emmaline secretly at the helm, the Whitmore fortune had grown considerably.

Of course, he realized, Charles had no idea she was Darcy's mistress, or he would never dare say such things.

"So, has that wily old Wu finally paid up?"

Darcy cleared his throat. "Yes."

"You don't look very pleased, Fitzroy."

"He didn't send it in silver."

"Oh? Silk?"

"No."

"Tea?"

"No."

"Jade?"

"No."

"Well, what, for heaven's sake?"

"He sent . . . a present, to me personally. Something that can't be traded for money."

Charles sat back in his chair. "A present? To you?"

"To me. I'll pay the debt from my own profit for this voyage." There was nothing else to do, although the thought of parting with a thousand pounds was like losing a limb.

"Well, that's good of you, I'm sure, old man. That'll make the bank very happy."

"I want to go to the ship later and check the rest of the cargo. Care to come along?"

Charles stood up. "No, thanks, old man. Hate the smell of those boats, don't you know? Besides, I thought I'd run up to the bank and tell 'em our ship's come in, eh?"

He laughed comfortably at his joke, which Darcy had heard every time one of their ships arrived safely.

Darcy nodded. "Fine. I'll bring the manifest to the office later."

Charles got up to leave, then hesitated. "I say, old man, you're looking rather done for. Feeling quite yourself?"

"I'm fine. Just tired."

"Oh, glad to hear it. Till later, then, Fitzroy."

Charles hurried out the door, closing it behind him and letting out his breath slowly. Every time he was in Darcy's presence, he felt as nervous as a schoolboy in front of the headmaster.

And every time he asked himself why he should be intimidated by a man who had come from nowhere, who had made his money in trade, who was his social inferior in every way. Why indeed... except for the incontrovertible fact that Darcy Fitzroy seemed to radiate raw power.

As Charles walked through the hall, he heard a rustle on the stairs above him. Turning quickly, he caught a flash of pink fabric and heard a door close quietly.

Pink. Mrs. MacTavish wouldn't wear pink. The maids' uniforms were all black.

What was Fitzroy up to? He already had Emmaline Whitmore for a mistress. No wonder the man looked as if he hadn't slept a wink all night. Probably hadn't.

Perhaps he could find out from that little maid, the one who'd been so extremely grateful for the job. It was good business to know your partner, and Charles knew everything there was to know about Darcy Fitzroy, or made it a point to find out.

The not-so-honorable Charles Horton-Smythe smiled to himself. Fortunately, Fitzroy seemed unaware of that piece of practical wisdom.

Chapter Three

"I missed you last night."

The words were simple and innocent enough, but Emmaline had long ago learned how to infuse even the most innocuous statement with a wealth of innuendo. She considered it one of her major assets, along with a beautiful face and a voluptuous figure that men had been noticing since she was eleven years old.

Darcy, seated on a sofa in her well-appointed parlor, smiled. His smiles were rare, and so this one was a good sign. Last night she had wondered if she had somehow lost his affection. Now she was sure she hadn't.

"I had some business to attend to. *China Lady* docked yesterday."

"Oh, Darcy, that's wonderful news." Her lovely face bloomed into a smile. She stood to gain considerably by *China Lady*'s cargo. "I was beginning to think bales of cloth and casks of tea were more important than me." She pouted prettily.

He stood up and came toward her, the animal grace of his movements exciting her. He had always excited her, from the first day she had seen him in the shipping office.

He had got up from his chair behind his desk, his eyes surveying her with impertinent curiosity. He didn't even

have the courtesy to stop when he realized she wasn't looking modestly away. She had been fascinated by him from
that moment onward and had used every means, every en-
ticement she knew to get him into her bed, to see if the
promise of his extremely masculine physique was borne out
by his lovemaking.

It was, more than she had even imagined.

Now he was properly attired in black frock coat and
trousers, but it took little imagination to remember him the
last time she had seen him. He had been gloriously naked,
the light of her bedside lamp flickering across the muscled
flesh of his broad shoulders, the tangled sheets wrapped
around his torso and hips leaving his long, strong legs exposed. He had been like a statue of a sleeping god. Apollo
or Zeus.

Darcy stopped a short distance from her, but tantaliz-
ingly close. "I'm sorry," he whispered, the intimacy of his
voice deliciously delightful. He put a small box on the table
near her, a box she recognized as being from a well-known—
and expensive—jeweler. She turned to him with a beguiling
smile.

If she could be sure when Frederick was coming home,
she would invite Darcy upstairs right now regardless of the
servants. But she didn't know when her husband might return from his club, so she dare not. A well-bred gentleman
might overlook some things, but finding another man in his
own bed with his wife was not one of them.

"Well," she said after a moment, toying languidly with
the leaf of a huge fern and incidentally showing off her
white, graceful hands, "I hope you won't miss my next
dinner party, on Tuesday week. I shall be feeling rather
lonely, since Frederick has to go to Kinverton on Monday
for a fortnight."

It never took much to persuade her husband to go to their country estate. She was always terribly bored in the country, unless they were accompanied by a large party of friends. And if one of those friends was a man of intimate acquaintance, a country visit could be quite titillating, what with the invigorating possibilities of long, secluded rambles.

Darcy took her hand and raised it to his full lips. Her limbs seemed to burn with liquid fire, the tongues of flame darting outward from his touch. "I promise I won't miss it."

She would definitely have to invite Darcy to Kinverton soon.

A middle-aged maid bearing a large tea tray came to the doorway just as they moved apart. With her face a careful blank, she set out the tea things on a low table in front of the sofa, then departed.

"Emmaline, I need a favor," Darcy said bluntly as she began to pour the tea.

"Anything," she replied softly.

He smiled slowly, his gaze raking her body in a way that made her heart pound in anticipation.

"I need a house, someplace secluded."

"Really?"

He cleared his throat. "Some cargo that came last night... I can't keep it in a warehouse."

"Is it valuable?" She handed him his teacup, letting her fingers brush his.

"Not particularly," he said casually. "But it's delicate."

"I see." She knew he was lying about its worth, and her curiosity began to grow. "I do have a small house, not too far outside the city. I was planning to rent it this month."

"I'll pay whatever rent you were going to ask."

She smiled and nodded. "Very well. I shall write you the address. You can use it right away, for as long as you like."

"Thank you."

As he finished his tea, she wrote the address down at her writing table, as well as the amount of the rent. He was sure she would inflate it, probably to at least twice the amount she was going to ask someone else, but he wouldn't quibble.

"There," she said, handing him the note. Their fingers touched, until Darcy withdrew his.

"I have some business to take care of now," he said, standing up. Emmaline rose gracefully, and he couldn't help being impressed by her beauty. Her hair, a charming golden yellow, framed a face perfect of feature and complexion, with pink cheeks and large, limpid brown eyes. Her lips, enticing and ruddy, seemed to be waiting for his kiss. His glance strayed to the swell of her bodice, the flesh of her breasts visible beneath the thin fabric of her chemisette, then disappearing into the pink silk of her gown. She moved toward him slowly, her full-skirted gown rustling as gently as leaves in a breeze. "I'm expecting some callers shortly, too."

He heard the regret in Emmaline's voice. Normally he would hate the thought of leaving her without making love, but today he had to get the matter of Fragrant Blossom and her servant settled. He wouldn't rest easy, in his house or Emmaline's arms, until those two were hidden away somewhere.

"Until next time, then," Emmaline said softly, her delicate lips turning up into a promising smile.

"Until next time."

Darcy spent the rest of the afternoon on *China Lady,* going through the manifest and making sure every item listed was on board. Captain Driscoll's log read like a catalog of every disaster known to shipping, from storms and damaged rigging to windless days and problems with port authorities. Nevertheless, the cargo was relatively good. The tea was past its peak, of course, but the cottons and silks were fine, with only a few bolts ruined by water. At least he would make a profit, and all hands had returned safely.

There were a few awkward moments when Driscoll asked him about the "damn women," but he had said only that they were taken care of. Mercifully Driscoll didn't press for more details.

His business concluded, Darcy headed down the gangplank toward the dock. One of the whores who frequented that area spotted him and sauntered slowly toward him as he went to get a cab. Her patched garments made her look like an ambulating rag shop.

"Evenin', deary," she said, her smile exposing rotting teeth.

He muttered a coarse expletive.

"Humph!" she snorted. "You ain't no gentleman!"

Darcy got into a cab quickly. As he headed home, he tried to put the whore out of his mind. Every time he saw one, he couldn't help remembering the fight with the pimp, whose teeth had been bared like a rat's, his eyes gleaming in the dark. Darcy closed his eyes as a shudder of revulsion passed through him. He told himself that it was all long ago, and if he had to do it again, he would have done just the same.

He forced himself to think about his business, thankful that the actual accounting was in Charles's hands. He had no head for figures.

Soon he was home. He jumped out and paid the cabbie as Powlett opened the door for him. The butler handed him a letter. "From Mr. Jeremy, I believe," he said solemnly, but there was the hint of distraction in his manner.

Darcy took his younger brother's letter and went into the parlor. Powlett hovered near the door, anxious as always for news of Jeremy.

Well, and so it should be, thought Darcy. His brother was happy and handsome and well-liked by everyone who met him, just as Darcy had planned from the day their mother died fifteen years ago.

Jeremy had been but three years old then and Darcy only lately returned from a voyage to the West Indies. That was the voyage that started Darcy's fortune, although the impetus to gain wealth had been implanted even before that.

The Fitzroys had once been wealthy country gentry, holding land since the Middle Ages. Times had changed, though, and through no fault of his own, Darcy's father had found himself with only a dismal, leaking house and a few pitiful acres. He had tried to make the farm pay, but he couldn't compete with those who had larger holdings and the new machinery. Little by little what money they had left had trickled away, and when his father died, there had been none left.

That had been when Darcy was fifteen, and his mother expecting the birth of his brother any day. When the pains started, his mother knew that something was wrong. The midwife, too, had been worried and sent Darcy from the room with a sharp reprimand. Darcy had waited helplessly as the hours and the pain dragged on and on, and listened as his mother's cries grew weaker and weaker. The midwife's daughter, wondering what was taking so long, arrived. Darcy eavesdropped at the door, making out little except despair, and one sentence, "Maybe she should have the doctor."

Darcy went at once to fetch the doctor, only to be told he was attending a dinner at a nearby estate. Through a driving rain, Darcy ran to the huge mansion. The footman, the butler and the housekeeper all tried to keep him from going inside, but he dashed around them, running into the fine dining room. He halted, momentarily blinded and silenced by the shining lights, the gleaming silver and the smell of food.

The finely dressed people stared at him. Then he saw the doctor and hurried to him, pleading with him to help.

The doctor looked down his fat, bulbous nose and said, "Go away, boy. The midwife will do for your mother."

It had taken four footmen to carry Darcy out of the house.

His brother arrived unharmed because the midwife was experienced and very skilled. His mother was not so fortunate. She did not die, but from that time on she was never the same. It was as if, in giving Jeremy life, she had pledged her own, bit by bit.

Later Darcy had realized the doctor would probably have done more harm than good, but it never lessened his hatred of people like the doctor. He had vowed that he would be rich one day, too. So rich that no one would ignore his requests.

His mother hadn't had much chance to experience the comfort he had been able to provide after a few successful voyages, but he had spared no expense in his care of Jeremy. He had hired the best nursemaids and tutors, then sent him to the best schools, including Oxford, where he was now reading history.

Jeremy would be everything his older brother could not, and when his education was finished, he would find a place waiting in Fitzroy Shipping.

Darcy opened the letter and read it as quickly as he could. "He's coming for a visit," he told Powlett, who almost smiled. "He says he has something very important to discuss with me." He sniffed. "He either needs more money or another horse."

Although he tried to sound annoyed, he really couldn't be. Jeremy was no spendthrift, despite the all-too-apparent temptations of life at Oxford among the moneyed class. In fact, Darcy was vastly proud of his brother.

Powlett was still distracted, which immediately struck Darcy as unusual. "Is anything wrong, Powlett?"

As if in response, a voice shouted, "No! No! *No!*" the words from upstairs echoing through the hall.

"Apparently, sir," Powlett said mournfully.

Frowning darkly, Darcy hurried up the stairs.

"I not wear such things. Never, never, never!" he heard a female voice shout, followed by a string of Chinese words that sounded suspiciously like curses.

When he got to the governess's bedroom, he found it strewn with ladies' garments like some sort of strange bazaar. There were petticoats and shoes, stockings and chemises, at least three dresses, two hats, a cloak and a muff. In the midst of this pandemonium, he barely recognized Mrs. MacTavish, who was more disheveled than he would have believed possible. The Chinese servant was standing in the corner of the room, grinning like a fool. And in the center of it all, wearing only pantalets and a chemise and gesturing wildly with a corset, stood Fragrant Blossom.

When she saw him standing in the doorway, she quickly kowtowed.

"What's going on?" Darcy demanded, trying not to look at the nearly naked girl, or, more precisely, her pert derriere.

"She won't dress properly," Mrs. MacTavish said, exasperation in every word.

"Get up," he said to Blossom. She got to her feet, staring at the floor, the corset limp in her hands.

"Why won't you do as Mrs. MacTavish says?" he asked, wishing Wu Wing Toi at the bottom of the China Sea.

Blossom knew she had no choice. "If *you* wish me to have air squeezed from my body until I die, then it must be so, honored lord," she said. It was a matter of face that she do whatever her master wished, even if it killed her.

Holding the disgusting body-binding thing, Blossom tried to subdue her confusion and worry, and to understand the strange ways of these people. Perhaps this instrument of torture was also intended to make her beautiful in his eyes. Whatever the reason, though, *he* would have to command it, not his *fan kow* servant.

"Forget the corset, Mrs. MacTavish," he said with a sigh. "I don't think she needs it anyway."

Blossom stifled a sigh of relief.

"But Mr. Fitzroy..."

"Just get her dressed, for God's sake."

Darcy turned and stalked from the room, all his previous good humor gone as if dashed by a wave. He strode into his study and slammed the door.

The sooner Fragrant Blossom was out of his house, the better.

After several minutes and two stiff drinks of whiskey, he heard Mrs. MacTavish knock on the door.

"What?" he bellowed. He wanted to be left in peace.

"I've got her dressed at last, Mr. Fitzroy," she said, opening the door.

Blossom stood on the threshold, wearing a gown of simple blue calico. It had a high neck, to please the conservative Mrs. MacTavish, no doubt. The full skirt hung from her narrow waist, petticoats making it as round as a bell. The full sleeves ended at her wrists, emphasizing her slender hands. Her hair was parted and arranged simply in a low bun at the nape of her neck.

She began to kneel, but Darcy spoke sharply. "Don't!"

Instead, she kept her eyes lowered and stared at the floor. Darcy stood up and went toward her as Mrs. MacTavish gave her a gentle shove into the room. "Much better," he said, and then realized it was a lie. To be sure she looked like a proper, modest young lady, but it was not true that she looked much better than she had in that transparent gown last night.

God help him, what kind of depraved animal was he becoming, that he could have such carnal thoughts about some poor girl who'd undoubtedly led a hellish existence as a prostitute? And how could he so easily forget that she was little better than that dockside dolly, and that he'd sworn never to touch another whore?

He forced his mind back to the present and saw the hint of a frown at the corners of her mouth. "Don't you like the dress?"

She glanced up at him sharply, her blue eyes snapping. "What evil barbarian lord decree such thing, honored lord? How can woman not fall when feet so hidden? How can woman sit? How can slave kowtow to master? These are impossibles."

For the second time in as many days, Darcy felt the urge to laugh. "Dame Fashion decrees these things."

"Dame Fashion is not right in head," she said with conviction.

This time Darcy did laugh. "You might have something there," he said. He glanced at Mrs. MacTavish. "Please pack up the rest of the things you've bought for her. She'll be leaving tonight."

Blossom's eyes narrowed. "I am to be leaving?"

Darcy went to his favorite chair by the hearth and sat down. "Yes, to a better place, in the country."

To his surprise, she turned deathly pale. "You send me away?"

"You cannot stay here, deary. It's not proper," Mrs. MacTavish chided.

"You send me away?" Blossom repeated, staring at Darcy until he actually began to feel guilty.

"Well, Mrs. MacTavish is right. You can't stay here."

"You . . . do not want me?"

The knowledge that he wanted her very much disturbed him profoundly. "No," he said harshly. "I don't want you."

She gasped. "I have no face!" she whispered, then turned and fled from the room, almost stumbling on her skirts in her haste. They heard her run up the stairs and a door close.

"Whatever did the girl mean by that, sir? How can she have no face?" Mrs. MacTavish looked at him as if he'd suddenly become a cannibal.

"I'm not sure," Darcy said, then he paused.

He remembered one of his shipmates, an old China hand, talking about a Chinese girl he'd lived with for a time. When he'd shipped out, she had hung herself. "She thought I'd deserted her, you see. They told me I'd taken away her face," Johnson had said, shaking his head. "Shame's worse'n death to the Chinese."

Apparently, he had just shamed Fragrant Blossom terribly.

Someone began an awful pounding, and he realized it was Ah Tup, banging on the bedroom door and crying out in Chinese.

Trying not to imagine what Fragrant Blossom might be doing behind a locked door, Darcy ran from the study and took the stairs two at a time.

Chapter Four

By the time Blossom reached the bedroom, her dismay had turned to a burning anger. Did the master think she was some stupid *fan kow* who would allow him to take away her face? Did he think he could send her away so easily, before she had fulfilled her duty...

She slammed the door behind her, realizing instantly that Ah Tup had not returned to the room. Together they had planned that Ah Tup should look secretly around this barbaric house to discover entrances and exits, to find suitable hiding places for valuables and people in times of trouble and to make spy holes to see into other rooms.

Blossom flung herself onto the bed. She would find a way to stay here, even though it was a strange, uncivilized place. She owed much to Honorable Wu, and she would not fail him.

At the same time she wanted to be back in Canton, where she knew what was expected of her. Even Precious Jade, her thin face contorted by anger, would be a welcome sight.

The remembrance of Precious Jade turned her thoughts. How Honorable Wu's *tai tai* would smile if she learned of Blossom's failure! That must never, never be.

But how to stay? She got off the bed, the gown dragging on her like a yoke of oxen.

Clothing! He could not send her away if she had nothing to wear! Especially here, where they seemed so concerned about proper garments.

She heard Ah Tup outside, banging on the door. But she wouldn't open it. Not yet. She alone should bear the burden of the destruction she was about to carry out.

Quickly she went to their trunk and found one of the cooking knives. She snatched it up and prepared to cut to pieces the detestable thing she wore.

At that moment, the door crashed open. "Stop!" the master shouted as he rushed in and knocked the knife from her hand, sending her reeling against the bed.

She stared at him. He looked as if he were possessed by an evil spirit.

"What were you going to do?" he demanded, his chest heaving.

"I . . ." She didn't know what to say. One look at his face was enough to tell her that this was not the time to tell him that she was going to destroy his property. She had never seen a man so furious. Quickly she kowtowed, hiding her face from his glaring eyes, desperately trying to overcome her fear. It was clear she had severely displeased him and she didn't doubt he would beat her.

"Were you going to kill yourself?" he asked, and she realized that he sounded a little less angry.

Didn't he know that it was a terrible thing to kill yourself, because you would be forever doomed to wander the earth as a ghost? She didn't answer, but risked looking at him. Deep in his eyes, she saw that he, too, was afraid. Of her? Ah, perhaps he was afraid that she would haunt him if she killed herself.

Suddenly she felt not only a great sense of averted disaster, but even the beginning of power over him.

And then another feeling came, one that surprised her.

She didn't want him to fear her, not even her spirit. She wanted him to like her. She told herself that his fear was a weapon in her hands that she shouldn't hesitate to use.

Ah Tup hurried inside. "*Ayee,* Little Mother! What is going on here? The man ran up the stairs as if pursued—"

Blossom signaled her to be silent. She needed to be able to concentrate on the man. With reluctance, she lied to him. "I could not live with my shame if you send me away."

"I can't live with the embarrassment if people find out I have somebody like you living in my house."

"So, one of us must die." She bowed her head again and waited.

She heard the swish of skirt and knew Mrs. MacTavish had come. "Is she all right, Mr. Fitzroy?"

"As you can see, yes." The man's voice was cool and composed.

"What are you going to do?" Mrs. MacTavish asked.

"I was going to send them to stay in another house."

Blossom pulled out the other weapon in her arsenal, the one Precious Jade called her unyielding nature.

Blossom sat up and crossed her arms, staring at them both defiantly. "No. I *not* go." He would have to drag her away, which would at least make him lose face before her and the other servants.

She glanced at Ah Tup, but Ah Tup looked at her as if she'd just offered to cut off her own head.

The man suddenly reached out and took her by the hand, pulling hard. "Get up," he barked, dragging her to her feet.

Ah Tup began to protest, but Blossom gave a quick shake of the head. This was between her and her master, and she wanted no one else to interfere, not even Ah Tup.

"Mrs. MacTavish, we'll be in the study. I don't wish to be disturbed," he said, tugging Blossom toward the door.

She let him pull her along the hall and down the stairs, knowing full well she had little choice.

He took her into a dim room that stank of stale smoke. The walls had many shelves filled with strange objects. The furniture was dark and old and very shabby for a rich man's house.

"Sit down," he commanded, pointing to a chair.

It took Blossom a moment to maneuver the strange skirts, but she managed it.

The man sat opposite her. "What was that all about?" he asked, his voice hard and cold as the ice in the courtyard pond in winter.

"I not go."

"So you keep saying." He leaned back in his chair, eyeing her speculatively. "I thought you were supposed to do whatever I wanted."

Her eyes widened for an instant. At least he seemed to understand something. "Yes, honored lord. I do whatever you command, except leave you. It is my duty to stay, to pay debt."

She would have failed Honorable Wu and suffered all of Water Lily's teaching and that awful journey for nothing. "If I go, what happen to debt?"

"Forget the God-rotting debt. You don't understand, do you? *A person can not be a payment.* Not in England. We don't have slaves."

"How debt to be paid then?"

"Wu will have to pay in silver. He's owed me for years."

Honorable Wu didn't have enough silver to feed his family before she was sold. That money would be almost gone now. Honorable Wu might be thrown into the streets penniless, and that she couldn't bear.

She crossed her arms, determined to be strong. "I not go."

The man's brows furrowed ominously, but she kept talking. "I *not* go. You say I can choose. I choose to stay here."

His mouth narrowed into an even tighter line. "You can't. It isn't right. You have to go."

She decided it was time for the truth. "I *want* to be payment."

She went and knelt at his feet, looking up into his dark, dark eyes. "Honorable Wu has no money, honored lord. He not make me do this. I *choose*."

He looked down at her, his expression unreadable. "You would sell yourself to help a man who bought you as a slave? Who beat you? Who..." He stopped.

She shook her head. "Honorable Wu not beat me. *Tai tai*—she hate me always. Honorable Wu...a kind man. Like Father. If you not want me in bed, I work. I cook. Please, let me be payment."

Darcy Fitzroy was not a weak man, but it would have taken twice his strength of character to resist the soft pleas of Blossom as she knelt at his feet, begging to repay the debt of Wu Wing Toi.

When he spoke, his voice was gentler. "You simply cannot stay in my house. If people found out, it would ruin me. No one would even speak to me."

"You would truly lose face?" Blossom said, still not quite believing that a wealthy man would be condemned for keeping a concubine. "It is shame to keep concubine?"

"You are not my concubine and you are never going to be, but even if I don't touch a hair on your head, people would still assume that you are. That is completely unacceptable to me."

"You do not like women?"

"I never said that."

"You are eunuch?"

"God, no!"

"You keep your women elsewhere? You go to special house or floating pleasure boat?"

"Yes, some men do that." Darcy began to blush, feeling as if he'd just gotten lost in a maze of morality. It was ridiculous that this young woman could sit here discussing men and their vices.

"That not sense. Why go far when concubine can be in same household? Much more easier."

"The only woman a man is supposed to live with is his *wife.*"

"Poor men keep only wives. Rich man gain face by having concubines. And he will be more contented, too."

"How is the wife supposed to feel?"

She looked dumbfounded. "Feel?" she asked after a moment of consideration. "That does not matter. She does her duty as wife."

"That hardly seems fair," he said, pleased to think he had won his point—until Blossom spoke again, her delicate brows wrinkled with thought. "If I were wife, I think I feel good. Less duties if shared, *heya?*"

"What about love?"

"Love? What is this, love?"

"Love is...the special feeling between a man and a woman. How would you feel if the man you loved brought home another woman?"

"I don't understand."

"Wouldn't you feel sorry that your husband, the man you chose to marry, the man you cared for, wanted to be intimate with another woman right in your house?"

"Ah!" she said, and he thought she was beginning to see his point of view. "*You* not understand. Husband's family pick wife, her parents agree or not, and she goes to live with husband's family. It is no shame to her if he takes a concubine. He did not choose wife, and she did not choose husband. Marriage is for the good of the family, not the man. The man chooses concubine for pleasure. Is it not this way here, too?''

Darcy was about to answer in the negative, until he realized that, for many people, marriage was entered into for exactly the same reason: wealth and family. And many men had mistresses for their pleasure.

Even he himself had thought of marriage in such light, until this moment. Startled, and feeling adrift in very treacherous waters, he decided to get back to the reason this discussion had started. ''We were talking about the necessity of you leaving this house. Fragrant Blossom, you simply cannot stay in my house. In England, it isn't considered proper for a man to keep unmarried women he isn't related to in the house without a chaperon.'' He moved toward the window.

''What is chaperon?''

''Another woman who protects her.''

''Protects from who? From you?''

He turned to her abruptly. ''No, for God's sake!''

''Ah Tup be chaperon.''

''No. It still wouldn't be proper. I simply cannot have an unmarried woman living in my house.''

''The other servant, Mrs. MacTavish. She is married?''

''No. That is, she was...''

''So she is unmarried woman living in household.''

Why was it every time he talked with her, he felt less and less in control of the situation? ''Will you please get up off the floor,'' he growled, ''and sit in a chair?''

Blossom complied, after another struggle with several layers of petticoats and skirt.

''What do you remember about your life before Wu bought you?''

If he surprised her with his abrupt question, she hid it well, looking up at him steadily with her big blue eyes.

"I was very small, honored lord. I remember almost nothing."

"Tell me what you do remember."

"I was on ship. Not so big as ship Ah Tup and I come on, with Father. There is trouble." Her voice grew softer and softer. "He is afraid and hides me. There is fighting, I am found and..." She looked at the floor.

"Go on," he prompted, not unkindly.

"Father lies dead," she whispered. "The men take me away."

"And sold you to Wu?"

She nodded.

He toyed with some papers on his desk. "I see." He came toward her. "You're free now, Fragrant Blossom. You're not a slave anymore. You can go where you choose with no loss of face."

As his dark eyes gazed into hers, she felt a stab of fear. If he did not want her and sent her away, what was to become of her? Were she and Ah Tup to fend for themselves in this strange country?

"I'll provide a house and food for you, and I'm going to try to find out about your family. Perhaps there's a relative who can take you."

"But Honorable Wu..."

"I'll forget about the debt."

If anybody ever heard him say that, Darcy thought ruefully, they would have supposed he'd taken complete leave of his senses.

Perhaps he had, with her looking at him with that captivating mixture of confusion and hope.

She came to him, reached forward and took his hand. "Thank you," she whispered, pressing her lips to it. The sensation went directly to his blood, sending it throbbing through his body.

"Don't do that!" he ordered, snatching his hand away.

"I tell Ah Tup we are to leave," she said, her voice filled with genuine sorrow.

It suddenly occurred to him that it might be better to have her here, where he could keep an eye on her. If she was in another house, who knew what she might say to one of the servants—maybe that she "belonged" to him. What if Emmaline, who was notoriously curious, happened to come by to check her property? What if she found Blossom there? She'd never believe any explanation, let alone the truth. At least here the extremely trustworthy and close-lipped Mrs. MacTavish and Powlett would be in charge.

He was due to make a trip to Liverpool to see about some business there. This would be as good a time as any. Before he left he'd come up with some excuse to get Charles searching for information about English people who had disappeared near China. While he was gone he could come up with a better plan to dispose of her, and in the meantime she would be with people whose discretion he could trust.

"Perhaps," he said slowly, "perhaps it would be wiser to let you stay here—temporarily."

Her eyes sparkled and her smile was lovely. Too lovely, as if she had been granted her dearest wish.

What the hell was he doing? And whose wish was he really granting?

"Many thanks, honored lord. I do all orders. I swear it!"

He looked away. "Well, see that you do. Mrs. MacTavish can teach you what you need to know."

She nodded eagerly. "*Everything*, lord?"

He assented. "Yes, everything. Now go and ask Mrs. MacTavish to come here."

The girl smiled exultantly once more and went out.

He picked up a cheroot from the box on his desk and struck a match.

God, had he taken utter leave of his senses? If anybody found out about this, his hard-won social standing would crumble like a ship thrown against a reef. Not even Charles's influence would help. And Emmaline might destroy him.

The match burned his fingers, and he cursed as he dropped it on the carpet. As he bent over to pick it up, he became aware of Mrs. MacTavish standing in the doorway. He motioned her inside. "They're going to stay for a while," he said bluntly. "At least until I can find out where they should be sent."

"Very well, Mr. Fitzroy," Mrs. MacTavish said after a short pause that seemed to imply she was wondering what the hell he was doing, too.

"Tell the servants they're my guests."

Mrs. MacTavish nodded and went out.

Darcy rubbed his hand where Fragrant Blossom's lips had touched it. For a moment he let himself think about touching her. Kissing her. Making love with her.

Stop! he commanded himself. He had already showed incredible weakness by letting her remain under his roof. If he was to give in to his baser instincts, who knew what she might expect then?

No. He would avoid her like rats in a plague year.

"We are to stay!" Blossom said triumphantly to a gaping-mouthed Ah Tup.

"Oh, Mother," she breathed, "I knew he would not be able to resist you! Did you cry?"

"Huh!" Blossom said contemptuously. "No. Besides, he would not be moved by tears. I told him the truth, about Honorable Wu. Water Lily said *fan kow* have hearts of cotton, and I believe she was right."

"Well, that must have been the correct thing to do, since we are to stay. And you are to be his concubine?"

Blossom sat on the bed. "I don't know. I'm not sure. I offered to cook, and I thought that was what he would prefer me to do, until I was leaving. He looked as if he might be thinking of bedding me, but—" she gestured helplessly "—who can tell with these foreign devils? Apparently it is considered a great wrong to keep a concubine in the house. And he talked about something called love."

"What is that?"

"I don't know, but it is a special feeling, he said, between a husband and wife."

"Perhaps he meant respect, *heya?*"

Blossom frowned. "Maybe."

"Could it be that he meant satisfying desires?"

"I don't know, but it seemed more than that, somehow." A touch of regret crept into her voice. "I think it is something they set great store in. I want to find out more about it."

Ah Tup looked skeptical. "It may be another stupid barbarian notion."

Blossom tried to tell herself that Ah Tup was probably right, but she couldn't help remembering the softness that had come into the man's voice when he talked of love.

"Do not despair, Mother. Maybe he needs more time. Or maybe, when we learn more of their ways, we'll know better what to do."

Blossom nodded, realizing that for the first time in her life, she might not be able to talk about something with her friend. She couldn't explain that, deep in her heart, she wanted to hear that softness in his voice every time he spoke to her. "Did you discover anything?" she asked after a moment of silence.

Ah Tup sniffed derisively. "They have no secret passage of escape. They have no spying places into any of the rooms—at least that I could find. There is another stairway that leads to the kitchen, though. Above us, under the roof, there is a place one could hide, I suppose. To see the street, you must use the master's bedchamber."

"So little protection?"

Ah Tup shrugged. "Everything here is so strange. There are many servants: cook, girls to clean, and the Crow Woman and Chief Eunuch. But only the Crow Woman and the Chief Eunuch *live in the house.*"

Blossom's face reflected her puzzlement. "Where do the others sleep? There is another building outside?"

Ah Tup shook her head. "They come from far away, every day. Outside there is only a tangled mess that is meant for a garden." Her mouth twisted with disgust. "It looks as if it has not been properly tended in ten years!"

"I hardly know what to do or think all the time," Blossom said. "It is so confusing and nothing seems to make sense. At least we are to stay. The man seems compassionate, for all his proudness and irritability."

"I would be irritable, too, surrounded by all this foolishness," Ah Tup said. "Do you think we will work in the kitchen, then?"

Blossom smiled. "I think perhaps not, if I have more time. I would not wish to go back to that." They both nodded, remembering the long hours of hard work and the lash of the willow rod if Precious Jade or the cook was displeased. "I will become his concubine and Honorable Wu's debt will be paid."

Blossom didn't tell her that she was beginning to believe she would enjoy the paying.

"Ah, Captain Driscoll!" Charles Horton-Smythe pushed closer to his quarry in the crowded pub. It took all of his self-control not to let his disgust of the place and the lower-class scum imbibing in it to show. The stench of stale beer, gin and unwashed bodies sickened him, reminding him of the times he'd had to drag his worthless father from similar places. The old sot and Charles's equally worthless elder brother, who was clearly bent on following in his pater's footsteps, couldn't even die so that Charles could come into the family title, practically the only thing they had to bequeath him.

He reached the captain. "Good to see you, old man," he drawled. "Delighted! Wonderful job, what, bringing the ship to port after all that trouble! We'd given you up for lost."

Driscoll, who'd been a seaman for nearly fifty years, barely nodded at Charles as he made his way toward him. The captain respected Darcy, as one seaman to another, but he clearly had no use for Charles Horton-Smythe.

Charles put a smile on his face. God, this place was almost as bad as the stinking chaos on the docks nearby, the myriad odors ranging from spices to tobacco to dry rot, and underneath it all the persistent stench of the river. A man could hardly think for the shouts of the dockworkers in a variety of tongues, not to mention the creaking of hawsers, the rattle of chains and the thudding roll of casks. But he was here to talk to Driscoll, and talk to him he would. "I say, Driscoll, interesting cargo, eh?"

Driscoll nodded, staring down into his ale.

"I never thought that damned rascal Wu would pay up." The captain shrugged his shoulders.

Charles pressed his lips together. The captain was obviously not loquacious even when drinking. "Must have been a hell of a voyage."

Driscoll snorted. "I hate havin' women on board. Bad luck, by God!"

"Women? What women?"

"Didn't Darcy tell you? That miserable Wu sent women to pay his debt."

Charles took a gulp of the terrible brew he held to cover his shock. Women! Wu Wing Toi had paid with *women!*

"Cursed creatures! Makes the men nervous, too, and they spend too much time dandifyin' themselves when they ought to be workin'. Kept 'em in their cabin, till Fitzroy took 'em off my hands."

Charles recovered sufficiently to speak. "Oriental girls can be quite fascinating, or so I'm told."

Driscoll looked at him sharply. "I don't think Mr. Fitzroy took quite that view on it, sir."

"No, I daresay he wouldn't." It was well-known around the business community that Darcy Fitzroy was notoriously upright, even to the point of prudery. Nobody but Charles, and the married women involved, knew about Darcy's liaisons.

Driscoll looked at his interlocutor. "I suppose he didn't tell you the rest of it then. They both wasn't Chinese."

This time Charles didn't even try to hide his surprise while Driscoll morosely gulped his ale. "What *was* the other one?"

"Don't know. Don't care to know. But them blue eyes don't belong to an Oriental."

"My, my, Captain. How astonishing! The things one encounters when doing business in a foreign country, eh?"

"I tried to tell that fool Mitchell I wouldn't take 'em, but he wouldn't take no for an answer. Threatened to go to the government. Threatened to have Fitzroy take my command away. God, the man thinks he's a bloody missionary!"

"Perhaps he felt sorry for them."

"Oh, he felt somethin' for the blue-eyed one, all right. Stupid young ass. Well, she's a pretty thing at that, but after years with the Chinese..." He left the rest of the sentence to Charles's very vivid imagination. "I wonder what Mr. Fitzroy aims to do with 'em."

"I really don't know, Captain, but I'm sure he won't do anything ungentlemanly."

Driscoll nodded his agreement as Charles set down his drink. "I must be going, Captain. Life of a man of business, eh, what? It's been a pleasure having a chat with you. Goodbye!"

Charles hurried out into the night air. So Wu had paid his debt with two women. And to think they were sent to Fitzroy, who wanted so much to be a gentleman that he'd probably send them to a home for orphans or some such thing.

What a waste. If they'd been sent to *him,* he would have known exactly what to do with them, preferably both at the same time.

His pulse began to quicken. Perhaps he would make a visit to the West End tonight to see if Warton had any new girls.

In the morning, he would pay a surprise visit on Fitzroy and see if the person in the pink garment had blue eyes.

Chapter Five

"This is a fork. This is a spoon. This is a knife," Mrs. MacTavish said, pointing at each article on the table in front of Blossom, who stared at the array of eating utensils and tried to concentrate. It was difficult with the man sitting at the other end of the table. To be sure he was ignoring her, reading some kind of paper thing covered in tiny writing, but she felt his presence nonetheless.

"Now, we'll begin with the porridge."

Blossom balked at the horrible mess in the bowl placed before her. "I to eat this?" she asked helplessly.

Mrs. MacTavish was clearly offended. "Of course you are. It'll make you good and strong. It sticks to your ribs."

"That I believe," Blossom said, shaking her head. She thought she heard a noise and looked up at the man, but he was now holding the paper thing in front of his face, so she couldn't see him. "This only for animals surely?"

"Animals?" Mrs. MacTavish said, sitting down on Blossom's right. "I should say not. Porridge is fit for the kings of Scotland."

Blossom gazed at the terrible gray lumpy food. She didn't remember what "king" meant, but it was probably some kind of farmer. Such a man might be expected to eat like one of his cows.

"Now, take your napkin and spread it on your lap."

Mrs. MacTavish demonstrated, and Blossom followed suit very carefully, picking up the large square cloth and placing it on her lap.

"You might like a little cream on your porridge." Mrs. MacTavish lifted a small pitcher and poured white liquid over top of the food in her bowl.

Blossom sighed and reached for the cream, pouring a liberal amount.

"Stop! That's enough! What are you trying to do?"

"Hide it," Blossom answered innocently. She may have to eat it, but she didn't have to look at it.

There was another sound at the far end of the table, and this time when she looked at the man, she realized his shoulders were shaking.

"You laugh, honored lord?"

The man put down his paper thing and she could see that she had guessed correctly.

"Now don't get upset or think you're losing face," he said, the smile disappearing. "I happen to agree with you."

Mrs. MacTavish gave him a fierce look.

"Don't *you* get upset, Mrs. MacTavish," he said. "Porridge may be the sacred food of the Scots, but even you have to admit it's not a pretty dish."

Mrs. MacTavish adjusted herself in her chair with an icy expression.

"Must I eat this, honored lord?"

"Well, you should try it. I guarantee it tastes better than it looks. And you simply must stop calling me 'honored lord.' I'm not a lord, and several people might even question my honor."

She found that incomprehensible. Sitting there, he was like an emperor or a general. Surely no dishonorable man could sit so straight, so proudly, so nobly, unless this place was filled with crazy people.

She had to admit that might be so, judging by her impressions so far.

"You should call me 'Mr. Fitzroy.'"

"Very well, Mis-ter Fizz-roy."

He smiled again, for a brief instant. "That'll do for a start."

The Chief Eunuch appeared in the doorway. "Sir, Mr. Horton-Smythe wishes to see you. I told him to wait in the drawing room."

"That's fortunate." Mr. Fitzroy stood up. "I wanted to see him first thing. I've decided to go to Liverpool."

"I understand you've had some very unusual guests?" Horton-Smythe smiled at the nervous little maid.

"I'm not supposed to say nothin' about that, sir," Sally said, shuffling her feet.

"Come, come, now, Sally," he said persuasively, moving a little closer to her in the drawing room, "I know all about them, of course. I *am* Mr. Fitzroy's partner, after all."

"Yes, sir," she said, clasping her hands over her stomach.

"Did you see them?"

She looked at him with wide brown eyes. "Oh, no, sir. They stay upstairs mostly."

Charles tried not to show his surprise. He wouldn't have thought Darcy would keep the "gift" here in his own house. "Are they upstairs now?"

"The servant one, she's havin' her breakfast in the kitchen. Th'other one, she's eatin' with Mr. Fitzroy in the morning room."

"Indeed? I believe I'll join Mr. Fitzroy in the morning room," he said, looking at the rather pretty young girl.

"Certainly, sir." She smiled innocently at him. "Thank you again for gettin' me this job, sir. I'm very grateful—and Mama is, too."

"Think nothing of it," he said. Her mother had been a servant of his family, left without a job when Charles's father had swallowed most of the family fortune in drink. He'd gotten Mrs. MacTavish to hire the girl after telling the kindhearted woman of the family's plight. Naturally he had counted on the girl's gratitude. It was very convenient having such a person in his partner's household, and already his idea was paying dividends. "Give my best to your good mother."

"Oh, I will, sir. I'll be sure to, sir." She curtsied.

"And I don't think you need mention this conversation to anyone else. They might misconstrue my attentions to you," he added with his most charming smile.

She blushed and for a moment he wondered just how grateful the pretty girl might be. However, at the moment he had more important matters to deal with.

"When will you be leaving?" Mrs. MacTavish asked.

"This afternoon," Mr. Fitzroy replied.

Blossom kept her gaze fastened on her uneaten porridge. Mrs. MacTavish got up. "Well, I'll have to get started with the packing."

"I did most of it this morning. I'll be taking my own carriage."

The housekeeper bustled to the door nonetheless. "I'll just make sure you've got everything, then. When should we expect you back?"

"In about a week."

Mrs. MacTavish left the room. Blossom had figured out that Mr. Fitzroy was going on a journey, but she had no idea where or for quite how long.

She felt miserable. She had truly failed. A lump came into her throat just as she realized Mr. Fitzroy was still standing by the door. She blinked rapidly, to subdue her tears, and looked at him.

The minute her gaze met his, he looked away. "Don't worry. Mrs. MacTavish will take good care of you."

Blossom stood up slowly.

"A week's not long, only seven days."

She walked toward him.

"I'll tell Mrs. MacTavish to follow your wishes, so that you'll be comfortable here."

She looked at his face, trying to see into the depths of his dark brown eyes.

"I'd better see what Charles wants and let him know of my plans," he said, but he stood absolutely motionless until they both heard footsteps approaching.

Mr. Fitzroy darted from the room. She heard him say, "Charles! How convenient of you to come this morning."

Left alone in the room, it was all Blossom could do to keep from shouting with triumph. She had not failed yet, not judging by the expression in his eyes when he looked at her.

She heard the men go into the study. Then she quickly went up the back stairs.

She had a week—what had he said?—seven days. In that time she could surely learn much about him, including what manner of gratification he most preferred in bed.

She went into the bedroom directly over the study, the first place Ah Tup had made a spy hole, under the rug. It had taken Ah Tup several minutes of working with the slender knife to create it. From above you could only see the area directly in front of Mr. Fitzroy's huge desk, but you could hear what was being said quite clearly.

She struggled with her skirt and petticoats until she could get down close to the hole.

"Liverpool, eh?" said a voice she didn't recognize.

"Yes," Mr. Fitzroy replied nonchalantly. "Oh, and there's something else I'd like your help with. I'm trying to locate an old friend, and I wonder if you know who I could contact."

"About your friend?"

"No, I meant someone to do the looking."

"Ah, detective or something, old man?" the other man said. "I might be able to find such a person."

"Good. The sooner the better."

"Not in any trouble, I trust?"

"Oh, not at all. Strictly a personal matter. Now, while I'm in Liverpool, I'm going to see about a new design for sails..."

The other man came into view. He was about the same age as Mr. Fitzroy but dressed in a much more flamboyant manner. His movements were graceful, almost catlike. In fact he resembled nothing so much as a cat eyeing the fish in the marketplace as if wondering when it could grab one.

The conversation became too complicated for Blossom to follow, and seemed to be all about ships and crews and provisions and goods. Nevertheless, she kept watching. As she did, she began to wonder more and more why Mr. Fitzroy dealt with this man. She had never seen a face less indicative of an honest nature. He reminded her of Li Chang, one of Honorable Wu's supposed friends. He had dined several times at Honorable Wu's house, praised his host's intelligence as a merchant and complimented him on his food. However, when Wu had asked Li Chang for help, the man refused.

This man below was like that, smiling only with his lips, while his eyes...his eyes made her feel as cold as a chunk of ice.

She would have to find out more about this Horton-Smythe. It was her duty to protect her master, as well as please him.

"What, may I ask, are you doing?"

Blossom scrambled to her knees, deftly pushing the rug back into place as she turned toward Mrs. MacTavish. "I...in China, it is custom to..."

Mercifully she didn't have to come up with a plausible lie, because Mrs. MacTavish interrupted. "You'll get your dress dirty, whatever you did in China. Now get up. You never finished your porridge."

Blossom obeyed at once, keeping her eyes respectfully downcast as they returned to the morning room.

She tried a spoonful of the substance in her bowl and, to her surprise, found it not unpalatable, although as thick as mud. "Mrs. MacTavish," she said, "who is Horton-Smythe?"

"The Honorable Charles Horton-Smythe is Mr. Fitzroy's business partner."

"What means that, bizz-nezz part-ner?"

"He works with Mr. Fitzroy and owns half of Fitzroy Shipping."

"Ah." He would have to be studied most carefully, if he had a position of trust. She took another spoonful of porridge. "Mr. Fitzroy said you are to teach me things."

"That's right, dear," the older woman said, eating her porridge with gusto.

"I wish to know what Mr. Fitzroy like."

"Oh, he's a fine man. Not very talkative, but fair and kind, really, underneath."

Blossom shook her head. "No, I mean, what he like in bed?"

Mrs. MacTavish's brow furrowed. "Crisp, clean sheets. But you're not to do any such work, I've been told."

Blossom shook her head again, searching for the words she needed. "I mean, what he like to *do* in bed. With women."

Mrs. MacTavish spluttered. "I'm sure I have no idea!" she cried, wiping her chin. "It's none of my business. And it's not *yours* either! It's simply not discussed...."

As the flabbergasted woman went on and on, Blossom stared down at the porridge. Clearly Mrs. MacTavish was not going to help her please Mr. Fitzroy.

She would have to find out these things for herself.

One week later, Darcy jumped from his carriage and hurried into his house. He was in good spirits, for his trip to Liverpool had been quite successful. He'd ordered two new ships at bargain prices and convinced one of the finest merchant captains to take command of one of the vessels. He'd also managed to sell some of the silk from *China Lady*.

"Good afternoon, Mr. Fitzroy," Powlett said, his deep musical Welsh voice betraying no emotion whatsoever when Darcy entered the house.

"Has Jeremy arrived yet?" Darcy asked, handing his hat to the butler.

"No, sir."

"Show him into the study when he does."

"Very good, sir."

Darcy hesitated, wanting to ask Powlett how the last few days had passed, but somehow Powlett's reticence forbade such a question.

Then Darcy realized something had changed while he was gone. There was a huge mirror—his bedroom mirror, unless he was terribly mistaken—on the landing of the stairs. He looked at Powlett.

"I understand, sir, it's to turn back harmful spirits or something of that ilk."

"I see." It didn't take a genius to know whose idea that must have been. He decided to ignore the mirror for now, and went to his study.

He halted on the threshold of his inner sanctum and stared in amazement. His room appeared to have been vandalized. Many of the books were missing from the shelves, replaced with a few personal items from his bedroom: a cigar box Charles had given him, a small framed cameo of his mother, a shrunken head he'd picked up in Borneo and right there, in the middle of the shelf behind his desk, a small statue of a satyr with enlarged genitalia. Emmaline had given it to him, claiming that it reminded her of him.

There were even a few flower arrangements, if the twigs and single blooms sticking out of vases could be called arrangements. Another large mirror, one he distinctly recalled banishing to the garret, now hung over the fireplace. And to top it all off, someone had tidied his desk.

"Mrs. MacTavish!" he bellowed, his anger surging like lava from a volcano.

His housekeeper appeared almost instantly. "Yes, sir?" She looked at the room, and her mouth fell open. Her expression would have been comical, except that Darcy was in no mood for humor.

"What in heaven's name have you done?"

Mrs. MacTavish moved her mouth, but nothing came out for a minute. Then she exploded. "Those two! I told them they were *not* to come into this room. I thought they understood the last time I caught them at the door!"

Now it was Darcy's turn to be surprised, and that lessened his anger somewhat. "You had nothing to do with this?"

"No, sir, and I'm very sorry that it happened. I'll talk to them right away."

"Never mind just now, Mrs. MacTavish. Come into the room for a moment, if you please."

Frowning deeply, the housekeeper complied.

"What else have they done?" he demanded.

"Except for this foolishness about some heathen notions of good and evil spirits and sneaking into this room like thieves, nothing that I know of. I thought they were being most congenial. And Blossom—that's what we call her, sir—her English is considerably improved."

He knew Mrs. MacTavish was scrupulously honest, but her answer did little to diminish his frustration. He felt as if his whole world had turned upside down since Wu's "payment" had arrived. Even in Liverpool, he couldn't stop thinking about Fragrant Blossom, and his dreams had been filled with images of her. "Send her to me."

"Yes, sir." Mrs. MacTavish took a deep breath. "But first may I ask how much longer they are to stay here?"

"I don't have any idea, but the sooner I can get rid of them both, the better."

"I must say, then, sir, that I think they should go to church."

Darcy glared at his housekeeper. Was everyone in his household going to start giving orders or complaining? "Why?"

"Because they're heathens. And some of the things she asks...I think church would do them both good."

"Mrs. MacTavish, if it keeps them out of my study and my mirrors in their proper places, I don't care if you take them to Timbuktu. Now *get her!*"

"At once, sir."

Darcy paced in his violated room and threw himself into his favorite chair. This was intolerable, really intolerable. He'd send them away tonight, to that house of Emmaline's if need be. Anything was better than having his household disrupted this way.

He picked up a cheroot and lit it. Besides, Jeremy was due to arrive soon. He couldn't have his little brother finding two strange—*very* strange—women in the house.

Yes, it was time he got them out of his house and out of his life.

When the housekeeper summoned her, Blossom suddenly felt overcome with nervousness. She had worked very hard since Mr. Fitzroy had gone, learning everything the Crow Woman and the Chief Eunuch could teach her. Of course, compared to Water Lily's teachings, theirs had been easy, but tiring nonetheless.

They had made a big fuss about her desire to move the mirrors, but she supposed that couldn't be helped. It was too bad they didn't know about the *ch'i* and *sha,* but that didn't mean the evil *sha* would keep away. She had persisted and would have kept at it for days, as they finally realized.

The worst had been getting into Mr. Fitzroy's study. She and Ah Tup had had to sneak downstairs in the middle of the night to make it ready for him. They had removed several dusty, dirty writings from the shelves and added what she assumed were personal mementos. These would make the beneficent *ch'i* linger in the room, and the mirror would keep it from leaving by the chimney.

Blossom hurried down the stairs and through the hall, not stopping to catch her breath. Surely Mr. Fitzroy would be happy with her now that she had made his room much more comfortable.

"Mr. Fitzroy, we so happy you have come home!" she cried, smiling brightly as she rushed through the door, her English the worse for her excitement.

Mr. Fitzroy didn't smile back.

Of course! She had forgotten to curtsy. It had taken her two days to master that. When he still didn't smile, she feared her effort was a failure.

Barely glancing at her, he gestured toward a chair opposite his imposing desk. She sat down, wondering what she had forgotten to do.

"Nobody but myself and Mrs. MacTavish comes into this room. Do you understand?" he said, his voice cold and his eyes unreadable.

She fought the tears that came into her eyes. Obviously her efforts to please him had had the opposite effect.

"I'm sorry you are not pleased, Mr. Fitzroy," she said, her careful choice of words and attempt to speak properly making her talk slowly.

Darcy suddenly felt like the worst dunderheaded fool on the face of the earth. He knew she was trying not to cry. He had acted like an overbearing brute. It wasn't reasonable to expect her to understand English ways after all those years in China. When he spoke, his voice was considerably calmer and gentler. "I realize you're only doing what you think is right, but I prefer this room as it was."

She nodded, and a single tear began to roll down her smooth, pale cheek. Quickly she wiped it away, but it had already burned his heart as if it had been acid. "Perhaps it is best that Ah Tup and I leave soon."

"That will be as soon as I can arrange it."

"Is it my big feet?"

"Hell, no!"

Another tear rolled down her cheek. He discovered that he hated being the cause of her sorrow, so he said something that he thought would make her feel better. "Mrs. MacTavish has been pleased."

She nodded, but she kept her gaze on the carpet. He found himself staring at her slender hands. Her fingers were intertwined and clasped together tightly.

"Mrs. MacTavish also thinks you should go to church."

She lifted her eyes and looked at him with a sad, bewildered expression. "What is church?"

"It's a place, a building, where we worship God."

"It is a temple?"

"Something like that."

"I cannot go to such a place."

Now *he* was bewildered. "Why not?"

"I make a promise to my father not to go into temples."

"I thought you said he was dead."

"Yes, Mr. Fitzroy. But I made a promise and I must keep it."

He heard her unyielding determination and decided it was best to drop the subject for the moment. "As you wish," he said. His idea that she might be the daughter of missionaries must be wrong. No missionary would make his daughter promise not to go to church.

"I go now, please, Mr. Fitzroy," she said quietly. The sadness in her voice smote him as completely as a sword through his heart. She stood up and turned toward the door.

"Blossom..."

She turned slightly toward him and he approached her. "Please try and understand."

"I understand," she said softly. "I understand that everything I do here is wrong. That I can never please you. That you do not want me. That I have failed."

He put his hands on her shoulders and turned her so that she faced him. "It has to be this way, for both our sakes."

She looked at him, her luminous blue eyes filled with unshed tears, her cheeks pale and her lips trembling. Without thinking, he pulled her closer and kissed her, lightly at first, then more deeply as she pressed against him.

It was like no other kiss in his entire life, at once somehow innocent and experienced. As if she'd never been kissed before but still knew exactly how to respond, moving her lips and body so that his passion ignited like lightning.

Of course, his mind shouted, she's been taught to be a whore!

He drew back as if she'd slapped him, horrified at the force of his response. She smiled at him, and it seemed a triumphant one.

"Please go," he said harshly, turning his back to her. If she cried, he didn't want to see her.

Blossom obeyed, hurrying upstairs and throwing herself on her bed. Ah Tup bent over her, speaking soothingly, trying to find out what had happened. After the first storm of weeping had passed, Blossom became aware of her friend's presence and sat up slowly. "We must leave here. I can never, never please him. Everything I do is wrong, even to a kiss."

Chapter Six

Darcy kicked the side of the fireplace and cursed himself for a weak-willed fool.

I must never forget what she is, he commanded himself. It didn't matter that she looked as innocent as an angel. That was undoubtedly a ruse.

Unfortunately, despite his efforts, in his heart he knew that he was weakening and might not be able to resist temptation much longer.

"Mr. Jeremy has arrived," Powlett intoned from the threshold of the study. "Shall I send him here or to the drawing room, sir?"

"Here," Darcy replied. He lit another cheroot to calm his nerves and wondered again what Jeremy wanted that was worth a trip to London.

He managed to smile as his brother strode into the room, an easy, affable expression on his face.

"How are you, Darcy?" Jeremy said, the refinement in his voice as pleasing as the casual air with which he wore his finely tailored clothing.

"Fine," Darcy replied, offering Jeremy a cheroot.

"No, thank you." Jeremy looked around the tidy room. "My word, what's happened here?"

Darcy scowled. "New maid," he lied. He sat on the chair behind his desk and motioned for Jeremy to sit, too. "Now, what brings you to the city before the end of term?"

"I would like you to give me something."

Darcy was rather surprised by the blunt nature of his brother's statement. "Anything—within reason, of course."

"Good. I want your blessing."

"For what?"

"I'm going to get married."

Darcy slowly got to his feet and walked toward the fireplace.

Jeremy smiled. "She's a lovely girl, Darcy. You'll like her. I would say you'd love her, too, but I reserve that right for myself."

"Who is she?" Darcy asked without turning around.

"Her name's Elizabeth Hazelmore. Her father's a minister at the most charming little church in a village just outside of London. I met her brother at school. They're as poor as the proverbial church mice, but Elizabeth is rich in goodness and beauty...."

Darcy, his face a mask of suppressed rage, slowly turned and looked at Jeremy. One hand rested on the mantelpiece; the other, truer to his emotional state, was bunched in a fist in the pocket of his trousers. He kept it there because he was very tempted to use it on Jeremy. "After all I've done for you," he said coldly, "all the money I've spent on you, this is how you repay me? By marrying some penniless parson's daughter?"

Jeremy stared at Darcy incredulously. "It doesn't matter that Elizabeth isn't wealthy."

"That's because you've never had to think about money. Or work for it, either."

"Whose fault is that? I never asked you to spend money on me. I never asked you for anything!"

"Damn right you didn't—because I've been looking after you since you could barely walk."

Jeremy got to his feet, thrusting back his chair so hard it hit the nearby table. "Look, Darcy, I appreciate what you've done for me. I'll say thank you as much as you'd like, but you're not going to tell me who I can or cannot marry!"

"And how far do you think you'll get without me running your life? What do you know about the world? All you know is the soft life you've been living at Oxford, thanks to *my* money and *my* hard work!"

Jeremy took a deep breath and tried to stay calm. By now he should be used to Darcy's easily aroused ire. "Maybe I don't know business," he said, his voice softer although no less determined, "but I can find myself a job. I can earn enough to keep Elizabeth and myself."

Darcy's expression became mocking. "Perhaps you should ask this Elizabeth how she'll feel living on what only *you* can provide."

Jeremy fought the anger building inside him at the sneer in Darcy's voice. "Love is more important than money, Darcy, as you'll probably find out some day. And we don't have quite your social ambitions."

It was a low blow in this fight of words, since Jeremy knew precisely how important his brother's social ambitions were, but he felt driven to say it, to hurt Darcy as much as Darcy was hurting him. All he wanted to do was marry sweet, gentle Elizabeth, whom his brother was accusing of being mercenary.

"It's a damn good thing you don't, then, if you're bent on marrying a penniless girl. She'll ruin you."

"You've never even met her!" Jeremy said angrily. "She's all I want out of life, Darcy. We're going to be very happy together. You'll see."

"No, I won't see." Darcy's fingers tightened on his cheroot until it broke in two pieces. "If you marry this girl, I'll never see you again."

Jeremy's eyes widened. "You mean it, don't you?"

Darcy didn't say anything. He didn't have to.

"I won't even try to reason with you now. I would be wasting my time. I hope you're willing to change your mind about this, Darcy, because I'm not going to change my mind about marrying the girl I love."

With a look that was the image of Darcy's own stubborn expression, Jeremy turned and stalked out of the room.

Blossom and Ah Tup gently rolled back the carpet in the bedroom over the study. They had heard the muffled sounds of angry voices when Blossom had stopped weeping. Wondering what could be happening, they had come to listen.

They crept back to their bedroom and looked at each other.

"The master was very angry, wasn't he? Even more than we have seen yet seen," Ah Tup whispered, as if they might be overheard as easily as they had listened to the quarrel in the study.

"So that is Younger Brother," Blossom said softly. "He is very like Mr. Fitzroy."

"The Chief Eunuch said he was to come today, but I don't think the Chief Eunuch expected the master to be angry. He almost smiled when he spoke of Younger Brother in the kitchen."

"Yet there must be trouble between them, since Younger Brother doesn't live here."

Ah Tup nodded her agreement. "I think you must be right, Mother. Unless it is just another unusual custom, like the servants who live someplace else."

"Perhaps that is the custom here, that each lives in a separate place, brothers, sisters, wives and concubines? Perhaps it is a sign of great wealth to own many houses." Blossom smiled. "It could be that I even gain face by living in a different place than Mr. Fitzroy!"

Ah Tup's face showed her admiration. "*Ayee!* You are so clever! We should have guessed that before!"

"Now if only I could be certain that I do not displease him," she said thoughtfully. "I seem to anger him even when I..." She hesitated, for some reason not willing to discuss the kiss with her friend.

"Maybe it is his nature to be always finding fault, like Precious Jade, who would find fault with the gods themselves if they were ever so crazy as to appear to her. If the master is quick to anger, that might explain why Younger Brother lives elsewhere, too, and why they fought."

Ah Tup began making tea, real tea, not the strange foreign brew. "Could you understand why the master was angry at Younger Brother?"

Blossom began undoing the back of her dress, wanting to get out of it. "It was about marriage."

"He doesn't like the master's choice for his wife?"

Blossom wriggled out of the gown and sighed deeply. "No, it seems Younger Brother has made his own choice."

Ah Tup stopped in the middle of pouring boiling water. "What? His own choice? No wonder the master was furious."

"I *think* that was the reason." Blossom drew on a robe and took the tea from Ah Tup. As she sat sipping it, she remembered that Younger Brother had talked of this thing "love" again. It puzzled her, because she couldn't decide what they meant by it. After several minutes, she gave up trying.

"I think we must find out more about this Elizabeth Hazelmore," she said. "It is my duty to protect Mr. Fitzroy and his family, and if this girl is not suitable for Younger Brother, the marriage must be stopped."

"Younger Brother was most lacking in proper respect, was he not? And Elizabeth—what an impossible name!"

"It is the way of brothers, I suppose, to lack respect."

"Do you think Mr. Fitzroy is annoyed because he wishes to marry before Younger Brother?"

Blossom set down her cup slowly. Mr. Fitzroy taking a wife! Another woman being kissed by him, being in bed with him, experiencing the zenith with him. She would feel like a beggar forced to only look at a rich man's feast.

After a long pause she said, "It will be hard to obey his *tai tai* after so much freedom."

Ah Tup got a conspiratorial expression on her face. "If you were to bear the first son, you would be in a position of great power in the household, despite a wife."

Blossom frowned. "To do that, he must take me into his bed."

Ah Tup looked at her. "You have been trained by Water Lily! Sooner or later—depending on these strange *fan kow* customs—he will."

Blossom knew that she wanted that very much, and it had little to do now with paying a debt. She wanted him because her heart beat with the fury of thunder when he stood near her. Her blood throbbed with desire when he looked at her. The house had seemed as empty as a tomb without him. The mere sight of him filled her with happiness. And the thought of him taking another woman filled her with agony.

"He will," she said with renewed determination.

Darcy sighed and leaned back into the tub of water until his back rested against the metal. There was nothing like a hot soak after a long journey—and a heated argument. He closed his eyes, letting his muscles relax.

He could fall asleep, if he could stop thinking about Jeremy and Blossom. He'd go to Emmaline's dinner party tonight and remind her again about renting that house. Then he'd be partly rid of one of his problems. Charles would probably be there, so he could find out if Charles had hired anyone to find information about the girl's origin.

He relaxed a little more and sank deeper into the tub. As for Jeremy, maybe it was a youthful infatuation that would end naturally. He really shouldn't have gotten so angry.

He heard a sound and opened his eyes lazily—then sat up abruptly, sloshing water over the edge of the tub and onto his bedroom carpet.

Blossom, wearing only her thin silk robe and an enticing smile, stood at the foot of the tub.

"What the hell!"

She let her robe slip to the floor. "I come to wash."

He thought she was about to step into the tub, but instead she picked up the soap and a cloth, letting it trail in the water as she walked toward the head of the tub.

"This isn't proper," he protested. He wanted to get up out of the tub, but his robe was just out of his reach. God, he was trapped!

She knelt beside the tub and leaned forward, her naked breasts almost touching the water as she rubbed the soap into the cloth.

"Put some clothes on," he said, trying to sound angry. Unfortunately, he only succeeded in sounding hoarse.

"Water would not be good for robe," she said, beginning to rub the cloth lightly over his chest.

Closing his eyes, he allowed himself to feel one moment of pure sensual pleasure before he reached out and grabbed her wrist. "Stop it. Right now."

"I wish only to please you," she whispered, leaning closer.

"I said..."

He never finished, because her lips touched his. Gently. Softly. Compelling him to respond.

It was as if the rest of the world and its rules and prohibitions ceased to exist. Suddenly nothing mattered except her. Her lips. Her tongue. Her breasts. Her body.

His mouth captured hers, sending dizzying waves of desire coursing through his body. Without breaking the fiery kiss, he twisted, put his hands under her arms and lifted her into the warm, soapy water. His hands caressed her slender body, cupping her breasts as she moaned with pleasure and longing, awakening a passion that was primitive and powerful. Slowly she inched her body upward so that he could kiss her silken flesh.

Her movement overbalanced the tub. It tipped sideways, spilling them and several gallons of water, onto the floor.

Panting, Darcy stood up and helped Blossom to her feet. They stood looking at each other's face, and in her eyes he saw the same blatant, primal desire that he felt.

He heard footsteps on the stairs. Quickly he turned and reached for her robe, tossing it to her before getting his own and hurrying into it.

"Get out of here before Mrs. MacTavish comes!" he ordered.

She obeyed as he picked up a towel and began mopping up the floor.

Blossom ran down the hall and closed the door just as she heard Mrs. MacTavish asking what had happened. She heard Mr. Fitzroy say something about falling asleep. Leaning back against the closed door, she let her breath out slowly.

"Well?" Ah Tup asked, taking note of Blossom's damp garment.

"Almost," Blossom replied, smiling triumphantly.

A few hours later, Darcy sat in his carriage on the way to Emmaline's large house in Mayfair. His nerves were still in what Mrs. MacTavish would call "a state," between his anger at Jeremy, the upheaval in his house and the lustful episode in his bedroom.

He scowled as he looked out of the window of the carriage, seeing little beyond the sooty fog that coated the city.

He vowed not to think about Blossom anymore tonight. Tonight he would concentrate on Emmaline. Perhaps that was what he needed: a night with his sensual, experienced mistress, a woman who could have had any number of lovers and had chosen him. She wasn't ordered to make love to him or trained to be a whore. Emmaline took lovers because she wanted them as much as they wanted her. Besides, she would make sure there was no scandal attached to their liaison, whereas if word got out that he was keeping a concubine in his house, all hell would break loose.

But he wasn't going to think about Blossom tonight.

He wouldn't think about Jeremy, either. He still couldn't believe that his younger brother would do such a thing to him—would disregard his advice and wisdom, and marry the daughter of a poor country parson without connections or fortune to recommend her.

Love wouldn't do them any good when it came to food or lodgings. Love wouldn't get Jeremy a position as fine as the one that awaited him at Fitzroy Shipping, provided he saw the error of his ways.

He had raised Jeremy with but one objective: to become a successful man. And to be a successful man meant acceptance into the highest level of society.

He had done his best to achieve such acceptance for himself, but even as he alighted from his carriage at Lord Whitmore's palatial mansion, he knew he was only tolerated by the upper-class people he would find there because investing in his shipping company had made some of them even richer, and because Lady Whitmore invited him. No doubt some wondered if her interest in him was more than financial, but no one would dare say so in public.

He handed his hat to the stiff butler at the door and went into the drawing room.

The spacious area was filled to capacity. The bright gowns of the ladies were as colorful as a market garden and highlighted the creamy complexion of their faces and shoulders. Around the edges of the room, in black coats and trousers, stood the most influential men in London.

Darcy's mood lightened. He was standing in the midst of the elite. Whether they accepted him or not, he was here.

Emmaline, beautiful in a gown of rose-colored silk trimmed with intricate lace, crossed the room toward him. Her lips smiled graciously.

For the first time since he'd met her, Darcy realized that Emmaline's eyes never smiled. They had never reflected any genuine joy in all the time he had known her. The realization made him think of other eyes, blue eyes that seemed to communicate their possessor's feelings better than any words.

But he wasn't going to think about Blossom tonight.

He smiled at Emmaline.

"Mr. Fitzroy! I'm so happy to see you," she said, meaning it in her own special way.

He had always admired the way she could make a crowded room feel as intimate as a boudoir. "The pleasure is all mine," he replied.

"Mr. Horton-Smythe is here already, with someone he told me you would be very interested in meeting. His name is Edward Thresham. His father is a very wealthy landowner. I also understand that his mother's quite an intellectual, although you'd never know it to judge by Mr. Thresham. He's very amusing." She took Darcy's arm and steered him toward the conservatory. "In fact, he's a bit of a wastrel, I think. He's been all over the world and tells the most fascinating stories. You and he should have quite a lot in common."

"As one seafaring man to another?"

She squeezed his arm. "As one *man* to another—and I'll expect you to tell me all his *best* stories."

Darcy grinned. Emmaline's taste in stories was decidedly unladylike, but their effect on her performance in bed more than made up for any reluctance he might have had recounting ribald tales to a woman.

"Charles wouldn't tell me why he brought Mr. Thresham here," she said offhandedly, again making her gracious, shallow smile. Nevertheless Darcy knew she was definitely not pleased that Charles hadn't told her more.

When they reached the conservatory, he saw Charles standing with another man beside a very large, no doubt rare and costly palm tree.

"Here he is," Emmaline said to Charles.

"Ah, Fitzroy, old man. Glad to see you. I'd like you to meet Edward Thresham."

Charles turned to the man beside him. His back was half to Emmaline. She frowned, and Darcy realized Charles had just blundered. No one turned even a part of his back to Lady Emmaline Whitmore.

Thresham made a slight bow and grinned. "Pleased to meet you," he said, his voice cultured and with a hint of laughter. "Charmed again, Lady Whitmore."

As Emmaline smiled at Thresham and Darcy wished the man had never been born, Charles leaned closer. "I've got a man looking into that little matter of a missing person," he whispered.

Darcy nodded. He was pleased, of course, that somehow he might solve the riddle of Blossom's identity, so that he could find some relative to relieve him of her. He was disturbed, he told himself, because Thresham was too handsome, too charming and altogether too well-bred. Now Emmaline wouldn't leave unless a disaster—or a spoiled dinner—threatened, and he couldn't ask Thresham the questions he wanted to, at least not without arousing suspicion.

"Knows lots about the Chinese, he tells me. Customs, trade, all that sort of thing," Charles said.

"Mr. Horton-Smythe says you're very interested in the Orient, Mr. Fitzroy." Thresham flashed a brilliant smile as much at Emmaline as Darcy.

Darcy felt a rush of jealousy but knew he wanted Thresham's knowledge of the Chinese, even if he wasn't going to think about Blossom tonight. "As a matter of fact, I am. We do quite a bit of trade in Canton, so I'm always looking out for helpful information. The Chinese are rather close-lipped about their customs, aren't they?"

Thresham laughed. Even the man's laugh was attractive, damn him. "That's one way to put it. Actually, they're xenophobic."

"I'm afraid you'll have to explain that to me," Emmaline said, somewhat to Darcy's relief, since he didn't have any idea what the word meant, either.

"They don't like foreigners, whom they consider barbarians. You see, they believe that they are the inhabitants of the only truly civilized country between heaven and earth.

That's why they call China the Middle Kingdom. And they don't want their country polluted by outsiders."

"Surely they can't mean the British?" Charles asked incredulously.

Thresham smiled at Emmaline before responding. "Oh, but they do. Any and all foreigners, I'm afraid."

"That's utter rot!"

"Not to them, Mr. Horton-Smythe. After all, they were making beautiful works of art when Europe was no more than a collection of warring savages."

"But the things we've heard. Eating dogs, killing babies, binding the women's feet. I hardly call that civilized!"

"They can't understand how we can keep dogs for pets, either. And I must say," Thresham smiled at Emmaline again, "that some people would consider corsets no less terrible than foot binding."

Darcy couldn't help remembering Blossom waving the corset like a flag of battle. A smile sprang to his lips until he realized Emmaline was looking at him.

The butler appeared. "The dinner is ready, Lady Whitmore."

"Oh, thank you, James," she said. "Mr. Fitzroy, will you be so kind as to escort me inside?"

"I'd be honored," he said, meaning it. To escort Lady Whitmore in the absence of her husband *was* an honor, especially when so many men at the party outranked him socially.

He turned to Thresham, who was obviously also invited to stay to dinner. "I'd like to ask you some questions. After dinner?"

"Delighted to be of service."

Darcy took Emmaline's arm. Thresham and Charles followed behind.

I should have been asked to take her in, Charles thought bitterly. He was much closer in rank to Lady Whitmore than that sailor Fitzroy.

Well, no matter now. He'd show them all for fools soon enough.

Darcy had never spent a more restless and boring time at one of Emmaline's dinner parties. He should have been flattered to be placed so near her as she presided at the head of the table, but he resented being so far from Thresham, who was entertaining those around him with stories of his far-flung travels. A few times he heard "China" and it was all he could do to keep still and try to look interested in the interminable rambling of the old man sitting beside him.

Across from Darcy sat Lady Gloriana Shrewtonbury, who was batting her cowlike eyes at him with great vigor and smiling insipidly every time he glanced her way. There had been a time not too long ago when he'd actually considered marrying her, despite her distinct lack of physical charms, because she was the eldest daughter of a very old, very wealthy family. Now, though, he thought he must have been temporarily insane to even contemplate such a step.

As he drank his wine it occurred to him that he really should be flattered to be the object of Lady Gloriana's flirtatious attention. It just went to show that money could force people to accept you or at least pretend to.

An idea struck him as forcibly as a rock. If they could accept him, perhaps they could accept a beautiful girl who had been raised in a foreign country. He scanned the table, taking note of several noble bachelors. Perhaps someone might even marry her if her dowry was sufficiently large. That would take Blossom off his hands completely!

He should have been very pleased with his brilliant idea,

but for some reason he wasn't. He glanced at Lord Blunderbast sitting beside him, who'd been droning on for the past several minutes. Probably his companion's babbling kept him from feeling a sense of relief.

Darcy sighed and tried to look as if he were paying attention to the elderly man, who had been quite the dandy and rake in his youth forty years ago. But forty years had rendered him more pathetic than dashing. Darcy couldn't help wondering if he'd seen anything quite like the man beside him with his powdered face, dyed hair, too-tight breeches and waistcoat, and blustery manner of speech that resembled a barrage of cannons firing haphazardly.

"I tell you," Lord Blunderbast went on, "it's nothing more than a demmed lure to foreigners and rogues of every description! A waste of money, too. A wretched monstrosity sitting smack in Hyde Park! Crystal Palace, indeed! The whole city's full of foreigners already." Darcy noted the man said "foreigners" as if each and every one carried bubonic plague and were thieves into the bargain. "And if it weren't for Prince Albert being so dashed set on it, the *smart* men in the city would have put a stop to it long ago!"

"But surely, your lordship, the exhibition will show the world the many accomplishments of the modern age, to the native born as well as to those visiting from foreign countries?" Emmaline said with her charming smile and slightly befuddled expression, as if she, only a poor woman, was having trouble comprehending the manly greatness represented by his lordship, demonstrating once again the shrewdness that had gained her the reputation as the finest hostess in London.

"A good point, madam, but I think this demmed government ought to make some restrictions, exhibition or not," Lord Blunderbast replied condescendingly. "You gels are bloody—beg pardon—ignorant of the mischief these people can get up to. And the whole blasted city seems too dashed like a child at a market fair to be paying attention!''

Blossom would make a fine hostess, too, even if all she did was sit and listen with that look of intelligent interest in her beautiful eyes. And if she chose to speak, it would never be ''Yes, my dear'' or ''No, my love'' or ''You know best, my darling.'' If she talked to Darcy, who was supposed to be her honored lord, the way she did, she wouldn't hesitate to tell her husband her opinions. A wife like that would certainly never be dull.

But he was not going to think about Blossom tonight.

Fortunately, dessert was concluded before Lord Blunderbast had an apoplectic fit which, judging by the increasing redness of his already florid complexion, was not an unreasonable worry. Emmaline rose gracefully. ''Ladies?''

All the other women got up and followed her to the drawing room while the men, led by Lord Blunderbast, headed for the billiards room and the comfort of a cheroot and brandy.

Since Lord Blunderbast had commandeered the brandy bottle, Darcy was forced to listen to more harangues against the foolery represented by the Crystal Palace. At last, though, he got his drink and moved away, closer to Thresham, who was surrounded by several men apparently hanging on his every word.

''Now, as for the women—'' Thresham paused and looked at the other men ''—they're quite—'' the men all leaned a little closer ''—*amazing.*''

The men's eyes widened with fascination. Even Darcy couldn't help being caught up by Thresham's manner, his easy familiarity and charm. Lord Blunderbast left the brandy bottle to come a little closer.

"Oriental women are generally quite small, but they have the most interesting techniques."

"Foreigners!" Lord Blunderbast snorted, but without nearly the vehemence he'd displayed at dinner.

"Well, they *are* different. For instance, a Chinese man cares more about the size of a woman's *feet* than any other portion of her anatomy."

The men looked incredulous.

"That's why they bind them, so that when the woman's fully grown, her feet are only about three inches long."

"Barbaric!" Lord Blunderbast interjected weakly.

Darcy noted that Charles seemed quite fascinated.

"The women suffer great pain for many years, and eventually some of their toes fall completely off. All in the name of beauty."

"Isn't it true they sell their daughters?" one of the other gentlemen asked.

Thresham, leaning against the mantelpiece, nodded. "As servants or concubines or to whorehouses."

"The poor creatures," Charles said solemnly. "It's as if they're something you can buy and sell like trade goods."

Darcy glanced at Charles quickly, but Charles didn't look anything other than curious.

Thresham shrugged his shoulders. "Girls aren't of much value in China, I'm afraid. Many times, during a famine or a financial disaster of some sort, they get sold or traded. Of course, some of the more beautiful concubines manage to live fairly comfortably, and if a girl is sold to provide money to help her family, she's even regarded as a particularly dutiful daughter."

"Really?" Lord Blunderbast seemed to have forgotten to condemn foreigners out of hand.

"I've heard some people talk about something they call 'face.' What is it, exactly?" Darcy asked, trying to look as if this were merely a quaint notion he'd heard of once.

Thresham grinned. "That's quite a complicated thing, face. It's all wrapped up in their version of society and doing what they perceive as the correct thing.

"Basically, it's about respect. Face can be determined by your actions, by acting correctly. If you act incorrectly, you lose face—much as we expect a gentleman to act like a gentleman and if he doesn't, we expect him to be ashamed of himself.

"But it's also based on your social standing. It's not enough to be wealthy or powerful, though. To have face, you have to have, well, a certain noblesse oblige. In that, they're not so different from anybody else."

"What if you lose face? Would it be so terrible a person might kill themselves?"

Thresham seemed rather surprised by Darcy's question, and Darcy resolved to be a little more circumspect in his probing. "Well, it is disastrous to lose face, but suicide in China is rather rare. They believe that if you do that, your spirit is doomed to be a restless ghost. That's something to be avoided at all costs.

"Of course, there are exceptions. For instance, if a woman is raped, they think it shows a proper sense of shame for her to kill herself. Or if a girl has a particularly nasty mother-in-law, she sometimes kills herself *hoping* her spirit will haunt the other woman."

"Tempting idea, eh? Might have considered haunting my wife's mother—terrible old battle-ax," Lord Blunderbast muttered. Apparently realizing he had just approved some blasted foreigner's idea, he cleared his throat loudly and moved back toward the brandy bottle.

Darcy needed another drink. It seemed he had been deluding himself like a besotted youth. To Blossom, making love was really nothing more than paying Wu's debt, just as her threat to kill herself was a lie. The desire in her eyes had no doubt been a lie, too. It was galling to think that he had been so easily duped by pity and a pretty face.

He tossed back his brandy. Tonight he would forget Blossom and show Emmaline just how much he regretted neglecting her.

Chapter Seven

Blossom fed another piece of coal into the bedroom grate. Afterward she went to the window and looked out onto the dark, damp street. It would not be long before the first faint light of dawn appeared in the eastern sky.

Perhaps Mr. Fitzroy had slept at the place called "club." Ah Tup had overheard the Chief Eunuch and the Crow Woman say he might, although neither Blossom nor Ah Tup had any idea what they meant by such a place.

Nevertheless, she would wait until he returned home, or the servants began their daily work. She knew it would not be good to be discovered here in Mr. Fitzroy's bedchamber.

With a deep sigh, she adjusted her ornately embroidered gown and settled into a chair beside the fireplace. She glanced at the spot where the mirror used to hang. It was good that she had moved it, even if it might have prevented *ch'i* from disappearing up the chimney, because it had faced Mr. Fitzroy's large bed. Everybody knew that a sleeper's soul might take fright at seeing the body's reflection and possibly flee. She had also been wise to move the screen from its place in the corner to a position in front of the door. This way the *ch'i* would stay in the room longer.

As she settled deeper into the chair, she let her mind rove back to China, where she knew what was expected of her.

Only a few days ago it would have been the Grave-Sweeping Festival, when Honorable Wu and all his family would tend to the graves of their ancestors, cleaning them and leaving offerings for the spirits. It was important that the spirits of the ancestors not be offended, and that they knew they were still remembered and revered by their descendents.

Of course, she had never been allowed to take part but had worked hard in the kitchen to prepare the food offerings. It had stung her to know that she had no graves to tend and that the spirits of her ancestors might be wandering the earth tormented. She knew exactly how they felt, for she, too, had wandered far and knew little contentment.

At least she should be happy that Mr. Fitzroy didn't beat her or make her work hard all day long as Precious Jade had. Many times Mr. Fitzroy seemed more frustrated than annoyed. Perhaps, in time, she could find ways to please him, starting tonight.

What if she never pleased him? Would he send her away? He had told her she was free, but what did that mean? If she was free to go, where would she live? How would she keep herself and Ah Tup? She knew only the life of a kitchen slave or a concubine.

To be the toy of a man was better than the drudge of a cook, but did she want to belong to any man but Mr. Fitzroy?

He was generous, providing her with clothes, detestable though they were. His servants seemed very loyal, despite his bad temper, so he must not be a bad master generally. He had even been most sympathetic in the matter of the terrible porridge.

She thought of the rare times she had seen him laugh and the way his eyes softened so wonderfully. She wanted to be near him, to watch for those precious moments.

She could not imagine another man caressing her. It thrilled her to know that she could find ways to break down the wall of his barbarian reserve. He was strong and powerful, but with her he was gentle and kind. Surely that meant she had touched his heart, just as surely as she knew she wanted to please Mr. Fitzroy and to be safe in his arms.

At that moment, Blossom made a decision. If he would not touch her, she would still stay and be his servant. It would be better to be a servant in his house than another man's concubine.

Of all things, though, the best would be to become Mr. Fitzroy's concubine. She let herself remember Mr. Fitzroy's naked body as he lay in the tub of water, the sensation of his lips on hers, the fire in his eyes when he looked at her.

The door opened. Half-asleep, Blossom automatically kowtowed.

"What do you think you're doing here?"

She stood up and smiled at Mr. Fitzroy. "I prepare your bed for sleeping," she said, poking at the coals until they grew brighter. She then proceeded to turn back the bedclothes while he stood motionless and watched. The room ready, she turned to him. "I go now."

"Blossom, I've decided you should learn more about English customs."

"As you wish, Mr. Fitzroy."

"I'll see about getting someone to teach you. Mrs. MacTavish doesn't have the time to spare."

She nodded.

"Good night, then."

"Good night, Mr. Fitzroy." She walked past him with great dignity, hoping he would look at her. When she was beside him, however, she detected a subtle odor that made her steps falter.

A woman's delicate scent.

She said nothing but continued out the door, closing it behind her. She realized from the pale light falling on the carpet that it was nearly morning. He had been gone all night and returned smelling of a woman's perfume.

A pang of disappointment hit her as she turned and looked at his closed door. Then a new feeling coursed through her body. If she had to do battle with another woman for him instead of some stupid barbarian notion of proper behavior, that she could understand.

That she could win.

She turned on her heel and marched back into the bedroom. Mr. Fitzroy spun around, his shirt in his hand.

The sight of his bare chest, the unmistakable ripple of strong muscles, the sudden seeming liquification of her own, made her speechless for a moment. Then, on his neck, she saw something that told her she had not guessed wrongly. It was a small, red mark, a thing Water Lily had described. It came from lips pulling gently on the skin.

He tugged on his shirt. "What do you want now?"

"Am I ugly?" she demanded. "Am I disgusting?"

"This is hardly the time or place to discuss your merits."

Blossom ignored him, went toward the bed and began to disrobe.

"What the hell do you think you're doing?"

"You have been with a woman tonight. Now you be with me."

Mr. Fitzroy folded his arms across his broad chest. "I prefer to choose with whom I go to bed," he said with a wry grin.

The knowledge that he found her amusing only made her more determined. "You cannot perform two times in same night?"

The grin disappeared and a frown took its place. "I mean I'm not going to go to bed with you."

"We don't have to go into bed. We can enjoy each other anywhere you like."

By now Blossom had reached the last layer of silk. "I will have to kill myself if you do not take me. I could not live with the shame of knowing you find another more pleasing than me."

To her shock, Mr. Fitzroy smiled. "Fine."

She stared at him. "You want me to kill myself?"

"I'll risk being haunted."

He knew. Somehow he had found out why she dare not kill herself. She had made a terrible mistake thinking she could control him with a threat. Water Lily would have heaped stinging curses on her head.

"No one forces me to do anything, especially not make love," Mr. Fitzroy said quietly. "And I can certainly do it more than once a night—if I want to."

There it was again, this thing called love. "What do you mean, make love? I thought you said it was a feeling. You make a feeling?"

Mr. Fitzroy didn't answer. Suddenly she understood. "Ah! This make love! It is man and woman..."

"Yes," Mr. Fitzroy said quickly. "Now go."

But Blossom was not to be dissuaded. This love, after all, was no great mystery. She had been taught all about it. "This *fan kow* woman you have been with, she pleases you, *heya?*"

"That's none of your business."

"Making love is my business, as you say. How can I please you if you always send me away? How can I learn what to do? What you like?"

"You don't have to please me. I thought I made it clear that I'm going to forget Wu's debt."

"I cannot live in your house and do nothing," she pleaded. She went close to him.

"Get out."

"No," she whispered. "I only wish to please you, honored lord. I wish to know how to do so. Please, teach me." Then she stood up on her tiptoes and kissed him.

At least, that was what she had thought she was doing. But the moment her lips touched his, a feeling of overpowering need and passion consumed her thoughts and sent them scattering like ashes. Instinctively her mouth pressed closer, harder, seeking his in union.

He pulled away, looking at her strangely, struggling with something inside himself. "Please..." she whispered.

Darcy gave up fighting. He wanted her desperately, passionately, more than he'd ever wanted a woman. Could it be so wrong, when she pleaded so sincerely? She didn't think it was wrong.

He took her in his arms with sure strength, pulling her tighter. Her hands moved up his chest to his shoulders, pushing the shirt off him.

His mouth trailed across hers, moving slowly down the tender satin of her throat, the excitement of the motion making her moan softly and clutch tighter. Lifting her easily, he took her in his arms and carried her to his bed, setting her down and lying beside her in one swift motion.

She looked up at him, seeing the naked need and blatant longing in his eyes. He loomed above her, so large, so powerful.

At that moment, she understood Water Lily's gleaming eyes when she explained the nature of the union between a man and a woman. The memory and knowledge, coupled with the burning, liquid feeling coursing through her own body, frightened her with its strength.

Suddenly his expression changed. Hardened. Grew cold. He moved away and stood up. "Get out," he said, his tone harsh and distant.

"Please, I . . ."

"Get *out!*" It was a shout, an order, an exclamation.

"As you wish," she murmured, wondering what had happened. Had she done something wrong again?

She heard the man's ragged gasp as he turned away. With slow steps, she walked past him. "Good night, honored lord," she whispered.

He said nothing. He never looked at her.

Slowly she closed the door behind her.

Darcy went to the pitcher and poured the water into his basin. He splashed his face and hair over and over again until he couldn't feel the throbbing of the blood in his veins anymore. Until he couldn't feel her kiss on his lips anymore. Until he could control his breathing, and his thoughts.

Then he went to the chair beside the grate and slumped down, running his hand through his damp hair.

"If she's not a virgin, I'm the Duke of Wellington," he muttered. How else could he explain the look in her eyes as she lay on his bed? Not experienced. Not sure of herself.

But frightened. Simply frightened.

Darcy stared at the glowing coals. If he hadn't seen it, he wouldn't have stopped. He would have taken her as surely as he sat there, like the worst undisciplined, lustful libertine in all of England, even though he had made love with Emmaline only two hours before.

What was happening to him, a man who had known the precise moment to stop before he crippled that pimp for life? Who could control a ship as if it were a toy boat in a pond. Who could tame a rough crew with a glance.

He had only been fooling himself when he thought her desire made it acceptable to make love with her. She knew only what she'd been taught as a slave. She couldn't understand free choice, or that she had the right to refuse him.

He couldn't go on like this, either, that was certain. He made his decision. He would abide by the plan he'd come up with at Emmaline's party: to have Blossom instructed in English social customs, then introduce her into society as his guest. Hopefully some young man would propose, she'd accept and he'd be rid of her forever, free to find himself a wealthy, socially prominent wife... who would probably bore him to distraction.

He shook his head. God, something was definitely happening to his ability to think clearly. The sooner he put his plan into action, the sooner it would be accomplished and the sooner he'd be free.

The next day Darcy went to Emmaline's the minute it was acceptable.

Emmaline was surprised to see him. It had only been a few hours since she had lost herself in his arms. Of all her lovers, Darcy Fitzroy was by far the most impressive and imaginative. Even here, in her drawing room, her pulse quickened at the sight of him.

He seemed distracted and she wondered if something was wrong when, without any polite preamble, he launched into his reason for coming to see her. "Emmaline, I need a chaperon."

She smiled, holding her delicate hand for his kiss. "I hardly think so," she replied, sitting down on a plush velvet sofa.

"Not for me, of course. A man who invests quite heavily in my ships wants to send his daughter to London for the season. He's got business in the West Indies he needs to attend to personally, and he's asked me if the girl could stay at my house."

Emmaline nodded, but inwardly she was trying to decide just how much of Darcy's story was a lie. It was all too obvious that much of it was a falsehood.

"I don't want to refuse, but as you know, I can't have a young, unchaperoned woman under my roof without causing a few comments."

"The girl's father isn't concerned?"

"Of course he is. In his letter he said that naturally her staying would be conditional on finding a suitable chaperon. He's very rich, so I don't want to say no."

Emmaline had never heard such a complete fabrication in her life. No father would trust a *man* to find a chaperon.

Nevertheless, she was intrigued. Who was this girl who would be staying with Darcy? He couldn't have any personal interest in her or he would hardly come to his mistress to ask for help in finding a chaperon. The whole thing was a mystery, and her life had become so boring lately a little mystery would be a welcome diversion.

"I do happen to know somebody who might be suitable," she said after a short pause. He looked at her with an eagerness that was almost boyish. So different from the man in her bed last night, when his eagerness had been of an entirely different nature. "I do have a female relation who might be acceptable. Mrs. Dulcibella Ditchett. She is a second cousin a few times removed, I think. She's not very well-off, although of course Frederick provides her with a living. I'm sure she'd welcome the chance."

Darcy smiled gratefully. "Thank you, Emmaline."

"She lives in Brighton, but I expect she could be here quite soon."

"That would be excellent."

She regarded Darcy thoughtfully, then decided. "Would you be able to spend the next fortnight at Kinverton, Darcy?" she asked softly.

His eyes glowed as he looked at her. "Are you inviting me?"

"Yes." She knew it was pushing her powers in social circles to admit Darcy Fitzroy as a member of a house party, but she enjoyed seeing the influence she wielded. Darcy would never be fully accepted by the upper class, but she liked to watch them maneuver around him when she was so obviously his sponsor, if not more.

"I'll come."

"Good. It will be my last visit there before the season begins. I hope to enjoy the tranquility." There could be no doubt in Darcy's mind how she hoped to enjoy herself, and with whom.

Darcy didn't linger. He did, after all, have a business to oversee, even with Charles's assistance, and if he was going to go to Kinverton, he had several things to put in order.

The minute Charles observed Darcy bounding up the steps to their offices, he began cracking his knuckles with consternation. It was obvious, even supposing one didn't know Darcy personally, to recognize that the man had recently had some good news.

"Never saw a luckier blackguard in my life!" Charles muttered to himself.

Outside, where the clerks worked, he could hear Darcy greeting them by name. Would the man never learn how to address one's inferiors? All the social varnish in the world could never hide what Darcy Fitzroy *really* was, lowborn and lower-class. Not like *him,* who deserved to be treated with the deference due to one of his rank.

Despite his thoughts, Charles opened the door of his office and entered Darcy's larger one with his face wreathed in charming smiles.

"Marvelous day, Charles, isn't it?" Darcy said, throwing his hat on a nearby chair and taking his seat behind the desk.

Charles began to crack a knuckle, then stopped himself. "Certainly," he said, while wishing Darcy and the day to perdition.

"I've been invited to Kinverton for a fortnight," Darcy said.

Smug bastard was the more gentle of the epithets Charles heaped on Darcy in his mind. To think that this upstart, this merchant, was being invited to the country home of Lord and Lady Whitmore, while he, the *Honorable* Charles Horton-Smythe, slaved in this building like, like some *coolie.* But he smiled and said, "Delightful."

"Is there anything here that needs my immediate attention?"

"There are some papers that need to be signed. I've already put them on your desk."

Darcy glanced at them. "And have you had any news on that investigative matter?"

"None, but the fellow's looking into missionary ventures to China."

Darcy nodded thoughtfully. "Ask him what he can find out about anybody else who might have had dealings with the Chinese."

Charles raised an eyebrow. "Rather like looking for a needle in the proverbial haystack, isn't it?"

Darcy shrugged his broad shoulders. "Perhaps, but ask him anyway."

The tone! As if he were the man's lackey! "Is that all?"

Darcy nodded and looked down at the papers awaiting his attention on his desk. "Yes."

"Anything else you'd like me to take care of particularly?" he asked, wondering if Darcy would finally mention Wu's tantalizing gift.

"No, nothing."

So, hc was dismissed.

Charles went back to his own little office and closed the door. He sat at his desk, staring for a moment at the wall between his office and Darcy's.

The arrogant bastard. Money had made him, but money could break him. The thought made Charles smile as he reached into the secret compartment in his desk and drew out his ledger. His private ledger for Fitzroy Shipping. The one that showed that Darcy Fitzroy was siphoning off funds for his own personal use.

The discovery would cause quite a scandal, of course. No doubt Fitzroy Shipping would be closcd down. Fortunately, Charles's uncle, old Phineas Horton-Smythe, would die in Madeira, leaving his money to his nephew. Of course, his nephew had been the one secretly depositing money in his uncle's name in a foreign bank, but no one need know that, just as no one need know that Phineas Horton-Smythe was nothing more than a convenient creation.

Charles chuckled softly and rubbed his hands together over the bogus ledger. In the dim light filtering through the high, narrow windows of his office, he looked like an evil genie plotting disaster.

And he most certainly was.

Chapter Eight

"Oh, my dear, you wouldn't *believe* the trouble I had with the cabdriver! Quite the highwayman, I do think. And such jolting and knocking about! It's a mercy I wasn't killed."

Mrs. MacTavish and Powlett did their best not to stare at the woman standing on the threshold. Mr. Fitzroy had said little about Mrs. Dulcibella Ditchett, but they had been anticipating a soft-spoken, plainly dressed gentlewoman in reduced circumstances.

They had in no way expected the species of outlandish plump middle-aged girlhood stumbling through the door that very moment.

Neither had Blossom or Ah Tup, who were crouched at the top of the stairs watching. They had been told to stay upstairs until called for, but the moment they heard a carriage stop outside, they had hurried to see.

The two looked at each other in astonishment. *This* was a woman of good character, suitable companion for proper young women? This apparition covered with bits of lace, fur, flowers, ruffles, flounces and jewelry all wafting about her stout form as if they were about to fall off at any moment?

Blossom pressed her lips together tightly. Dismayed by Mr. Fitzroy's abrupt change of mood the other night, she had decided to learn all she could about English ways. Then she might understand what was preventing Mr. Fitzroy from making love with her.

Powlett's arm shot out to assist Mrs. Ditchett.

"Oh, thank you, my good man. Be so good as to bring up my bags, please. And mind the small one—it's got breakables. And the middle-sized brown one—hats."

Powlett deposited her beside Mrs. MacTavish, who had recovered her usual demeanor. "Good day, ma'am."

"I do hope I'm not too late for tea! Abominable cab-driver—quite ignored my pleas to hurry. And the language…oh, my dear, quite unacceptable! But *have* I missed tea? I'm quite done for."

Mrs. Ditchett paused for breath and Mrs. MacTavish stepped into the breach. "I'll ring for tea at once. Would you care to walk into the drawing room, or would you prefer to go straight up to your room?"

"Oh, the drawing room will be lovely, I'm sure. I'm so tired I can barely speak. Tea will be quite reviving, I'm sure. And if there's a bit of brandy…my doctor recommends it for fatigue and really it's quite amazing the effect it has…" The woman rustled off into the drawing room, followed by Mrs. MacTavish, whose expression was such a mixture of deference and incredulity that Blossom had to cover her mouth so she wouldn't laugh out loud.

Blossom went back to her room, followed by Ah Tup waddling in imitation of the woman.

Ah Tup stifled a snort of laughter. "Did you ever see anything like Crow Woman's face?"

Blossom shook her head, smiling broadly. "Still—" her expression grew somber "—this woman may be able to show me what I have done wrong."

"It is impossible to imagine *her* with a man, *heya?*"

Blossom couldn't suppress a giggle. "He would hardly be able to find her precious valley under all those ornaments and clothes!" Together they shared a companionable chuckle. Blossom smiled at her friend. "Ah Tup, I would be so miserable if you weren't here to make me laugh."

"Well, Mother, I would rather laugh than be sad. After all, have we not survived that terrible *fan kow* boat? And do we not know everything about this house, more than even the other servants? Are you not beautiful and desirable to our master, despite this strange custom of one wife to satisfy a man? Surely we have more to be happy about than sad, especially now that you have a new teacher."

There was a timid knock at the door, and Sally stuck her head into the room. "If you please, you're wanted in the drawing room."

Blossom glanced at Ah Tup, adjusted her gown and went downstairs.

Mrs. Ditchett's hand, holding a pastry, stopped halfway to her mouth when she saw Blossom. Her eyes narrowed and she surveyed the girl slowly, starting at her head and working her way down. Instantly Blossom realized that, whatever first impression this woman made, she was no fool.

"Well, my dear, I believe you'll do very well for yourself," the woman said. "Looks, bearing—yes, we should be able to find you a suitable husband with no trouble at all."

"Husband?" For a moment Blossom's heart soared with the hope that Mr. Fitzroy was going to wed her. Such a thing was not unheard of and would not only please her greatly but give her vast face.

The pastry found its mark, but a full mouth didn't deter Mrs. Ditchett from talking. "Why, yes, my dear. I quite believe we may have to fight the young men off."

Blossom stood as straight as a column of stone. Mr. Fitzroy was going to give her in marriage to another man!

Such a thing would still increase her face, since it was better to be a wife than a concubine. But not for her. Not if it meant marriage to another man. She spoke firmly. "I am not to marry."

The older woman stared at her as if *she* did not understand the language, then waved her hand dismissively until it lit on another pastry. "Oh, that's what many young girls say, but wait until a few balls, a few dances, some young man whispering flattering comments out in a garden in the moonlight..." She sighed. "I assure you, you'll change your mind. And why else would your father want you to spend the season in London?"

"My father?" Blossom was now completely puzzled. "My father is—"

"An old friend of mine," Mr. Fitzroy said, stepping into the room quickly. "You must be Mrs. Ditchett. I'm Darcy Fitzroy."

"Charmed to make your acquaintance, sir," Mrs. Ditchett said, half rising from her chair.

"I see you've met my ward."

Blossom stared at him, but he turned so that only she could see his face. He glared at her. It wasn't hard to tell that he wanted her to be quiet.

"I must say this air of charming confusion is most becoming, my dear. Most becoming." Mrs. Ditchett reached for her tea. "I understand you've made quite a fortune in the shipping business, Mr. Fitzroy?"

"I've made some money, yes."

"My dear Emmaline—oh, I suppose I should call her Lady Whitmore although we were quite close when she was growing up and even as a child quite the loveliest thing you ever saw—told me about your dilemma."

"I am not worthy to be married."

Mrs. Ditchett stopped chewing and looked at Blossom, who was keeping her gaze on Mr. Fitzroy.

He strode over to the fireplace and leaned an arm on the mantel. "Your modesty is most becoming, Miss Flowers. Isn't it, Mrs. Ditchett?"

"Yes indeed. It should quite captivate the young men—"

Mr. Fitzroy interrupted. "I'm happy you were able to come on such short notice. I leave for Kinverton tomorrow morning."

"A most charming estate. Emmaline—Lady Whitmore— was very fortunate in her choice of husband. I hope we can do the same for Miss Flowers."

Mrs. Ditchett looked at Mr. Fitzroy significantly. By now she had consumed everything on the tray and her second cup of tea. "If you'll excuse me, Mr. Fitzroy and Miss Flowers, I'm quite exhausted from the journey. A good rest tonight and we can begin in earnest tomorrow. I think, yes, I think the proper use of a fan would be the best place to begin." She rose to her feet. "If your housekeeper could show me to my room?"

Mr. Fitzroy tugged the bellpull and Mrs. MacTavish quickly appeared at the doorway. She looked at the empty tray and frowned slightly as Mrs. Ditchett rustled toward her. Together they went up the stairs.

As soon as they disappeared from sight, Blossom spoke. "My father is dead and I am not worthy to marry."

Mr. Fitzroy didn't look at her. "I'm sorry you had to find out about our ruse that way, but I had to come up with some story to explain your presence here."

"Ah. You tell a lie."

He glanced at her and she saw a hint of a smile. "You seem to be learning English well enough."

"I am not worthy to be married."

He began pacing the room and she watched his every move. "I'm afraid there isn't much else for a young woman to do in England, except work long hours at horrible tasks, or get married."

"I can be your servant."

"No, you can't." His tone was final, and it went to her heart like a knife.

"I do not wish to be a wife. I wish to be your concubine."

"For the last time, you will *never* be my mistress. Mrs. Ditchett is here to teach you how to behave in English society. I've told people that you're the daughter of a man I do business with, and that you're staying with me for the season. Whether or not you find a husband is up to the young men, but most people will assume, rightly or not, that the intention of your visit is to get you a husband." He cleared his throat. "Besides, I can't afford to keep you and it would cause a scandal if people found out about you. I've already explained all that."

She heard the finality in his tone and thought of something else, something that increased her dismay. "Is that why you stopped last night, so that I stay a virgin and you will be able to give less money to husband's family?"

He didn't answer right away, and when he did, he stared out the window. "Yes."

She had no choice but to believe that he meant her to become the wife of another man. Her eyes burned with tears and she tried to tell herself that she should be feeling honored that Mr. Fitzroy wished to provide a marriage for her.

No, no, no! her heart protested. Do you give up so easily? Blossom felt the fire of determination flare up. She would not surrender. Not yet.

Unfortunately, Water Lily had never told her what to do if she wanted a man and he appeared reluctant.

She *had* told Blossom what to do if there was a rival woman in the house. She should find a way to make herself unavailable to the man, since it was well-known that men desire most what they cannot have.

"I will do as you wish," she said softly.

"You choose your own husband, you know. I'm sure many young men will . . ." He turned to look at her and she saw that he had not expected her to agree so easily.

"This is a wonderful barbarian custom, I think, choosing."

"Yes, yes, it is."

"Will there be many men for me to pick from?"

"I assume so."

"Will they be rich?"

"Probably," he muttered, turning back to stare out the window.

"I am honored you arrange a marriage for me."

"Fine. Good night, Blossom."

"Good night, Mr. Fitzroy."

As she left the room, Blossom glanced covertly at Mr. Fitzroy. She would not give up as long as she was still in his house.

"No! No! No! That will *never* do! You must move all in one motion, gracefully, like a willow bending in the breeze!"

Blossom watched again as Mrs. Ditchett demonstrated a curtsy, one hand holding a fan fluttering in front of her face.

Blossom sighed and gripped the fan in her right hand tightly. This woman was worse than Precious Jade, Water Lily and Mrs. MacTavish combined.

"Better, better—no, dip! dip! Not bend! From the knees, my dear! Once more!"

Blossom had never spent a more horrible time in her life. Every morning the lessons began, sometimes even before breakfast, then continued all day and into the night until she crawled wearily into bed. Who would have thought Englishwomen had to know so much! Things like how to move as if all those cumbersome skirts were so much air and how to sit and how to eat and how to speak and what a certain motion of a fan meant . . . on and on and on, until she was exhausted.

"I quite despair of your ever understanding, I must say," Mrs. Ditchett said with another long, mournful sigh. Blossom had come to despise those sighs, almost wishing for a beating instead of that tone of utter defeat. "But enough of the curtsy. Let's discuss . . . general deportment."

"What is this 'deportment'?"

"How one behaves in society, generally, my dear."

"Ah."

"Well, sit down, and I'll begin."

Blossom complied, glad of the chance to sit down.

"Now, it's absolutely *vital,* my dear, that you never look a gentleman quite in the eye."

Blossom shuddered. "Why would anyone except a doctor wish to look inside a man's eye?" she wondered out loud.

Mrs. Ditchett shook her head. "Really, my dear, you have such a literal mind! You must make an effort to curb these rather startling speeches!

"I mean, you mustn't ever look at a man while he's looking at you. Such a thing would be considered very bold. Very bold, indeed!"

"Where, then, am I to look?"

"Well, I believe the best place is the floor, so that your eyes are suitably downcast." Mrs. Ditchett smiled conspiratorially. "It also shows one's eyelashes off to great effect."

That was so like something Water Lily had told her that Blossom almost smiled.

"I begin to see we understand each other, my dear. Now, can you flutter your eyelids, like this—" Mrs. Ditchett proceeded to demonstrate.

Blossom stared in fascination. The woman's eyelids twitched as if she had something embedded in each eye, and her mouth looked as if she had just bitten into something sour but was trying to smile nonetheless.

"I assure you men find this sort of modest expression absolutely irresistible," Mrs. Ditchett said when she finally stopped. "Try it."

Blossom did her best to comply.

"Well, my dear, it needs a little work. Let's try something else.

"Oh, I know. When a man asks you a question, especially if it's a man you particularly fancy, you should act pleasantly ruffled."

"I am to wear more skirt?"

"No, no. Like this." Mrs. Ditchett fluttered her fan rapidly, panted like a servant who had just carried in two large jugs of water and looked at Blossom while turning her head to one side. "Oh, my! I don't know...I may be engaged...but I think not!" She instantly became her normal self. "Men find confusion so captivating!"

Blossom stifled a yawn and hoped Mrs. MacTavish would soon arrive to order her to retire. Ever since Mrs. Ditchett's arrival, Blossom had seen little of Mrs. MacTavish, who seemed to have taken an instant dislike to the other woman, as was all too evident in the next moment, when Mrs. MacTavish walked into the room.

"It's ten o'clock," she announced.

"She'll have to get used to late hours if she's going to be attending balls and parties," Mrs. Ditchett complained, barely glancing at Mrs. MacTavish.

"She's not at a ball tonight. She should go to her bed."

"Oh, very well, since you're so persistent, although I'm sure Mr. Fitzroy would agree with me." Mrs. Ditchett gave the housekeeper a sour look. "Good night, Mrs. Mac-Tavish."

Mrs. Ditchett didn't watch to see if Mrs. MacTavish left or not, clearly determined to assume she had the last word, and instead turned to Blossom. "Let's see you do what I've told you," she said.

Blossom waited until Mrs. MacTavish was closing the door. Then, trying to imitate the fluttering movements of Mrs. Ditchett, she said, "Oh, my. I don't think so...I really don't know..."

"Perfect! You're so perfectly coy! The men will be standing in line to dance with you."

Blossom gasped. "*I* am to dance?"

"Why, my dear, certainly."

"I am not trained!" It took years of study to become a dancer even in one of the lowliest pleasure houses.

"I've engaged a dancing master. He's coming tomorrow."

"I...there is not time!"

Mrs. Ditchett smiled condescendingly. "As long as you don't step directly on a gentleman's feet, I don't think it matters too much, in your particular case."

"I am to dance with a *man?*"

"My dear, it's clear to me you've led a very sheltered life. It's been quite acceptable for several years now."

Blossom tried not to cringe at the thought of learning how to dance with her big feet, and then having to dance with a man. She would surely be clumsy.

"You'd best go upstairs to bed now," Mrs. Ditchett said, not unkindly, "before that horrible woman who doesn't know her place comes back."

Blossom got up, curtsied—Mrs. Ditchett eyed her performance critically but didn't say anything—and went up to her room. Ah Tup was waiting, as always, but Blossom was too tired to say much.

Ah Tup was full of her usual gossip and good spirits, talking of the Chief Eunuch and his attempts to tell Ah Tup what to do. He never seemed to learn that under her benign smiling face, Ah Tup had a mind as sharp as a needle and an unshakable belief that any Chinese person, even a kitchen slave, was vastly superior to any *fan kow*—just as Ah Tup couldn't seem to understand that Powlett had equal faith in the supremacy of the Welsh. However, Ah Tup soon realized that Blossom wanted to go to sleep. Once she had helped her mistress undress, she lay down on the floor beside the door and fell asleep.

Slipping into a delightfully soft silk robe, Blossom sighed. She was so tired of having to learn new things all the time. It would be nice to simply spend a day walking out in the garden or sewing with Ah Tup.

Then, as she had done every night of her life for as long as she could remember, she made sure Ah Tup was asleep, knelt at the side of her bed, pressed her palms together and whispered, "My father, who is in heaven, haloed be your name..."

Downstairs in the kitchen, Mrs. MacTavish frowned at Powlett. "I'm going to speak to Mr. Fitzroy."

Powlett's face betrayed slight disapproval. "It was he who engaged the services of Mrs. Ditchett, who was recommended, let us not forget, by Lady Whitmore."

"I don't care if she was sent by the queen herself, she's not teaching the poor wee thing properly."

Powlett sipped his nightly brandy and water. "How do you mean, Mrs. MacTavish?"

"I mean, sir, she's teaching her to...to..."

"To what, madam?"

"It's improper, that's all." Mrs. MacTavish's teacup rattled against the saucer as an external sign of her inward agitation.

"I believe you will have to be more explicit with Mr. Fitzroy. She's not condoning wanton behavior, I trust?"

"Not that. But teaching her all kinds of affectations and coyness. It's terrible!"

"Perhaps we should let Mr. Fitzroy judge for himself."

Mrs. MacTavish stared down at her teacup as if trying to decipher the tea leaves for guidance. "I suppose you're right, Mr. Powlett. There's nothing I can say she's doing wrong *exactly*." The last word conveyed a host of meaning.

"Then I suggest we await Mr. Fitzroy's return. It will only be another week."

"Very well." The silence grew for a few moments, then Mrs. MacTavish spoke again. "Has she said anything to you about Ah Tup?"

Powlett's face remained as impassive as ever, and Mrs. MacTavish didn't see the slight tip of his glass that threatened to spill some of the contents onto the spotless table. "No, Mrs. MacTavish."

"Well, it's my opinion that she wants to send the poor girl off."

"Off where?"

Mrs. MacTavish frowned darkly, reminding Powlett of a performance he had once seen of *Macbeth*—the witches particularly. "I don't know. But she said to me that she wondered if the Oriental servant, as she called her, was an appropriate one.''

"What do you think she meant by that?"

Mrs. MacTavish, whose feelings toward the two girls now bordered on maternal, frowned. "Why, man, I think she means to send her back to China and get a maid of her own choosing." For an instant Mrs. MacTavish thought Powlett paled, but put it down to the flickering light. "I'd like to see her try it!" she said emphatically.

Powlett nodded solemnly. "I don't think Mr. Fitzroy would approve."

Mrs. MacTavish leaned closer still, and this time Powlett inclined slightly toward her. "We'd best keep our eyes open and our ears, too. It's my opinion that Mrs. Ditchett's going to bring nothing but trouble!"

Powlett, his face still impassive despite his now rapidly beating heart, signified his agreement.

Darcy, standing beside the hearth in the drawing room of Kinverton, could barely suppress a scowl.

In one corner, two middle-aged women and two middle-aged men played whist. In another, a small knot of well-dressed men discussed the state of hunting this spring.

Over by the piano, a subdued group listened as the insipid, skinny Lady Gloriana Shrewtonbury and equally insipid, but stout, Lord Neville Northrup played what Darcy assumed was a duet. The notes were so tentative and light it was hard to tell *what* they thought they were doing. Certainly it couldn't be flirting. If that young man called his pathetic attempts flirting, the English nobility was in direct danger of dying out.

Not that Darcy proposed to set an example of how to attract a woman's attention. There wasn't one woman here worth even the slightest bother, although judging from some of the sly looks the other men had given him, it was clear they expected him to act like some kind of rabid stud.

Two or three females had looked at *him* a few times as if they might find him dangerously tempting, but he gave them absolutely no encouragement.

In fact, he hadn't even gone near Emmaline for the past week. He might have, but the moment he had arrived, he had realized that something had gone wrong. Or rather, was not going the way he had planned.

She had acted aloof, distant, paying most attention to her dolt of a husband. Then the carriages containing the other guests arrived and he had discovered why.

He was the only man there who wasn't titled.

Apparently even Emmaline's ability to flout convention had a limit, and inviting him had come perilously close to it. Rather than pass that boundary, she had retreated behind safer lines.

Well, he couldn't blame her. Her influence had already enabled him to reach far above his "deserved" social station; he couldn't fault her for wanting to protect her own achievements.

But it had been a hellish week. The men had deftly ignored him after the dinners, except for smirks whenever he happened to say anything to a female. Occasionally one would make some reference to their club or school, and seemed to be shocked to have to be reminded that Darcy didn't belong or hadn't attended. Their ploy to remind him that he wasn't of their class of society had all the subtlety of a boom in the face.

They also contrived to exclude him from any activities in the day. He supposed if he'd wanted to, he could have forced them to include him, but he doubted it was worth the effort.

So he'd spent much of the time riding alone when weather permitted and brooding indoors when it didn't.

He walked to the tall windows and looked out over the elaborate garden. Emmaline's estate was tended by more than twenty gardeners, and the results were certainly impressive, as they were meant to be.

A paved walk led the way down from the house through artistically designed flower beds toward a huge lawn. On one side of the house there was a shrubbery with charming little rustic seats, all the way from Italy, for weak-limbed females to rest upon. A brook ran along the other side, seeming to promise a hint of unhindered nature, but he had heard Emmaline describing the building of the waterway, including the exact placement of rocks to get the best babbling sound.

He had a sudden urge to see some wild shoreline ravaged by wind and wave, untouched by humanity.

Lady Gloriana made an insipid little exclamation. He glanced toward the piano.

"Oh, good gracious, Lord Northrup! I'm so clumsy! Forgive my fingers." She must have touched his hand, but she was acting as if she'd touched something rather more private.

"It is I who should be asking your forgiveness, dear Lady Gloriana! Although how could my fingers not help but wander, drawn like a bee to the sweet honey of your fingertips!"

God, how pathetic!

The girl glanced at Darcy with her watery, vapid eyes. He smiled back, a slow smile that made the skinny girl blush. Lord Northrup, also blushing but not from embarrassment, stared at him stonily.

Darcy casually walked toward the piano. "Perhaps you would favor us with some more music, Lady Gloriana?" he asked, knowing that Lord Northrup was probably wishing him halfway around the world.

Lady Gloriana blushed again and glanced at her mother, who was playing whist. However her mother had just won a rather tricky rubber and was too busy commenting on her cleverness to take immediate notice.

"Please, Lady Gloriana?" Darcy said, transfixing her with his gaze.

"I say..." Lord Northrup stammered.

"What does the lady say?" Darcy interrupted.

After looking again at her preoccupied mother, Lady Gloriana began to play.

Lord Northrup withdrew to the other part of the room where the talk was now of fishing. Darcy, tired of his little game, gradually wandered away from the piano and out into the garden.

From old habit he surveyed the night sky, seeking first the North Star and then the other constellations. At the same time, he was taking note of the scent of the air, realizing it would rain before morning. Damn. Another day shut up with this collection of tiresome, arrogant imbeciles.

And to think he had once thought of something like this as the pinnacle of life! God, he couldn't have been more wrong if he'd supposed mud was gold.

"I say, there, sir!"

He turned to find a red-faced Lord Northrup glaring at him like a little boy in a fit of temper. "Yes?" he said coolly.

"I say, there! I must ask you to keep your attentions to yourself!"

"Oh?"

"I say, the young lady in question doesn't want 'em!"

"No?"

"No, sir. Not a bit. And if you don't leave her alone, I'll..."

Darcy smiled. This threat was sure to be fascinating. "Yes?"

"I'll . . . I'll . . . that is, you'll be sorry!"

Darcy advanced toward the stout young man whose excess of emotion was making him puff and pant like a steam engine about to blow. "*You'll* make me sorry?"

Lord Northrup would have turned pale if he wasn't already beet red. "I say, that is, well . . ."

Darcy kept advancing. "*How* will you make me sorry?"

"I'll . . . I'll . . ."

By now Lord Northrup was actually quaking. Darcy decided to be merciful. "Very well. I won't speak to her again."

Lord Northrup stared a moment, panted some more, then drew himself up so that his large stomach flattened—a little. "Well, see that you don't!" he said majestically, then turned and went back into the drawing room.

Darcy watched him as he walked toward Lady Gloriana with the air of a conquering hero.

"That wasn't very nice, Darcy."

He turned as Emmaline came out of a nearby doorway. He shrugged his shoulders. "That boy's an idiot."

"That *boy* comes into two hundred thousand pounds a year in a few months."

Darcy shrugged again. The past few minutes' amusement might have cost him an investor, but there were plenty of others.

"I've missed you," Emmaline said.

Perhaps it was the general atmosphere of his stay at Kinverton, but for once Emmaline's soft, suggestive voice failed to move him.

"I know I haven't been very attentive," she said, coming closer.

Darcy discovered that he really didn't care one way or the other. He wanted to go home, back to his own house and his own business, where *he* made the rules. He didn't acknowledge, even to himself, that it might also be pleasant to be welcomed by a beautiful girl who seemed delighted to see him.

"I'm leaving," he said, the decision made in that instant. "Tomorrow."

Emmaline looked disconcerted. "But..." Then she seemed to think better of protesting. "As you'd like."

"First thing."

She nodded.

He went a little nearer, but still far from close. "Thank you for inviting me, Emmaline."

She smiled her charming, empty smile. "You're welcome, Darcy."

He knew that she realized their liaison was at an end.

Chapter Nine

The great City of London lay on the horizon like a huge monster waiting for its meal of human beings. They would disappear into its maw, to poverty, disease and a thousand other fates. Perhaps one in a hundred might have the ambition and skills to become successful, but for the other ninety-nine there awaited only a slow, lingering death of heartache and despair, of mud and filth, of sickness and starvation.

All along the road into the swelling metropolis, Darcy passed the hopeful in his carriage. Some called out to him for mercy as he went by, ignoring the clumps of dirt stirred up by the horses' churning hooves. Some glared with undisguised hatred and envy at the fine carriage going past.

The hate he could understand better than the begging. He, too, had been such a one long ago, determined to provide—and provide well—for his mother and brother.

Darcy attributed much of his success to luck. To finding a ship willing to take an untrained youth. To having the strength to survive his first voyages and the quick intelligence to learn everything the older seamen could teach. And the fact that he had never been on a ship that had gone down.

What Darcy Fitzroy didn't see was that whatever part luck played in his success, there was a still larger part due to his intelligence, his ambition and his single-minded perseverance, which had kept him from the many easy distractions that might have led him astray. It was also due to his fierce willingness to fight for himself. He knew he had survived many a brawl, but he didn't know how many more rogues and villains had decided it wasn't worth the risk to accost a man like him.

The carriage stopped at an inn, and Darcy went inside to eat a brief meal while the horses were fed and rested. Coming outside in the dim light of early evening to smoke, he saw a young girl with brilliant red hair, her face pinched with starvation, staring at him from the shelter of the stable. Her clothes were a collection of rags. Beside her on the ground sat an equally dirty and ragged old woman, whom the girl spoke to quietly before turning her eyes back to him. The old woman, leaning against her, seemed to draw on the girl's quiet strength.

He couldn't help watching her and the play of emotion in her eyes. She was unsure and frightened, eyeing the stamping horses and men milling about the courtyard as if she had come from someplace faraway and vastly different.

He wondered if they were headed for the city and what their fate would be once they arrived.

Darcy began to wonder what would have happened if he'd been born a girl. He would have had little hope beyond the most menial of employment. Perhaps, if he'd been desperate enough, hungry enough and cold enough, alone and unprotected, he might even have sold his body.

Quickly he stubbed out his cheroot and strode toward the stable. The red-haired girl, who appeared to be about fourteen, looked at him warily, trying hard to mask her fear when she saw that he was coming toward her. Her slender hand grasped the old woman's tightly.

Did Blossom look like that when she was all alone in a foreign land? Only she had been completely alone, without mother, brother or friend. Would he have had the strength to survive that?

Blossom had not only lived, she had kept some part of her pride. In that, she was as strong as any man he had ever met. Perhaps stronger. Now he could understand how Wu Wing Toi might have taken pity on her and had no other thought than to protect her from a terrible fate at the hands of other men.

Without saying anything, Darcy handed the girl a few coins, although he had never before given anything to a beggar.

The girl said nothing, but for a moment he thought she was going to give him back his money until the old woman muttered something. The girl turned away and showed the coins to the woman before turning back once more to him. "Thank you, sir," she said softly, her voice surprisingly melodious.

He smiled briefly.

A groom appeared. "Your horses are ready, Mr. Fitzroy," he said. Darcy nodded and went to get inside his waiting vehicle.

Soon the noise and the myriad odors that assaulted his nostrils told him he had entered London. As he got closer to home, the sounds and smells grew less and less noticeable from inside the carriage, and soon the carriage rattled over the cobblestones near his house.

Different indeed the city from the leafy lawns of Kinverton. It was the only thing Darcy missed about his recent sojourn in the country.

When he arrived at his house, he quickly got out of the carriage and hurried inside—narrowly avoiding a collision with Powlett. "This is an unexpected pleasure, sir," the implacable man intoned.

"The country, Powlett, may be pretty, but it's a damn bore," Darcy said, feeling rather lighthearted. Perhaps it was hunger.

"Indeed, sir?"

Darcy threw open the doors to the drawing room. It was empty. "Where's Blossom?" He hadn't meant to ask that question. It had just...popped out.

"Upstairs with Mrs. Ditchett, sir."

Darcy nodded. "Send her to me. And bring me something to eat. Tea, too."

Powlett hesitated for a fraction of a second. "Whom do you wish to see, sir?"

Now it was Darcy's turn to hesitate. After a long moment, he decided to pursue the wiser course. "Mrs. Ditchett, please."

"Very good, sir."

Darcy walked around the drawing room. More things were different now, he noticed. Although Mrs. MacTavish had always kept everything spotless, the tables and woodwork seemed to gleam as if they had been covered with glass. Vases filled with flowers sat in every possible space, their fragrance subtly permeating the air. It could, of course, be Mrs. Ditchett's influence, but somehow he doubted it. Just as he sat down, the rustling of skirts made him get to his feet.

"Ah, Mr. Fitzroy, I trust! Home so soon? How delightful!"

Darcy tried not to frown at the woman charging into his drawing room like a train with a full head of steam. Her round face was not unlike the front end of an engine, and she was puffing and panting like one, too. However, her clothes, a miracle of ruffles, flounces, lace and ribbon could only belong to a female.

"Pray tell me, how is Emmaline—my dear Lady Whitmore, I should say?" The plump woman simpered, smiling at him in what he supposed was intended to pass for coyness.

"Very well," he said coolly. "I trust everything has been satisfactory in my absence?"

"Delightful! Charming—once we got the little matter of the coal straightened out."

"Coal?" Darcy gestured at a chair. Mrs. Ditchett sat down.

"Yes, Mr. Fitzroy. I must say," her voice dropped to a whisper, "that I wish I had been forewarned about your housekeeper."

"Mrs. MacTavish?"

"An excellent woman in her way, I'm sure. But stingy, like all the Scotch. She told me I wasn't to use more than one scuttleful a day. I told *her* that I was sure that that might be the rule for servants, but certainly not for guests!"

"That is the general rule of the house, ma'am."

Mrs. Ditchett had the grace to blush. "Oh, dear, well, of course, if those are *your* wishes."

Darcy really didn't want to hear about domestic matters. "How are you getting along with Miss Flowers?"

"A charming young lady, I must say. And very quick to learn."

"Ready to go out in society?"

"Well—" Mrs. Ditchett hesitated "—perhaps in another week or so, as was, I believe, the original idea. She has not the least idea about dancing. That's what comes of being abroad all one's life, I suppose. Really, Mr. Fitzroy, I wonder at her parents, I must say. Some of the things she says!"

It was a struggle to sound nonchalant, but he managed it. "For example, Mrs. Ditchett?"

"Well, she might as well have been living in a barn for all she understands of society."

That was all. He stifled a sigh of relief. "I see."

Mrs. Ditchett leaned a little closer. "I must also tell you, sir, that I consider her servant rather . . . inappropriate."

"How so?"

"The way they chatter on in that abominable language! I'm sure it's impeding Miss Flowers' progress."

"What do you suggest?"

"I think the Oriental should be discharged at once."

"I see."

"Yes, and replaced with a proper English maid. I'm sure the right sort of girl would be a great help to me. It's very troublesome to have to repeat my instructions or wait for Miss Flowers to tell the girl in that infernal tongue. And of course the servant knows *nothing* about the proper care of garments or hairdressing."

"I understand, Mrs. Ditchett," Darcy said, keeping his tone noncommittal.

It appeared that Mrs. Ditchett considered her point won, judging by the rather smug smile that crossed her plump face. "I must say, Mr. Fitzroy, that I think you'll be quite pleased with Miss Flowers' progress. I'm sure she'll be ready for the start of the season." Mrs. Ditchett cleared her throat. "Pardon my boldness, Mr. Fitzroy, but may I take the liberty of suggesting a ball here to introduce Miss Flowers to society?"

Darcy frowned. He could think of nothing more guaranteed to disrupt his peace than a ball, but he had to defer to Mrs. Ditchett's superior knowledge of what was done in the upper levels of society. The realization that he was at the mercy of this overweight, overbearing bundle of middle-aged coyness was galling, but he could do little about it. "I think a ball will be suitable," he said. "I assume I may leave all the details to your capable hands?"

Mrs. Ditchett beamed. "Indeed you may, Mr. Fitzroy. And I believe you may expect an invitation to Emmaline— Lady Whitmore's—costume ball. It's sure to be one of the events of the season."

"I'd like to see Miss Flowers now."

"Just one more thing, Mr. Fitzroy. She'll need some more gowns, sir."

Darcy frowned. "Very well—but nothing extravagant."

"I assume her father has provided for her in that way. May I ask which shop we should patronize?"

Darcy could have groaned at his own stupidity. If he was to continue the ruse of acting for a loving father gone on business, he would have to provide yet more money for clothes and God knows what else. "I don't think it matters," he said, trying not to sound annoyed.

"Ah, sir, well, I'm sure I know just the dressmaker we'll need. If it's Mr. Flowers' intention to get his daughter married off this season, we must take every measure at our disposal, and Madame Stitsokova's taste and fit are not to be equaled. She makes all of Lady Whitmore's gowns and mine, too." She looked at him coyly, clearly expecting a compliment.

"Lovely," Darcy said, but inwardly he was getting more and more upset. Emmaline's gowns cost a small fortune!

He reached out and gave the bellpull a strong tug. Sally appeared at the door.

"Would you mind asking Bl…Miss Flowers to join us?"

The maid curtsied nervously and disappeared behind the door instantly.

"I am pleased to see you, Mr. Fitzroy. I am pleased to see you, Mr. Fitzroy." Blossom recited the words over and over again as Ah Tup finished arranging her hair.

Instead of an elaborate Oriental coiffure, or the simple bun of the past days, her hair was parted in the center with long ringlets down each side. Her back hair was in a high bun. Mrs. Ditchett had insisted on having Ah Tup master this particular mode of hairdressing, even if Ah Tup had almost burned both Blossom and herself with the curling tongs, and despite Blossom's belief that the whole style looked absolutely ridiculous.

"I am pleased to see you, Mr. Fitzroy."

"It is perfect, Mother! The words are like those of Mrs. Dish herself!"

"Do you really think so?" Blossom bit her lower lip in consternation and adjusted the sleeves of her dress once more. This pale green gown was more fancy than the blue one, with lace at the tight cuffs that seemed to be forever in the way.

"Yes, I do. Besides, he will not care how you *talk*."

Blossom nodded, wondering if Ah Tup was correct. She felt as nervous as that night on the ship when she had first seen Mr. Fitzroy, only this time she must be certain to make no errors, for Mrs. Ditchett would be watching with her all-seeing eyes. She hoped he would think her improved!

"Stop twitching! I will make a mistake," Ah Tup commanded.

Blossom sighed and sat perfectly still so that Ah Tup could finish.

Sally's head popped around the doorway after a brief knock. "Mr. Fitzroy sent me to fetch you," she said softly.

"I am finished," Ah Tup said.

Taking a deep breath, Blossom stood up and went down the stairs. Toward the bottom she could hear the voice of Mrs. Ditchett and the blunt answers of Mr. Fitzroy.

At the sound of his voice, her heart leapt and her blood began to throb in her veins, sending heat through her body and surely reddening her face. She hesitated a moment, trying to "compose herself" as Mrs. Ditchett had told her to do. But she couldn't rid her mind of the memory of his warm flesh under her fingers, his soft moan of pleasure or the taste of his firm, sure lips on her own.

With a determined shake of her head that set her ringlets bouncing, she entered the drawing room, making certain she walked slowly with her eyes downcast, the way Mrs. Ditchett had shown her.

"Hello," Mr. Fitzroy said.

She raised her eyes for a brief glance. He was looking directly at her, and she caught a look in his face that puzzled her.

She curtsied. "I am pleased to see you, Mr. Fitzroy," she said softly, still keeping her gaze on the carpet.

Darcy didn't know quite what to think.

What had happened? Where was the flash of determined fire in her eyes, the proud lift of her delicate chin, the air of unconquerable will he had noticed the first moment he had looked into her face?

He tried to tell himself that her meek demeanor was much better. She seemed like every other well-brought-up young Englishwoman, which was why he had engaged the services of Mrs. Ditchett. With a manner like this, Blossom was much more suitable to his plan to get her married.

So why was he not much more pleased?

At that moment Mrs. MacTavish arrived, and behind her came Sally, bearing a large tea tray. "Good evening, sir," his housekeeper said, her eyes narrowing at the sight of Mrs. Ditchett. It didn't take much perception to realize that there was no love lost between the two women.

Mrs. Ditchett gestured for Blossom to sit down. She complied, sitting barely perched on the edge of the chair with her back rigidly straight.

"How have you been, Miss Flowers?" he asked after an awkward silence.

"I have been very well, sir," she said quietly, her words pronounced accurately, but with all the enthusiasm of a quartermaster listing ship's stores.

"Learning many things, I trust?"

"Ah, la! She's very quick to learn, Mr. Fitzroy."

Blossom saw his feet move slightly, betraying his impatience. So far she was unsure if she had pleased him or not, so he was not the only impatient one.

Mrs. MacTavish and Sally, having deposited the tea things, left the room. By her expression, Mrs. Ditchett felt triumphant for having taken over the responsibility of pouring from Mrs. MacTavish.

Mrs. Ditchett began to hand around the tea. "We were not expecting you for another week, sir."

"No, I decided to come home early."

Blossom heard something in his tone that made her risk another glance at his face. He had not been happy at this country place. Mrs. Ditchett had made it very clear that it was an honor for Mr. Fitzroy to go to Lady Whitmore's, and Blossom had realized that Mrs. Ditchett wasn't quite sure if Mr. Fitzroy was deserving of such an invitation. Perhaps he had been as out of place there as she was in London.

She knew she shouldn't feel happy if his journey had not been pleasant. She told herself she was merely glad he had returned.

"I've been telling Mr. Fitzroy, my dear, that you've been making excellent progress."

Blossom nodded. Mr. Fitzroy sat beside Mrs. Ditchett and reached for some tea.

She watched his strong, masculine hands that were capable of arousing so much pleasure. She had missed his presence very much. It was as if the house were asleep when he was not there.

Mrs. Ditchett cleared her throat loudly. Blossom started and almost dropped her teacup.

"Mr. Fitzroy is amenable to having a ball, my dear."

"Thank you, Mr. Fitzroy," Blossom said, noting his scowling face. He no more wanted this ball thing than she did!

She began to hope that he no longer wished her to marry someone else. Perhaps all her efforts with Mrs. Ditchett *had* made a difference already.

"I trust you will try to keep down expenses, Mrs. Ditchett," he said coldly. "It isn't necessary to spend a fortune to introduce Miss Flowers to society."

"As you wish," Mrs. Ditchett said with a frown. "I shall do my best." She brightened. "After all, I'm sure Miss Flowers will be the greatest attraction. The young men will simply flock around her."

"I'm sure they will, which is, as you so correctly surmised, the purpose of this enterprise."

Blossom wanted to run, to hide, to get away from him. He was so cold and distant, and his last words left little doubt that anything she saw that made her think his feelings toward her were changing were only in her own imagination.

However, she sat motionless, blocking out the rest of their words as they talked of the ball.

She imagined herself back in Honorable Wu's kitchen, late at night when the rest of the household slept. She remembered how she and Ah Tup would complain and laugh and talk of what they would do if they were rich. She had been happy then, and the two of them had made their own little world apart from Precious Jade and the other servants.

It was useless to pretend that she could make another world, with another person who could understand her the way Ah Tup did.

Then Powlett appeared. "The Honorable Horton-Smythe," he said, standing back to allow that gentleman to enter.

"Fitzroy!" the man exclaimed, coming inside. "What a pleasure this is!"

Blossom's gaze darted to Mr. Fitzroy. He was not feeling pleasure, of that she was certain.

With sudden unease, she realized the other man was staring at her in a way that reminded her of those other men in the marketplace when she was a little girl.

Mr. Fitzroy spoke. "Miss Flowers, allow me to present the Honorable Charles Horton-Smythe, my business partner."

Remembering what Mrs. Ditchett had told her, Blossom held out a hand. Horton-Smythe took it and pressed it to his lips.

Try as she might, Blossom could not help feeling sickened by the touch of his lips on her skin. She knew that here to touch another's flesh in such a manner was not grossly improper, but she remembered how this man had scrutinized Mr. Fitzroy. Blossom glanced upward, wondering if Ah Tup was watching now.

"And this is Mrs. Ditchett," Mr. Fitzroy said.

"Charmed, I must say."

"Really, sir, thank you, but it is I who ought to be charmed to meet a friend of Mr. Fitzroy's, I'm sure," Mrs. Ditchett oozed.

"Is there something I can do for you?" Mr. Fitzroy asked.

"Well, old man, I came to drop off some papers. Nothing vital, but I thought to save you some time when you returned next week. Quite a shock to have Powlett tell me you were back, don't you know?"

"Yes, well, I had enough of the country."

"Did you?"

Blossom had the distinct feeling a snake might sound like this other man, his words winding around his tongue.

Mr. Fitzroy nodded toward the door. "Let's go to my study, shall we? Excuse us, ladies."

Mr. Horton-Smythe turned to Mrs. Ditchett and bowed slightly. "Delighted to make your acquaintance, ma'am." He bowed toward Blossom and smiled. "Charmed, I'm sure."

The girl didn't acknowledge his words, but nodded with an inscrutable expression.

As he followed Darcy out of the room, Charles tried not to smile too broadly. He knew the moment he had seen the girl that he had at last met Wu Wing Toi's "payment."

She was without doubt one of the loveliest girls he had ever seen, and he had seen several in his pursuit of pleasure. There was a certain air of submission about her, but no truly submissive female had so proud a carriage, or eyes that looked at him in quite that enigmatic way.

In short, she was fascinating.

It was also fascinating watching Darcy Fitzroy practically squirming like a mouse in a trap. He was going to find Darcy's explanation of this girl's presence entertaining.

"A dashed charming young lady, Darcy," Charles began the moment they were in the study. "Who is she?"

Darcy, obviously trying not to scowl, turned toward him. "She's the daughter of an old friend."

"Really?"

"Yes, she's staying here while her father's in the West Indies. He's asked me to look after her and introduce her into society."

"Well, she's an astoundingly beautiful creature."

Darcy glanced at him, and Charles realized he might have sounded much too interested. "Here's the papers I was leaving. Nothing important. How was the charming Lady Whitmore?"

"Charming, as always."

"And her ass of a husband?"

Darcy smiled. "An ass, as always."

His partner chuckled companionably.

"I'm thinking of having a ball, Charles."

"Now that's surprising news, old man. Is this in honor of the lovely Miss Flowers?"

Darcy sat down, looking discomfited. "Mrs. Ditchett tells me that's the right way to launch Miss Flowers."

God, the man made the girl sound like a ship about to get christened. Charles had never seen a figure less like a boat's—although there were certain figureheads, of the mermaid type, that she might resemble. Minus some articles of clothing, of course.

Charles forced himself to concentrate on Darcy. "Wonderful idea."

It suddenly occurred to Charles that if the beautiful, inscrutable "gift" was going to mingle in society, it was very possible that he could become quite friendly with her. Intimate, even, especially if Darcy wanted nothing to do with her. Obviously he didn't, or he would have kept her presence a secret.

Instead it seemed Darcy was going to try to pass her off as some kind of ward. With what goal?

What other goal did a guardian have when he introduced a ward into society other than marriage? Of course. The ever-upright Darcy Fitzroy would try to pass her off as honorable marriage material. The girl was so lovely the man might even succeed.

Unless, of course, it happened to get about that Darcy's apparently innocent ward was really a whore.

Chapter Ten

In a few short days Darcy wished Mrs. Ditchett had shot him after he agreed to the ball for Blossom. That would have been the merciful thing to do.

Leaving all the arrangements and invitations to her was proving to be one of the major mistakes of his life. For instance, he would have done well to inquire of Mrs. Ditchett what exactly she meant by a "small number" of guests. He had assumed ten at the most; Mrs. Ditchett seemed to be thinking of at least fifty. She had apparently consulted with Emmaline, with the result that even that detestable little toad Lord Northrup had been invited. Worse, the toad had replied that he would attend. Darcy thought he detected Emmaline's influence in that response, for which he supposed he should feel grateful. After all, the toad was going to be very rich.

Even Mrs. MacTavish seemed to be conspiring against his peace, although she maintained a belligerent attitude toward Mrs. Ditchett. Mrs. MacTavish had announced that if he didn't want to be ashamed in front of his guests, he'd need new wallpaper in the drawing and dining rooms and new linens on the table. Reluctantly he had given in, to find scaffolding all over the lower floor when he returned from the office the next day. He felt like an intruder in his own house, less important than food and clothing.

A new cook, engaged from only God and Mrs. Mac-Tavish knew where, had arrived and was always demanding to show him menus, as if he gave a damn what they ate.

Some fop of a Frenchman was coming every day to teach Blossom how to dance, the music repeating and repeating until Darcy thought he'd go mad.

And there was the sudden flurry of bills from dressmakers, milliners, bootmakers, jewelers…which he had to pay, since he was apparently acting for Blossom's father.

For all he saw of Blossom, however, she might have been a figment of his dreams. Mrs. Ditchett was obviously drilling the poor girl as thoroughly as any sergeant major. They even ate upstairs so he wouldn't be disturbed by the "corrections."

Several times he wondered if it wouldn't have been wiser, not to mention cheaper, to send Blossom back on the first ship bound for the Orient.

As for Blossom, she was beginning to feel as if her life in China, despite the beatings, had been infinitely more pleasant than her life under Mrs. Ditchett's tutelage. Indeed, if it wasn't for the strong memories of Mr. Fitzroy's arms about her and Ah Tup's constant pleasantness, she might have been very tempted to run away. As it was she was constantly being told what to do, how to do it, and what was wrong with the way she had just done it.

In vain she looked for evidence that Mr. Fitzroy had even the smallest concern for her. The few times she saw him, he looked as if he suffered from indigestion, and considering the vast quantity of food barbarians consumed daily, that would not have surprised her. She found herself wondering if Water Lily had been wrong about making a man jealous. Perhaps that worked in Canton, but not with Englishmen.

Perhaps he no longer wanted her at all. Rather than give in to the despair such thoughts provoked, Blossom decided to concentrate on all she had to learn for the ball. That was not easy, for simply thinking about Mr. Fitzroy usually made her make more mistakes than ever.

She was vastly relieved when the night of the ball arrived at last.

"You tremble, Little Mother!" Ah Tup said, holding out a petticoat for Blossom to step into.

Blossom tried to smile. "I have so much to remember and I am afraid of all those barbarians!"

"Afraid? You are never afraid!"

"I fear I might lose face, by doing something wrong or saying the wrong thing."

Ah Tup nodded understandingly. "*Ayee,* so much to think about! I am glad to stay upstairs. But I do not think you will make a mistake. The Dish woman has taught you well, of that I am certain."

Blossom sighed and tugged gently on her chemise as she stood up. "I wish I were as certain of it as you are."

She glanced at the pink ball gown she was to wear and couldn't help frowning. Mrs. Ditchett had wanted her to wear a white dress, but Blossom had refused. She would not wear the color of mourning. She had wanted a red dress, since that was the color of good fortune, but Mrs. Ditchett had said Blossom would look like a "trollop" in it, whatever that was. At last they had agreed on pink.

The gown was the same strange shape as all the dresses the barbarian women wore, with a skirt even larger than any Blossom had yet seen. Mrs. Ditchett had personally supervised its making, so it had several rows of flounces and tucks around the bottom of the skirt and an abundance of lace at the low-cut bodice.

Involuntarily her hand went to her neck. She still couldn't understand the appeal of the naked skin on arms and chest or why a man would find a woman attractive if she wore a dress that looked in danger of slipping off. How much better to wear the soft caress of silk, which fit to one's body like a second skin yet flowed as smoothly as water in a placid stream.

Sighing, she let Ah Tup help her into the dress, guiding it carefully over the petticoat. "You look beautiful," she said approvingly.

Blossom drew on one of the long white gloves she was to wear. The fabric was so fine and delicate she was afraid they would tear. "You will be watching?"

Ah Tup's eyes were as sharp as a fox's, and Blossom knew she would see and remember things while her mistress was too busy trying not to lose face. "Of course. I want to see how the barbarians do this, men and women dancing together."

"You watched me and the *monsieur*."

Ah Tup sniffed. "Now *that* man I am certain is a eunuch! Or perhaps a woman pretending to be a man. I wish to see the master at this dancing with you."

Blossom felt her face flush hotly. "He may not dance. Not once has he come into the room while I learned, and I know Mrs. Ditchett asked him to. Perhaps, since he wishes to find a husband for me, he wants me to dance only with other men."

Ah Tup wasn't fooled by her excuses for a moment. "Come, Mother! Even though their dances are strange, you are as graceful as a willow in the wind! Besides, didn't the Dish woman say he would ask you for the first one since he holds this ball for you?"

"Yes, but..."

The servant girl sniffed scornfully. "Mother, all this barbarian nonsense has disturbed your harmony and addled your brain. You are beautiful. You are graceful. You have been trained by the best, most famous concubine in all of Canton. There is no man who could resist you, especially not such a virile man as the master. It seems to be their way to play love games. But I promise you, he will find you irresistible tonight."

Blossom put on her other glove. "I hope you are right, Ah Tup. I begin to think that perhaps I will be wed to another man after all."

"Huh! Convince yourself first, and then perhaps you will be able to convince me."

Blossom said nothing, but pulled her bodice as far up as it would go.

Mrs. Ditchett pounded on her door. "Are you ready, my dear? It's time to go down."

Ah Tup smiled and spoke quickly. "Go now, and I will watch from upstairs. Remember what I said. You are *irresistible.*"

Blossom smiled back nervously and went to the door. Mrs. Ditchett, wearing an elaborate gown of bright blue with several flounces and ruffles, an enormous lace bertha over the bodice, several ostrich feathers in her hair and gloves so tight they seemed in danger of splitting asunder at any moment, was waiting impatiently. "That's enough of that Chinese chattering for tonight," she said rather harshly.

Blossom nodded, biting back an angry word. She must try to be on her best behavior tonight.

As they went toward the drawing room where they would receive their guests, Blossom saw Mr. Fitzroy pacing the hall the way Honorable Wu had when he was beset by many problems. From above she noted the formfitting perfection of his black coat with the things called tails down the back and his long, black-trousered legs. Then he turned around.

She tried to remember everything Mrs. Ditchett had said about not looking directly at a man, but all the woman's admonitions might have been chaff in the wind. Blossom could no more withdraw her gaze from Mr. Fitzroy's face than she could command the house to rise into the air.

He did not smile. Instead, his eyes narrowed and he looked at her with an expression that was scornful at best, full of aversion at worst. What little confidence she had vanished instantly, and she had to blink to hold back tears.

With desperation she reminded herself that she was Fragrant Blossom of the Middle Kingdom, raised in civilization, trained by Water Lily. She was irresistible.

She was miserable.

"Ah, Mr. Fitzroy, I'm so glad we're all ready on time."

Blossom started. She had actually forgotten that Mrs. Ditchett even existed, let alone stood just behind her. For once she was glad to have the woman there, since she could turn to her and ignore the face of Mr. Fitzroy.

"It's the height of impropriety to be late. I do hope the cook has got the supper well in hand. You can never trust these hired people, as I told the housekeeper. And I'm happy to see that the orchestra is here, although I suppose a violin, cello and piano hardly constitute an orchestra, but they should do very nicely for this."

Mr. Fitzroy held out his hand to Blossom. She placed hers on his arm, her fingers barely touching the fabric of his coat.

Together they went into the drawing room, Mrs. Ditchett chattering along behind them.

Darcy glanced absently around the drawing room, now almost empty of furniture except for some chairs along the wall and the places for the orchestra at the far end. They took up their places to receive their guests. His mind, however, was not on the altered state of the room but on the altered state of his thoughts.

If someone had asked him what he had expected when he was waiting for Blossom at the bottom of the stairs, he probably couldn't have put it into words. But it wouldn't have been this...this puppet in an overelaborate gown with her hair in a ridiculous style that resembled string beans hanging off her head. She moved as stiffly as a wooden doll and seemed about as vivacious.

Good God, what had that Ditchett woman done to her?

Darcy was still scowling when Charles Horton-Smythe arrived.

Charles realized at once that something was amiss. Darcy looked like a man who was forced to stand next to his worst enemy, and the girl seemed petrified with fear.

How interesting, he thought, greeting them and moving into the drawing room.

Next to arrive were several business associates and their families, but Charles paid scant attention to them. However, when Lord and Lady Whitmore appeared, he maneuvered closer to the door, watching carefully.

"Lord and Lady Whitmore, may I present Miss Flowers?" Mr. Fitzroy said, his face cool and expressionless.

Blossom found herself on the receiving end of two very different types of scrutiny. The man, Lord Whitmore, held a round glass thing in front of his eye and smiled blandly, as if she were no more than a gown on a stick. His wife's gaze, however, was quite another matter.

As Blossom curtsied toward the woman in the lovely blue silk gown and the handsome, rather stupid looking man, she caught the faint scent of the woman's perfume. It was the same one she remembered from the night in Mr. Fitzroy's bedroom, when she had known he had been with another woman. Blossom deliberately returned Lady Whitmore's slow scrutiny.

Mr. Fitzroy took Lady Whitmore's hand politely and kissed it in a chaste, gentlemanly fashion.

Lady Whitmore smiled. "I do hope you're planning to attend my costume ball, Darcy, to commemorate the opening of the Crystal Palace. With your charming guest, of course."

Mr. Fitzroy nodded. "We'll be delighted."

As the golden-haired Lady Whitmore went into the room, Blossom watched her covertly. To think a woman would have the audacity to appear in public at the home of her lover! Of course her husband, who appeared to have the intelligence of a carp, must have no knowledge of her adultery.

Despite her revulsion at the woman's moral laxity, Blossom couldn't help comparing herself to the woman. Lady Whitmore's gown, simple yet of very fine silk, was infinitely better than the garment Blossom wore, and Lady Whitmore moved as if she'd been born wearing such a dress. It could be that Englishmen preferred that strange yellow-colored hair, too. Suddenly Blossom felt hopelessly ugly and clumsy.

Then Lady Whitmore glanced back.

It might have been the look in the woman's eyes or the hint of a frown in the woman's full lips, but at once Blossom knew that this woman feared her. Clutching Mr. Fitzroy's arm a little tighter, she lifted her chin and smiled at the next couple who entered the room.

"She's a pretty little thing, eh, my love?" Lord Whitmore said to his beautiful and graceful wife.

"Yes, very pretty," Emmaline replied. She had measured the girl quickly against her own criteria, based on experience and hard-won skill. She had seen a very lovely girl who had the face of a madonna, but whose eyes were far from innocent. Miss Flowers was somehow old for her years, despite the bloom on her cheeks, and her eyes had been shrewd and discerning. Standing next to Darcy, she had seemed right at home. A quick survey of the gentlemen in the room revealed that most of the men were quite captivated by Mr. Fitzroy's guest.

As she glanced back, Emmaline realized she had just met a girl who could blossom into the most dangerous rival she had ever known.

Charles watched Lady Whitmore glide into the drawing room. He was mildly surprised by the almost bored greeting she had exchanged with Darcy. Had something happened between the two lovebirds? Was that why Darcy had come back from Kinverton early? Charles had been puzzling over that for days, almost tasting the curiosity to know what would compel Darcy to leave what should have been a glowing scene of social triumph.

Lady Whitmore moved toward Mrs. Ditchett, the chaperon, and it was immediately clear that they were old acquaintances.

That would seem to prove that Darcy had indeed kept away from the charming little Miss Flowers, or whatever her real name was. Surely no woman would send a relative to chaperon a usurper to a lover's bed. Or would she? Emmaline Whitmore was a very clever woman, and perhaps she knew more about the girl than he guessed. It could be that Lady Whitmore had sent Mrs. Ditchett with the sole purpose of insuring that she had no rival for Darcy's affections.

If so, Lady Whitmore's plan was working. It was obvious to anyone who knew Darcy that he was upset about something, and having a girl like that in the house without being able to touch her would certainly upset any full-blooded male.

His gaze moved to Miss Flowers. Despite the hideous gown and even more hideous hairstyle, there was no denying that she was beautiful. Her bodice left ample creamy skin showing, and her figure was virtually perfect.

Of course, Darcy could be a sanctimonious bastard, as Charles recalled from the first and only time he suggested that Darcy accompany him to a well-known brothel. Darcy had looked at him as if he'd just suggested castrating himself with a dinner knife.

No explanation. Darcy never explained anything. But Charles never invited him again. For a brief period of time, he had wondered if Darcy was merely a typical middle-class righteous idiot, or perhaps something a little more unusual, but then he found out about Darcy's liaisons with various married women. It seemed his scruples allowed for adultery but not prostitution.

Jeremy Fitzroy, a younger, softer version of his brother, entered the drawing room with a delicate young woman holding on to his arm demurely. Charles surveyed the girl slowly—pale, pretty in a delicate way, but nothing to get a man's blood stirring—and noted the way her grip tightened on Jeremy's arm when he presented her to his brother.

The two men glared at each other like two knights about to joust. Sidling casually closer, he caught the blond girl's name: Elizabeth Hazelmore. Unfamiliar. She must not be anybody special.

He saw Jeremy look down at her with great tenderness as they were presented to Miss Flowers.

So, that was the way the wind was blowing, eh? Charles wanted to laugh out loud. Darcy had made no secret of his grandiose plans for his brother, as if education and money could make up for lack of social standing, not to mention how Darcy planned to push Charles aside and hand his place to Jeremy, even if Darcy had never said it out loud.

And now here stood Jeremy, the delight of his brother's eyes, with a girl from God knows where on his arm. Jeremy looked at her as if she were some kind of angel. No wonder Darcy looked like he could do murder.

As the musicians began taking their places at one end of the room, there was a commotion by the door. Moving closer, Charles realized Darcy had refused to take the first dance with Miss Flowers.

Of course. Darcy never danced.

Charles grinned and quickened his step. Here was an opportunity much too good to miss.

Chapter Eleven

Mrs. Ditchett spoke quickly, panic in her voice. "We assumed you would lead the first dance, Mr. Fitzroy. It's only proper."

Mr. Fitzroy glared at Mrs. Ditchett, then at Blossom. "I don't dance," he repeated brusquely.

Out of the corner of her eye Blossom saw Lady Whitmore smile with what looked like triumph. One of the other female guests, with the impossible name of Shrew-something who was clutching the arm of the plump lord named Northrup, giggled shrilly. It seemed as if everyone else was frozen motionless, staring at her. There was only one exception, and that was the girl with Younger Brother. Her expression was friendly, but in her eyes Blossom saw pity.

Instantly Blossom forgot her fear and embarrassment. She straightened her bare shoulders and held her head high as Mr. Horton-Smythe appeared beside Mr. Fitzroy. "Will you allow me the honor, Darcy?" he said, smiling.

Blossom thought he looked more like a snake than ever and would dearly have loved to refuse him, but she stepped forward. "I would be delighted," she said, not worrying about how the words sounded.

Mrs. Ditchett eyed Mr. Fitzroy with still-shocked disapproval. "Well, *someone* had better take the first dance."

Blossom allowed Mr. Horton-Smythe to escort her to the center of the room while other couples formed behind them.

The music began and she started to dance, finding it surprisingly easy now that she knew she could not be interrupted and berated for clumsiness. Only the urge to see Mr. Fitzroy disturbed her pleasant surprise, but he never seemed to be looking at her at all.

"Enjoying yourself, m'dear?"

She glanced at Mr. Horton-Smythe and tried not to show her distaste as he leaned closer.

He smiled knowingly. "Making some conquests already, I think."

She turned away, but she could still feel his hot breath on her bare shoulder.

"Darcy will be pleased. He should make a pretty penny with your marriage settlement."

They circled and turned, and Blossom said nothing. The evil man spoke again. "You don't understand, do you? Let me explain, my dear. When you marry, the man will make a marriage settlement upon you. That's when Darcy plans to get back the money Wu owes him."

Another turn as the music grew louder and the room grew hotter. "Mr. Fitzroy honors me by arranging a marriage."

Mr. Horton-Smythe's pale hazel eyes gleamed. "Is that what he told you? Hate to enlighten you, my dear, but I assure you the only person Darcy's thinking about is himself. He's selling you, my dear. Right now you're on display and then, when he gets the best offer, he'll sell you."

She opened her mouth to call him a liar, but the words stuck in her throat. It might be so, and it would explain why Mr. Fitzroy was spending so much money. And yet she understood this man. Had, indeed, from the first time she had seen him. He was the kind of man who would do anything, say anything, to further his own ambitions.

She need not trust a word he said.

As the dance finished, Mr. Horton-Smythe moved uncomfortably close. "I would be delighted to offer you my protection."

The thought of being near this man another moment longer chilled her. She said nothing, curtsied and tried to walk away, but he took her hand in a grip of iron, placed it on his arm and began moving toward Darcy.

"You're a charming dancer, *Miss Flowers,*" he said softly, "although I understand that's not really your name."

Blossom looked at him sharply.

"It's a pity Darcy doesn't appreciate you and all your many talents."

"You must forgive my ignorance," she said quietly. "I am not sure what you mean, but I think you are mistaken. Mr. Fitzroy appreciates me, and my skills, very much."

She had little concern about lying to such a man as this, and was pleased to see his surprised expression.

"Darcy is a very lucky man," Mr. Horton-Smythe said slowly, drawing her back out onto the dance floor.

"I wish to rest," she protested, but he ignored her.

She wondered where Mr. Fitzroy was, then spotted him over in the corner, talking—or arguing, to judge by his expression—with Younger Brother.

"Does he treat you well?"

She looked at Mr. Horton-Smythe and tried not to frown. "Yes, very."

"If anything should ever go amiss, my dear, please remember that you can always come to me."

Blossom would sooner slit her own throat. She could easily guess how this man would treat a woman. "Thank you," she said softly.

Mercifully Mr. Horton-Smythe said no more, and when the dance ended, she hurried over to Mrs. Ditchett before he could monopolize her again.

"A most unusual man, my dear," Mrs. Ditchett said, nodding toward Mr. Fitzroy. "I quite wonder at your father leaving him in charge. He barely takes an interest in the proceedings. Why, I recall when dear Emmaline—Lady Whitmore—had her first ball, her father was a perfect menace making sure everything was done properly. Well, I suppose it's different, since Mr. Fitzroy isn't your father."

"No, he is not," Blossom replied, watching his back as he spoke to his brother and the pale, pale girl he had brought with him. She glanced up at the ceiling and saw the spot from which Ah Tup was watching. She hoped Ah Tup could hear everything.

The short, plump Lord Northrup waddled up to her. "I say, Miss Flowers, may I have the honor of a dance?"

Blossom nodded, for she had no excuse to refuse, and took his arm.

As they began to dance, the young man stepped heavily on her foot. "Oh, I say, I'm terribly sorry, Miss Flowers! How clumsy!"

She muttered something—she wasn't sure quite what—as she watched Mr. Horton-Smythe walk toward Mr. Fitzroy.

"Miss Flowers, I understand you're in London for the season?"

Blossom, intent on Mr. Fitzroy, smiled absently at her dancing partner.

And quite unknowingly captured the affection of Lord Neville Northrup, future heir to two hundred thousand pounds.

"Darcy, this is Elizabeth."

Darcy didn't bother to hide a scowl as he looked down at

the girl holding on to his brother's arm like a barnacle. He couldn't deny there was a certain pale, helpless attractiveness to her, if you liked that sort of female. Jeremy would. When he was a boy he was always bringing injured animals home and nursing them better.

"What are you doing here?" Darcy asked bluntly, ignoring the girl.

"I was invited," Jeremy replied.

"What?"

Jeremy turned an exasperated face to him after glancing at the crowded room. "Please, Darcy, not here."

Darcy kept his feet firmly in place. "Here's as good a place as any for anything you have to say to me."

Jeremy looked at Elizabeth, but she only tightened her hand on his arm.

"All right," Jeremy said, his mouth becoming a hard line that matched his brother's. "Elizabeth and I are getting married."

Darcy laughed harshly. "And what are you planning to live on, air?"

A flickering expression of pain passed over Jeremy's features, and for a moment Darcy's heart softened. For a moment.

"We aren't going to ask you for anything, if that's what you're afraid of. We won't get married until I have a suitable income. I . . . I wanted you to meet her, Darcy."

"So now I have. Please leave me to do my duties as host." *Whatever the hell they are,* he finished in his thoughts, with another frown.

"All right, Darcy. If that's the way you want it."

Jeremy, with Elizabeth beside him, walked across the room to where an old business friend sat with his elderly mother.

Darcy looked for Blossom. She wasn't hard to find, dancing in the center of the room with that idiot Northrup. The imbecilic nobleman was staring at her like a lovesick puppy and she was smiling at him.

He turned away quickly and came face-to-face with Charles. "Lovely girl, Darcy."

"Yes." He watched her dance. "But I'll be glad when the season's over."

"Ah. She goes back to her dear papa then?"

"Or gets married."

"Quite a charming little thing. Might be tempted myself."

Darcy glanced at Charles to see if the man was in earnest, but Charles had moved off toward Lord Whitmore.

Darcy strode down the side of the room, heading for the garden. The house had suddenly become unbearably warm.

Mrs. Ditchett sighed rapturously. "You were quite a success, my dear. Really *quite* a success. I'm certain Lord Northrup was absolutely captivated!"

Blossom tried not to trip on the stairs as they proceeded upstairs. All the guests had gone. Mrs. MacTavish was downstairs directing the servants who were cleaning up from the supper, Powlett was supervising the kitchen staff, and Mr. Fitzroy had disappeared into his study after saying he needed a drink.

Blossom was utterly exhausted and wanted nothing more than to go to bed and sleep. She had eaten almost nothing at the dinner, her appetite for English food not noticeably developed. The dancing, however, had made her rather thirsty, and the drink called champagne had been very good. She had finished five or six glasses.

Mrs. Ditchett followed Blossom inside her bedroom.

"Your dear papa would have been so proud if he'd seen you here!"

"Yes," Blossom said, wondering why the floor seemed to be on a curious angle. Perhaps the dancing had made the house tilt.

Ah Tup, waiting to help her disrobe, smiled broadly. "*Ayee,* Little Mother! What a night!"

Mrs. Ditchett's eyes narrowed suspiciously. "Please be so good, Miss Flowers, as to remind your *servant* that no one has addressed her yet."

Blossom nodded and, keeping her back to Mrs. Ditchett, who had collapsed into the nearest chair, spoke to Ah Tup in Cantonese. "Ah Tup, please. We'll talk later, when we can be alone." The tone was severe, but Ah Tup saw Blossom attempt a conspiratorial wink—and not quite succeed.

"You have had too much rice wine!" Ah Tup said, trying not to giggle. She looked at Mrs. Ditchett and feigned to be ashamed. Then she moved away, until she stood behind Mrs. Ditchett's chair.

"Just think of it, my dear!" The rapid movement of Mrs. Ditchett's fan betrayed her excitement. "Lord Neville Northrup! His fortune's *immense,* my dear. Simply astounding—and his parents are both dead, so there's no one to interfere...that is, come between two young people."

Blossom tried to look serious, but it was very difficult. Ah Tup was making faces, imitating Mrs. Ditchett behind her back. Finally Blossom found a chair and sat down dizzily.

"I saw at once, of course, that that horrid Gloriana Shrewtonbury had her heart set on catching Northrup. Those Shrewtonburys were always like that—an eye out for the best catch. Huh! The women in that family all look more like horses than most horses! Such noses—really, they're almost an embarrassment to the human race! It was her mother who even tried to lure my first husband away from *me*—without success, need I add. And now the daughter's set her cap for Neville Northrup!'' By this time Mrs. Ditchett was talking mainly to herself. Blossom swayed in her chair as if she were back on board ship. ''We'll see about *that*. But I see you're fatigued, my dear. I'll leave you. Tomorrow we must be ready to receive callers, and I'm certain Lord Neville Northrup will be one of the first!''

Blossom nodded as Mrs. Ditchett left the room. The minute she was gone, she spoke eagerly. ''Ah Tup, who was the girl with Younger Brother?''

''She is the girl he wishes to marry.''

''Mr. Fitzroy does not agree?''

''No, he does not.''

''Ah,'' Blossom nodded. ''And yet I saw no harm in her. Of course, if Mr. Fitzroy says it is not to be, it will not be.''

Ah Tup shook her head. ''They have no sense of filial duty, these barbarians. They argued. I think Younger Brother will marry her anyway. And as for the girl—she looks sickly, don't you think?''

Blossom shrugged. ''I caught a glimpse of her feet. They are enormous. But if Younger Brother wants her, I think Mr. Fitzroy should consider it.'' She remembered how the girl had looked at her across the room. ''She smiled at me in a most friendly way. I like her.''

''You may be right.'' Ah Tup grinned broadly. ''Now, Mother, about this dancing. Although we know that barbarians are shamefully ignorant and uncivilized, I think perhaps their idea of dancing is not so foolish after all.''

Blossom remembered the tight clasp of Mr. Horton-Smythe around her waist and the heavy tread of Lord Northrup on her toes. ''It is very tiring.''

"With the wrong man perhaps. But with the right one…it looks almost as good as reaching the zenith, with not nearly so much effort."

"Maybe," Blossom said slowly, thinking once more of Mr. Fitzroy's embrace. It would be quite wonderful to dance with him.

"Well, it must be, or why else would the master look at you with such jealous eyes as you danced with other men?"

Blossom glanced at Ah Tup sharply, the effects of the champagne momentarily vanishing. "He did?"

"*Ayee!* If ever I saw a jealous man, it was him! Why, he looked as if he would kill them all!"

"He never danced with me."

"No," Ah Tup admitted slowly. "Maybe he doesn't know how?"

That idea had never occurred to Blossom, but it did make sense. "Mr. Fitzroy—he was really jealous, do you think?"

"Have I not eyes? Am I a fool?"

Her words made Blossom feel even more giddy. "Perhaps I should go downstairs and thank him for the ball?" she asked softly.

Ah Tup nodded sagely.

Without another word, Blossom went out, tiptoeing to the top of the stairs.

"That will do for tonight, girls," she heard Mrs. Mac-Tavish say, and then Powlett spoke from outside the study.

"Mr. Fitzroy," he said, "will you need anything else tonight?"

She didn't hear Mr. Fitzroy's reply, but hurriedly ducked into the first bedroom where she waited until she heard the housekeeper and the butler pass by.

She continued downstairs. When she reached the study, she took a deep breath, almost fell over, recovered her balance and knocked softly.

"What?"

She opened the door. Mr. Fitzroy's jacket had been slung over a chair, and he stood beside the mantel, his necktie hanging undone and his shirt partly unbuttoned. He held a glass of brandy in his hand and straightened when she entered.

Blossom closed the door and turned toward him, suddenly very aware of the naked skin that the gown did not cover and the heat coursing through every particle of her body.

She moved nearer, drawn by the expression of desire in his face as if she were a moth and he a flame.

Without a word he set down his drink, strode across the room and pulled her into his arms. His lips found hers as surely as if they had touched a hundred times. Her desire swept everything away except sensation as his lean strong hands caressed the bare flesh of her back. There was no art in her response, no remembrance of what she had been taught. She acted on the most basic human instincts—and that was more than enough.

His lips moved slowly across her cheek to the throbbing pulse of her neck, making her moan and arch against him.

She tugged at his shirt, wanting to feel his heated skin, to bring it closer. Her lips followed their own path, touching the tender skin of his ear. She heard him groan and the sound thrilled her, making her even more desirous to fulfill the needs of their bodies.

His hands found the soft swell of her breasts, plunging inside the gown as she gasped with shock and delight. She pulled away for an instant, letting his hands move where he willed, enjoying the pleasure he aroused in her until she could stand still no longer. She pressed forward, pulling his shirt open and letting her tongue tease his nipples.

She felt her bodice loosening, his fingers hurriedly undoing the constraining garment. "Yes, oh, yes, honored lord!" she whispered, her hands pushing the shirt from his body.

He stopped. Bewildered and filled with hot desire, she looked at him and tried to read the strange expression on his face. "Why did you come to this room?" he asked, his voice quiet but hard at the same time.

"I . . . I came to thank you for the ball."

He stepped back, and she spoke quickly. "It was lovely, and I know it cost much money . . ." She stopped, halted by the expression of loathing in his eyes.

"And this—" he gestured at her partly-unlaced bodice "—is how you intended to thank me? I thought you said you were not a whore."

His words stung, as full of poison as a serpent's fang. Her face flushed with anger and shame and pride. "I have never been a whore." Her hands balled into fists. "It is *you* who wish to sell me."

"What the hell are you talking about?" he demanded, but his face burned red.

"You think I do not know about marriage settlement? You think I am some lowly, foolish servant you can cast out? I have done my best to please you, but now I learn that you have lied to me. You will get your money by selling me in marriage."

She angrily wiped away the tear that fell on her cheek. "Perhaps I am stupid fool after all, when I dared to think I could make you care for me."

Mr. Fitzroy took a step closer. "Blossom, I'm—"

"You think to make me a whore?" She turned her back to him and in one swift movement tugged down her garment so that he could see the scars on her back. "Look and know that no one can make me do a thing against my will!"

She turned back, clutching her bodice over her breasts, her chest heaving with anger, her eyes blazing. "But if I have no other choice than to be a whore in this awful, terrible place, I will go to the richest man I can find. And I will never, *never,* let you touch me again!"

He heard her sob as she ran from the room.

Darcy picked up his drink and threw the glass into the fireplace, where it shattered into tiny pieces.

Chapter Twelve

Dear Mr. Fitzroy:

Pray excuse the haste and untidiness of this letter, but I have little time before the ship sails for England, and I wish to inform you of the information I have been able to attain regarding the young lady recently arrived (I trust) in London. You will know of whom I speak.

I have made several inquiries among the English community here in Canton and am delighted to tell you that I believe I have solved part of the mystery. I have been told by an elderly gentleman that there was once, in a nearby missionary post, a Yorkshireman who lived there with his family. He was an Anglican minister and was awaiting the chance to go into the interior.

Before that could be accomplished, his wife took ill and died, leaving him the sole parent of a little girl, then aged five years. There was some talk at the time of sending her back to his parents in England, but the father refused until he himself suffered a near-fatal illness three years later. He then realized that the child would be better off in her native land, and the father decided to accompany her on the journey. They set off from Canton in the spring nearly eleven years ago, and neither they, nor anyone else on the ship, were ever seen again.

I believe, sir, that you will agree that the date of departure, as well as the age of the little girl who had, I was told, dark hair, make it highly likely that she must be the unfortunate daughter of this man, the Reverend Saul Cooper. I hope this information allows you to find the young lady's family, and I trust she is safe in your care.

If you would be so good as to inform me of the arrival of the young lady and her present state of health, I would be eternally grateful.

> Yours very sincerely,
> Elias Mitchell

Charles Horton-Smythe frowned as he refolded the letter addressed to his partner. "Mitchell is an enterprising, zealous young man," he muttered, tapping the letter on his chin. "He should remain in China indefinitely."

He put the letter in the secret compartment of his desk. Perhaps later he would pass it on to Darcy, but for now it suited his purposes if the girl's identity remained a mystery.

Someone entered the outer office. Charles peered out the door and saw that it was only a clerk arriving, not Darcy. Since the evening of the ball nearly a fortnight ago, Darcy had grown increasingly haggard in appearance, and increasingly tardy in his arrival at the office.

It was also Charles's opinion that Darcy was drinking rather too much wine. With a girl like Miss Flowers in the house, who couldn't be touched whether because of Darcy's own stupid morality or the presence of Mrs. Ditchett, it was no wonder a man had to find refuge someplace.

Charles closed the door, momentarily thinking of the little dark-haired whore he'd found in his favorite brothel, the one who looked so much like Miss Flowers.

But there was business to be done. Scooping up a handful of documents, Charles headed for Darcy's office.

Before he got there, however, someone else came in, this time the soon-to-be-wealthy Lord Neville Northrup, who was accompanied by Lady Emmaline Whitmore. Charles approached them at once.

"How wonderful of you to grace our humble offices!" he said to Lady Whitmore. "This is truly an unexpected pleasure!"

"Is Mr. Fitzroy in?" Lady Whitmore asked, arching her exquisite eyebrows questioningly.

"Not just at present," Charles replied. "Perhaps if you care to step into my office, I may be of assistance?"

Lady Whitmore inclined her head and followed. Lord Northrup, looking around with the fascinated gaze of a man in a curio shop, came after—once he'd realized they were walking away without him.

Inside his office, Charles held a chair for Lady Whitmore and gestured toward another for Lord Northrup.

"Now, how may I be of assistance?" he asked, sitting down behind his desk and looking studiously at Lady Whitmore, who turned to Lord Northrup.

"Well, the fact is, I come into my inheritance next month, don't you know," Northrup said, "and I want, that is, should, I suppose, invest some?"

Charles smiled kindly. "Ah, would that all young men were as wise, eh, Lady Whitmore?"

With a very slight smile, she inclined her head again.

"And I thought, well, might as well invest in shipping as anything else, eh, what?"

"A very good choice, I must say." It was all Charles could do to keep from rubbing his hands with glee. There was nothing quite so wonderful as a very rich, very stupid investor. "We're currently planning our shipping schedule for the next six months. Approximately how much were you planning to invest?"

Lord Northrup's face went blank, then red. "Well, that is..."

"Not a large sum, just at present," Lady Whitmore said.

Lord Northrup looked relieved. "Yes, not a large sum, just at present."

"I see. Well, I'll have one of the clerks draw up a list of the ships and trade goods. There's some that are quite regular voyages, and we're planning one or two that are really very exciting. One thing to remember, old chap, the greater the risk, the greater the profit, eh?"

Lord Northrup's eyes gleamed with excitement, but Charles realized Lady Whitmore was looking at him with a very shrewd expression. Very shrewd indeed.

He'd heard the rumors that *she* really made all the decisions, but he'd never believed a woman that beautiful could have a head for business. Now he could.

Obviously he would have to get Northrup alone if he was going to convince him to risk major capital. "Well," he said with a friendly smile, "there's no rush. Time and tide wait for no man, but there's always ships at sea, eh? I'll just get that list started, shall I?"

When he came back, Lady Whitmore and Lord Northrup rose to leave. "Do you expect Mr. Fitzroy back soon?" Lady Whitmore said.

"I'm not sure when he'll arrive. He's a very busy man these days." He thought her eyes flashed for a moment, but the expression was gone in an instant. "Tell me, what do you think of Miss Flowers?"

"A very charming young lady."

Lord Northrup beamed. "Isn't she, though? Such a pretty little thing, too!"

"I understand Mr. Fitzroy's taking her to see the Crystal Palace tomorrow."

"I say, is he really?"

"I believe so. Have you been already?"

"Went opening day. I say, it's jolly incredible, all the stuff they've crammed in the place. Really amazing. Have you seen it yet, Mr. Horton-Smythe?"

"No, I haven't had the time."

"Well—" Lord Northrup cleared his throat self-consciously "—I really don't think one visit is enough. Do you, Lady Whitmore?"

Lady Whitmore, who'd been standing quietly beside the door, shook her head. "No, I don't believe it is. I should like to view the exhibits once more myself."

Darcy paced in the drawing room. He'd probably already marched the equivalent of five miles in the past half hour, but Blossom was getting as bad as any female, keeping him waiting for longer and longer periods of time as they prepared to go out.

As if the waiting weren't bad enough, he had no more desire to see the blasted Crystal Palace than he would an iceberg. He hated crowds, especially gawking, talking crowds of people marveling at overgrown toys and cheap baubles. Crystal Palace indeed!

At last he heard Blossom and Mrs. Ditchett coming down the stairs. Without a word, he went past Powlett and strode down the steps to the waiting cab.

All the way to Hyde Park, the only person who did any talking was Mrs. Ditchett, but it had become obvious over the past two weeks that the woman would talk to a statue.

Darcy and Blossom might as well have been two ivory figures for all the talking they did. From the way the woman occasionally looked at the slender girl sitting beside her, it was easy to guess that the chaperon believed all her admonitions about how a proper young lady conducts herself, along the lines of being seen and not heard, had finally taken effect, to her chaperon's glory.

Darcy, who knew better, was finding Blossom's silence much more unnerving than he would have believed possible. They had gone out a few times, twice to dinner parties and once to a theater. At first he'd been worried that Blossom would say or do something that would make it abundantly clear that her upbringing had been unusual, to say the least. Perhaps he should be grateful that she felt the way she did about him now, because she rarely said anything at all in his company.

Darcy stared moodily out the window of the hansom cab, oblivious to the cries of the street sellers. Over and over again he kept telling himself that things were much better this way, as if by constant repetition he could come to believe it.

Blossom tried not to look at Mr. Fitzroy and to concentrate on the sights and sounds of the huge city. After all, she had never been allowed outside the walls of Honorable Wu's house, rarely outside the stuffy cabin aboard the ship and only been to a few social gatherings at night. London by daytime was a noisy, smelly, incredible sight.

Mr. Fitzroy crossed his long, muscular legs that were so close to hers that she could have nudged him with her knee. But she was never going to touch him again.

When she said those words, she had meant them with every fiber of her being. She had been hurt and angry, dismayed and determined.

Only later, when she thought of the look on his face when she faced him, did she realize he might have been regretting his words. He looked sorry and ashamed, as well he should.

She had not gone to him to thank him with her body, and in her heart she knew there was no shame in what had happened between them. If there was something wrong, it was that he could not admit that there was a bond, a feeling, growing between them.

As for herself, she knew that she needed him. Without him her life would be as empty as a storehouse during a famine.

She had never before met a man who made her feel so safe and protected, not even Honorable Wu. When Mr. Fitzroy smiled at her, it filled her with joy, and hope that she might yet find happiness for herself. When he touched her, she felt as if her spirit could soar into the clouds.

That was finished.

Now Mr. Fitzroy never smiled at her and barely spoke to her except to give orders. Around other people, he stood near her, but she might have been in another country for all the attention he paid to her.

That foolish boy, the plump lord, was always at her elbow. If Mr. Fitzroy cared anything at all for her, he would have seen that she wanted to be rescued from the lord's annoying attentions. It had become all too obvious that he didn't even care that much for her.

She sighed softly and tried to pay attention to Mrs. Ditchett.

In the distance the weak sunlight, struggling to shine through low gray clouds and the ever-present pall of coal smoke, made something sparkle. At first Blossom was too lost in thought to notice, but when they drew closer, she gave a little cry of delight as she realized it was an entire building made of glass.

"I don't know when I've ever seen Hyde Park so crowded!" Mrs. Ditchett exclaimed, leaning out the window.

Mr. Fitzroy grunted an acknowledgment and leaned back against the cushions.

Blossom ignored him and spoke to Mrs. Ditchett. "Who owns all this place? Surely he must be a great lord."

"Who owns Hyde Park?" Mrs. Ditchett chuckled. "Why, my dear, no one. Well, I suppose you could say the people of London."

Blossom stared incredulously. This place belonged to no one? "And the great glass building?"

"Waste of people's money, I think."

Blossom pretended she didn't hear Mr. Fitzroy and looked at Mrs. Ditchett.

"Well, to be sure it was a costly undertaking, but what a wonderful way to show the world the might and ingenuity of the British Empire."

Blossom's eyes narrowed. She didn't quite know what Mrs. Ditchett meant, but she didn't like the smug, assured tone of the woman's voice.

"I mean, really, to think of all the latest inventions under one roof and displays from so many foreign countries—which of course won't hold a candle to the British exhibits—well, it almost takes one's breath away."

Mr. Fitzroy looked at her as if he'd like to take Mrs. Ditchett's breath away permanently, but he said nothing.

"There will be things from many countries?"

"Oh, yes, my dear. According to the papers, there are over seven thousand British exhibitors and over six thousand foreign exhibits. I should think just about every civilized country will have sent something."

Blossom nodded. Then of course there would be something from China, the most civilized country in the entire world.

The cab finally came to a stop. Mr. Fitzroy jumped down and offered his arm first to Mrs. Ditchett, then to Blossom.

The Crystal Palace loomed ahead like some marvelous creation of the gods, one hundred and eight feet tall at its apex. The sheer multitude of glass panes held in place by a framework painted orange, scarlet and pale blue almost overwhelmed Blossom. For the first time she began to believe that the British might not be quite so inferior after all.

They made their way inside and immediately saw the enormous elm that had been enclosed by the structure and beyond that a beautiful crystal fountain nearly thirty feet high. Blossom was much too impressed to utter a sound, and when she looked at Mr. Fitzroy, she saw that he didn't seem nearly so indifferent as he had in the cab.

"Now, Mr. Fitzroy, let's find the Textile Section first, shall we? I understand from Lady Whitmore that there's some velvet there that simply has to be seen to be believed...." Like a ship making headway through high waves, Mrs. Ditchett began pushing her way through the crowd, leaving Blossom and Mr. Fitzroy to follow along behind.

Mrs. Ditchett seemed to know exactly where to go, so they found the Textile Section quickly. It teemed with all kinds of fabric, from velvet to silk to cotton to fur to feathers and even hair.

Darcy, after the initial shock at the magnitude of the place, knew he would soon be bored by this feminine section of the exhibits. Maneuvering his way to a corner, he leaned against a wall and wondered what would happen if he lit a cheroot. As he scanned the crowd aimlessly, he saw a little girl staring at him as she held on to a plump woman's hand. The woman was fascinated by the cloth she was looking at, but the little girl was apparently fascinated by him.

She had large, blue eyes and a delicately pointed chin. Her skin was smooth and pale and her face was framed with curling dark hair. He realized, as he returned her scrutiny, that the little girl reminded him quite forcibly of Blossom.

All at once the girl smiled. Darcy began to smile back until he realized she was smiling at the man beside him. Then the girl's mother spoke and she turned to answer.

"Your daughter?" Darcy ventured, looking a the dark-haired, rather short man dressed in a simple coat and breeches beside him.

"Aye, sir."

"She's very pretty."

"Aye, so she is." The man's accent told Darcy at once that he was a Yorkshireman. "Ding! The women'll be all day about it." He sighed and Darcy nodded. "I'll be lucky to get out with a ha'pence in my pocket. Any road, I suppose if it'll keep them happy for a while."

Darcy grinned. "I've just resigned myself to spending half the day right here."

"Aye," the Yorkshireman said, a companion in misery.

"Father," the stout mother said as she turned to them, "why don't you go and see the big machines? We'll meet you at the fountain in a little while."

"Now that's a fine idea," the man said. He turned to go but glanced back at Darcy. "Wouldn't mind somebody to talk to, if you're not wanting to stay here."

Darcy thought that was one of the best invitations he'd had in years.

He found Blossom and Mrs. Ditchett examining some expensive silk, which he knew he would probably be paying for later, told them of his plan to see some of the exhibits on his own and to meet him at the crystal fountain in two hours.

"Now, shall we?" he said when he rejoined his new-found companion.

Ever since Blossom had arrived at the Crystal Palace and moved slowly through the mob of incomprehensible voices, knowing that somewhere in the vast glass building there was a Chinese stall, she had been filled with homesickness. She wanted to hear a familiar tongue, to see familiar features, to feel once again a part of the ancient civilization of the Middle Kingdom.

She knew that it could take a very long time before Mrs. Ditchett was ready to leave all the fabrics and move on to another exhibit, so she waited until Mrs. Ditchett had moved far inside the stall selling velvet and other fine cloth. Then, cautiously, she moved away, out into the vast passageway. She didn't really know where to go, but she would find the Chinese exhibit if she had to take the whole day.

It occurred to her as she kept to the edges of the stalls and crowds that Mr. Fitzroy might see her. She reached up to undo the veil on the top of her hat. She could at least hide her face, and she doubted Mr. Fitzroy would recognize her dress since he paid so little attention to her now.

After walking what seemed like miles, she finally spotted a stall with a giant porcelain vase outside. Her steps quickened, for she was certain she had found what she was looking for.

She had, to her profound disappointment. Inside the stall was simply junk, the things the beggars made for foreign devils. Even more disappointing, there wasn't one Chinese person in the booth. Instead there was an immensely fat man seated on a stool that barely seemed of a strength to support her, let alone him.

Slowly she went inside the stall and discovered that all was not quite so bad. There were some good examples of porcelain and some silk, but compared to the British exhibits—and indeed, most of the rest—this was embarrassingly pathetic.

"Is this all?" she finally asked the fat man, loath to believe it.

"Yep," he said, reaching into his pocket and producing a clay pipe. "And what a time we had gettin' this!"

He saw that she didn't understand and began filling his pipe. "See, they asked them Chinese to send some things, and they said they would. Never did. What a hullabaloo!" He leaned back, struck a match on the sole of his boot and began to light his pipe. When it began smoking, he took a long draw and exhaled, the smell almost making Blossom fall over. "Yep, not a thing they sent. So they rounded up this here stuff. I'm just a watchman, like."

"Oh," Blossom said weakly, her face burning with shame. What could her countrymen have been thinking of?

She knew almost at once. They thought the English and their exhibition not worth the trouble.

If only they had understood how this would be, all the hundreds of people going past. If they had, they could have sent so many wonderful, marvelous things. Beautiful silks such as only the very wealthy could afford, silks like no English person had ever seen. Why, even one of her simplest and least costly gowns was better than anything here. They could have sent carved furniture so ornate that it seemed only a god could have created it, and porcelain as fine and delicate as a breath. They could have sent clocks so intricate you watch them for hours.

They could have shown the whole world that they were truly the greatest nation on earth. Instead all that was on display was trash, so obviously inferior that people simply walked past.

Angry at her countrymen and ashamed, too, she turned away. It was better, at least, that she had seen this alone, without Mr. Fitzroy and Mrs. Ditchett.

As she turned to go down the corridor, she stopped. Lord Neville Northrup and Lady Whitmore were heading her way. She had no wish to see Lord Northrup. Not now and certainly not here. She went into the Chinese stall, and, with her back to the entrance, began to examine some silk.

Mercifully they passed by the booth.

Not wasting any time, she pushed past the fat watchman and went down the corridor in the opposite direction to Lord Northrup. She hurried on until she reached the farthest end of the pavilion and sat panting on a small bench. As she tried to catch her breath, Blossom suddenly realized that she was quite lost.

"Did you come all the way from Yorkshire to see this?" Darcy asked as he and his new friend made their way to the civil engineering section.

"Aye, partly. Come to London to visit my wife's sister and see the Palace."

"What do you think?"

"Think I should've stayed at home on the farm."

His tone and words were so like Darcy's own feelings that he laughed.

"You're a Londoner, then, are you?" the man asked.

"I live here, yes."

"Businessman?"

"Shipping."

By this time they had reached their destination. They spent several minutes in companionable silence examining the model of the Liverpool Docks, complete with sixteen hundred fully rigged model ships. There were also various models of bridges, railways, lighthouses and canals. Then it was on to the raw materials section containing almost every substance that could be used in manufacturing; next came the weaponry, with guns and models of warships and even a strange vessel that was called a "submarine."

"Incredible what some men think up, ain't it?" Darcy's friend muttered. "Who'd want to be under water like that? God, gives me the cold creeps thinking about it."

Darcy nodded. "Except you wouldn't be at the mercy of the weather, I suppose."

"No, suppose not."

By now they had reached what were called the "Philosophical Exhibits."

"Never saw a stupider idea in my whole life!" the Yorkshireman muttered as he looked at the Anhydrohepseterion. "What's it meant to do?"

"It says it's a device to stew a potato in its own juice."

"My God! Some men got too much time on their hands."

As they shared a companionable chuckle, Darcy realized he was having a very enjoyable time. The Yorkshireman was practical, sensible and pleasant. "I'm Darcy Fitzroy," he said, offering his hand.

They shook heartily. "Sam Cooper."

Darcy nodded and then realized Sam was staring at something behind him.

"Here comes your lady friend," Sam said.

Darcy turned as Mrs. Ditchett came rushing up. "Oh, Mr. Fitzroy, thank heavens I've found you! Miss Flowers has disappeared!"

Chapter Thirteen

Blossom tried not to panic. The fabrics were at the other end of the building. She could go to a different level to avoid Lord Northrup, and since she was watching for him, she could surely hide again if she saw him. If all else failed, Mr. Fitzroy had said to meet at the crystal fountain. It was so large it should be quite simple to find. Feeling slightly relieved, she stood up and prepared to head back to the fabric.

"Elizabeth, my darling, don't cry."

Blossom halted abruptly. The voice was like Mr. Fitzroy's, but she recognized it as Younger Brother's. She glanced over her shoulder and saw Younger Brother with the pale yellow-haired girl he had brought to the ball going into one of the least crowded stalls, which was full of some strange animal statues. She hesitated for a moment, then followed cautiously. Pretending to look at the statues, she hovered near the entrance.

"But Jeremy, we *must* end our engagement. I won't be the cause of a break between you and your brother."

"I'm not worried about Darcy. He's just being stubborn and selfish. Once we're married, he'll come round. I promise."

Blossom moved a little closer and heard quiet sobs.

"You do love me, don't you, Elizabeth?"

"Oh, Jeremy, more than my own life!"

Blossom had never heard anything like the emotion in the girl's voice. It was at once sad but happy, weak and strong. Younger Brother's voice was soft and gentle, but filled with intensity. Blossom closed her eyes and imagined how Mr. Fitzroy would sound, saying such words to her.

"Your brother loves you, too, in his own way. You owe him so much."

This Elizabeth was no grasping woman, no Precious Jade in an English body. She was willing to give Younger Brother up rather than come between the two men.

"My brother's been good to me. I won't deny that. But I love you too much to let you go, even for his sake. Please, Elizabeth, marry me!"

"Oh, Jeremy, yes, yes!"

Their tenderness, their passion, their desperate longing for each other was so clear in every word that Blossom hurried out of the stall, a lump in her throat.

All at once she realized she had misunderstood this thing love. It was more than the mere physical union between a man and a woman. It was a feeling so strong it transcended filial duty and so powerful it could turn even a pale, weak creature into a determined woman.

It was the way she felt about Mr. Fitzroy. But he felt no love for her.

Her eyes filled with tears as she pushed her way through the crowd. She didn't see Mr. Fitzroy come storming toward her, his brow furrowed in anger.

"Where the hell have you been?" he whispered harshly.

Oh, how different from the way his brother had sounded moments before!

Before Blossom could answer, Mrs. Ditchett hurried up, her handkerchief, veil and hat shaking with agitation.

"Oh, my dear, what a turn you gave us! We didn't know where you had gone!"

"Well, I guess I'd best be off, seeing that you've found her."

Blossom bit her lip to subdue her tears and turned to the man who had spoken. The short stocky man, whose words she could barely understand, was looking at her with a most peculiar expression.

"It's been a pleasure." Mr. Fitzroy shook hands with the man. "Here's my card. Perhaps you'll be in London again."

The man nodded. "Aye, maybe. I don't have a card, but if you're ever in Haxby, ask anybody at the Saracen's Head Inn and they'll tell you how to get to my farm." Then, with one more nod and another searching look at Blossom, the man drifted off into the crowd.

Mr. Fitzroy turned to her and looked about to curse when another voice cut through the crowd.

"Oh, I say, Miss Flowers! This is a pleasant surprise, eh, what?" Lord Northrup came trundling up, looking like a boy who had just finished a dish of sweetmeats. Behind him came the stately and lovely Lady Whitmore.

Blossom tried to smile at Lord Northrup but couldn't. All she could do was stare at the floor and wish herself far away from this place.

Mr. Fitzroy nodded to Lady Whitmore. "Enjoying the exhibitions?" he asked nonchalantly.

"I'm getting some more ideas for my ball next week," Lady Whitmore replied. "You are still planning to attend?"

"Definitely," Mr. Fitzroy replied.

"Oh, I say, that's wonderful! And you, too, Miss Flowers?"

"I am honored to be invited," she whispered.

"Oh, the pleasure is all mine, my dear," Lady Whitmore said, smiling coldly. "Really, all mine."

Mrs. Ditchett sat or, rather, reclined on a sofa in the drawing room after dinner. Blossom watched to make certain she was asleep, then stood up and went toward Mr. Fitzroy, who was seated at the far end of the room reading a newspaper.

"Mr. Fitzroy," she said softly.

The force and speed with which he moved the paper away and the intensity of his gaze almost unnerved her. "Well?"

"I am sorry I wandered away like a lost sheep today," she said, determined to get her apology out of the way.

He moved the paper back in front of his face.

"Mr. Fitzroy?"

Again the paper moved rapidly, but this time he just looked at her.

"While I was walking back to you in the Palace, I overheard Younger Brother speaking to the girl he wishes to marry."

Mr. Fitzroy's eyes narrowed. "You eavesdropped?"

"I dropped nothing, Mr. Fitzroy. I *heard* them talking."

"Same thing. That's considered very rude."

She cleared her throat. "I think you should let Younger Brother marry her."

Mr. Fitzroy's face hardened. "It's none of your business."

Blossom didn't let his cold tone deter her. She might never find love, but she could at least help Younger Brother. "It *is* my concern as long as I am of this household."

"If Jeremy wants to marry that penniless girl, that's his trouble, not mine. He understands that, even if you don't."

"You are right. I do not understand things here, but I do know that it would be better to be friends with your brother than enemies. Is it not better," she asked softly, "to agree and help? Then they will bless you all their days."

She saw that he still did not agree with her and decided to try a different way. "I do know that he is as determined to marry as you are to stop it. Think, then, Mr. Fitzroy, if you were in your brother's place. Would you obey?"

Mr. Fitzroy looked away.

"You should let them marry. They will anyway. And I think she is a woman who would make a fine sister-in-law, for she understands proper filial duty. She does not wish to make trouble between you." She hesitated for a moment, looking intently at his face. "They love."

Mr. Fitzroy made no sign that he heard her.

"I am sorry if it was not in my place to speak of such matters, but I only seek to make your way smooth."

Slowly Darcy turned to her, seeing an expression in her deep blue eyes that told him she meant what she said. Why should she care about his family? She had made it amply clear in the past fortnight that she cared nothing for him. Indeed, by the apparent reciprocity of her feelings for that oaf Northrup, it seemed all her previous emotions had been only sham.

And yet, when she spoke of love, he began to wonder....

Mrs. Ditchett stirred, snorted and sat up. "Oh, dear me, I seem to have fallen asleep."

Blossom moved away and Darcy tried not to notice, especially as Mrs. Ditchett was looking at them suspiciously.

"Well, obviously it's time to retire," Mrs. Ditchett said, heaving herself upright. "Come, Miss Flowers."

Without a murmur of protest or look in his direction, Blossom walked toward the door.

"Oh, by the by, Mr. Fitzroy, I understand the costumes will be ready for a fitting tomorrow."

"Costumes?"

"For Lady Whitmore's ball."

Darcy went to a cigar box, selecting a cheroot. "I'm not wearing any costume."

Mrs. Ditchett made a disapproving sound. "But you must! *Everyone* will be in costume!"

"Not me."

The tone of his voice made it clear even to the less-discerning Mrs. Ditchett that there was no point in further protest. "Is Miss Flowers not to wear a costume, then, either, sir?" she said meekly.

"I don't give a damn what she wears."

"Well, *that's* something, I suppose," he heard Mrs. Ditchett say as she went out the door. "Good night," she said a little more loudly.

He turned and watched Blossom's slender form go out the door and up the stairs, remembering the soft, intent expression she had fixed on his face moments before. He slumped down in a chair, lit his cheroot and reached for the bottle of port at his elbow.

After the third drink, he became aware that Mrs. Ditchett was standing in front of him.

"What?" he said, not bothering to sound polite.

"It's about the servant, sir," she said equally bluntly.

"What servant?"

"The Chinese girl, Ah Tup." Mrs. Ditchett sat down across from him, her voice now conspiratorially quiet.

"What about her?"

"I think we should consider finding a replacement."

Darcy glared at Mrs. Ditchett, who seemed to be swaying oddly. "What's she done?"

"Nothing specific, I must admit. But her continued presence is not helping Miss Flowers to shed her, shall I say, peculiarities?"

"Peclu . . . percu . . . what do you mean?"

"I mean, sir, that I think it would be more conducive to Miss Flowers's father's plans, especially as they pertain to finding a husband, to hire a more suitable ladies' maid."

Darcy finally got Mrs. Ditchett in focus. "Bl...Miss Flowers likes her."

"That may very well be, but I think we have to consider the larger scope. After all, a young lady may like to eat, but a plump one will have a more difficult time to catch a husband."

"I suppose you would know about that," Darcy said, not noticing how Mrs. Ditchett's face reddened. "Well, I shall think about it."

"There is something else I should like to discuss with you, sir."

"What?"

"You'll excuse me for mentioning it, but I really feel it would be better if you could manage not to use such coarse language around the young lady."

Darcy's mouth hardened. "I'll talk any damn way I like. This is *my* house."

Mrs. Ditchett got to her feet quickly. "Very well, but I'm forced to say it's having a rather disturbing effect on the young lady's conversation. Only yesterday she asked Lord Northrup if he didn't think the theater a damned pretty place."

Darcy gave a loud snort of laughter. "Good for her!"

"Really, sir, this is not going to further the relationship, which I'm certain we're both desirous to promote."

He frowned. "Very well."

"Good night, then, sir."

"Good night."

As Mrs. Ditchett waddled toward the door, Powlett hurried silently down the hall to find Mrs. MacTavish.

* * *

The next day Jeremy stood before his brother in the study, his stance defiant and his face hard. "Well, what do you have to say to me? Or do you just want to remind me that you don't approve of my choice of wife?"

Darcy gestured to a chair. "Sit down."

"No, thank you."

Blossom was right, Darcy reflected as he looked up at his younger brother's face. Jeremy *was* quite as stubborn as he was. "All right. Stand up then. I simply wanted to tell you that I remove all my former objections to your marriage, and I still want you to come into the business when you're finished school."

Jeremy sat down with a thump in the nearest chair. "What brought on this sudden change of heart?"

"Well, I've never seen you quite so determined to do anything as you are to marry this girl, so I realized there was no point trying to dissuade you. I decided it would be better to be your friend."

Jeremy's face mirrored the changing of his thoughts. First there was shock and surprise in his eyes, then a smile burst onto his lips and lightened the rest of his features. "That's wonderful, Darcy!" Jeremy jumped out of the chair and grabbed Darcy's hand, shaking it vigorously. "This is wonderful! You'll like Elizabeth, really! She's just the most wonderful girl! I have to go tell her right away! Really, she's just the most wonderful girl, Darcy!"

He rushed to the door, then paused on the threshold, turning back to his brother. "Darcy, I know you wanted me to marry well. Believe me when I say I couldn't marry any better than this, if love is any guide, and I *know* it is. I can only hope, now, that you'll find a woman as kind, as sweet, as loving as Elizabeth. God bless you!"

Darcy went to the door of the study as Jeremy bounded out of the house like a dog off the lead at the hunt.

Love was for young fools. Boys with their whole lives ahead of them, who had no worries about business. Who were perfectly free to choose a woman who could make them happy for the rest of their lives.

He would find a socially advantageous wife. He'd been meaning to do just that for some time, but he'd always put it off with one excuse or another, secretly counting on Jeremy to fulfill that objective while he lived a free, bachelor existence.

Such a marriage wouldn't mean anything more than a convenient hostess and an occasional moment of husbandly duty in the nuptial bed with a woman who would probably put up with that distastefully.

At least Jeremy would be happy.

"Oh, Miss Flowers! I'm so sorry, but you must forgive me. I'm in great haste!"

Younger Brother was smiling so broadly that Blossom had to smile back even though he had almost knocked her flat as she reached the bottom of the stairs. She watched him career out of the house and into the street.

When she turned back, she saw Mr. Fitzroy standing in the hall. He looked at her for a moment with an expression that made her heart begin to beat rapidly. She thought he was going to speak, but instead he turned and went back into his study.

Blossom guessed what had just happened. Mr. Fitzroy had given Younger Brother permission to marry. He had listened to her! He had taken her advice!

Without stopping to think beyond the excitement such knowledge gave her, she hurried down the hall and burst into the study.

Mr. Fitzroy spun around quickly and ran his hand across his eyes, but not before Blossom realized what she had seen.

A tear running down his cheek.

In that instant she forgot how angry he had made her, forgot the terrible things they had said to each other, and only knew that her heart smote her as she saw the pain in his eyes.

"Oh, Mr. Fitzroy!" she whispered, going up to him and putting her hands on his still-damp cheeks and looking into his dark eyes.

He pushed her hands away. "I . . . I got some soot in my eye. That's all."

Blossom had had all she could stand of English reticence. "No, there was no soot in your eye. You are ashamed to tell me that you have a tender heart!"

"That's completely wrong!" He strode over to the window and stared at the back garden.

"Very well, Mr. Fitzroy, you have no tender heart. You did not reconsider Younger Brother's marriage and did not listen to my wisdom. You asked him here to argue and protest, and so he left looking as happy as it is possible for a man to look, *heya?* Clearly I was most mistaken. Forgive me."

Mr. Fitzroy turned his head slightly and glanced at her. "Maybe I asked my brother here as a means of getting you to speak to me again."

Blossom opened her mouth, but nothing came out.

He turned around and looked at her steadily. "Tell me the truth, Blossom. Will you marry that idiot Northrup if he asks you?"

At that moment, with him looking at her that way, she hardly knew which way was up, let alone what she was going to do about the foolish lord.

"I realize he would be quite the catch, of course." He came a few steps closer. "Since I just approved one marriage, I won't stand in your way, either."

"I have not been asked yet," she said, trying not to show her dismay in her voice or expression.

"I see. Mrs. Ditchett seems to think he's tottering on the brink."

"Is he?"

The cool tone with which Blossom replied, as if she had been planning and considering the marriage like any business proposal, chilled him as much as her inscrutable expression frustrated him.

Ever since he had first laid eyes on Blossom he had fought to keep his emotions under control, and yet he knew he had not been successful. The more time he spent with her, the more he realized he was perilously close to falling in love. Apparently, however, she cared little for him now that she felt free of any obligation to him.

God, what a fool he was! The sooner she was married and gone from him, the better. And the more she hated him, the easier it would be to forget her.

"Mrs. Ditchett also thinks I should get you a new maid."

Blossom stared at him. "What of Ah Tup?"

He tried to ignore the frightened, bewildered tone of her voice and he didn't dare look at her face.

"What of Ah Tup?"

"Don't you think she would be happier back in China?"

Out of the corner of his eye he saw Blossom's hands clench into tight balls, the same hands that had caressed him so gently only moments ago.

"Ah Tup's home is with me. She will not go."

"She won't have any choice," Darcy said, going out of the study and leaving her there, alone.

Chapter Fourteen

Blossom rolled over in the small bed and looked at the shape of Ah Tup on the floor next to the door.

What would she do without her friend? She had no doubt that Mr. Fitzroy meant to send Ah Tup away. He had been so cold, so cruel.

It would be a pain worse than torture to see Ah Tup go away. Yet as long as she was in Mr. Fitzroy's house, he had the right to send Ah Tup back to China.

She had failed in her duty to Honorable Wu, failed to fulfill her own desire and now she was failing Ah Tup.

It was not hard to guess that Mrs. Ditchett was responsible for this idea. She had never liked Ah Tup, making no secret that she disliked anything or anybody who was not English.

Blossom turned over and stared at the ceiling. She had to think of a way to keep Ah Tup with her.

She could do nothing about Mr. Fitzroy or her own wants, but perhaps if she married Lord Northrup he would let Ah Tup stay with her. He was always very anxious to please her.

To manipulate Lord Northrup reminded her so much of Precious Jade that the idea at first repelled her. At the same time she found herself sympathizing with Precious Jade. She could understand something of the woman's bitterness and hatred. As with all Chinese marriages, hers had been arranged by her parents. Neither Precious Jade nor Honorable Wu had seen each other until their wedding day. Although Honorable Wu was kind, he was not a man to inspire passion. It could be that the emptiness of her life had made Precious Jade what she was.

Blossom didn't want to marry Lord Northrup and become another Precious Jade.

Perhaps there was another way. Perhaps she could convince Mr. Fitzroy that Ah Tup was vital to his household, or someone in it.

She thought of all the servants and quickly realized that although Ah Tup knew enough English to joke with them, she was never anything but respectful with the Chief Eunuch, just as he was always very polite to her.

Respect was sometimes the road to a more tender feeling. She remembered a look Powlett had given Ah Tup once as the girl laughed merrily over her work in the kitchen. The man was surely not a eunuch.

"Ah Tup," Blossom said innocently the next morning, "have you never thought of being married?"

The maid giggled. "Of course not, Mother! How could I be your servant if I had a husband?"

Blossom toyed with the ruffles on her gown and glanced surreptitiously at Ah Tup, who was embroidering one of Blossom's robes. It was of a fine, serviceable silk, but plain. Having little to do, Ah Tup had decided to decorate it. "But suppose you were free, what type of man would tempt you?"

Ah Tup took her time selecting a pale blue thread and frowned slightly. "A dead one. Then I would be a widow and still have my freedom."

Ah Tup was not answering at all seriously. Knowing how important this conversation was and having to keep the secret that Mr. Fitzroy might be planning to send Ah Tup away made Blossom feel like crying instead of laughing. "Really, Ah Tup. If you had to marry, what kind of man would you choose?"

"One like you are choosing. Rich."

"He must have much money?"

"Of course. And preferably many concubines, so he will leave me in peace."

"I don't suppose you would consider a foreign devil?"

Ah Tup snorted. "*Ayee!* Why not? They seem to treat their women very well—although they seem most backward in this business of concubines. Still, I would see that he had one and then I would be left to run the household without anyone's interference."

"What of, perhaps, someone like the Chief Eunuch?"

Ah Tup looked at her, her face a picture of surprise. "The Chief Eunuch?"

"Yes. I think he has money."

"Money he may have, but he is too proud and pompous."

"I think he likes you."

"I don't."

"He looks at you when you laugh."

"Probably condemning me for having some joy in this awful country."

"Once I thought he was going to smile at you."

"Impossible. He does not know how."

"You never tease him."

"It would be a waste of effort."

"I think I'm right."

"I think you are mad."

Blossom decided she had pursued the matter far enough, for if she asked many more questions, Ah Tup might begin to guess her plans. But she also knew that Ah Tup, for all her protestations, liked the Chief Eunuch, or she would have made endless jokes on the matter. Instead, she sewed as if her life depended on the completion of that one gown, and was most uncharacteristically silent. "I do not like the dress I am to wear to this costume thing," Blossom said after a long moment.

"Huh! Nor should you. Indeed, it is the most hideous garment I have ever seen in my life."

"Mr. Ditchett says it is Eliza-beet-an."

"To be sure somebody should have been beaten for making it. What a jumble of colors and patterns—not to mention the way it flattens your breasts!"

Blossom sighed. "She says the Eliza-beet-an was a 'glorious age of British history.'"

"That is like her, to say such a thing. She believes the British do everything best. Fool!"

Blossom thought about the Crystal Palace. Before that, she would have quickly agreed with Ah Tup's estimation of the British as bragging fools; now she knew that their high opinion of themselves had some merit, however small. It still rankled that the Chinese exhibit had been so embarrassingly pitiful. Why, even the gown Ah Tup was working on was better than anything else in that stall.

Suddenly Blossom had an idea. She got to her feet quickly and hurried over to the trunk in the corner.

"What is it, Mother? What do you seek?" Ah Tup put down her sewing and joined her.

"My best gown. The beautiful one from Honorable Wu. And my best silk undergarment. And my lovely shoes."

"Why?" Ah Tup asked as Blossom took an armload of clothing and laid it on the bed.

"I will show these British what the Chinese can do. I will wear *this* to the costume ball." She held up the beautiful robe she had worn that night on the ship, the first time she had seen Mr. Fitzroy.

Ah Tup smiled broadly. "Ah, Mother! Surely this will impress them all!"

"But we must say nothing to Mrs. Ditchett or she will put a stop to our plans."

Ah Tup frowned. "Am I such a fool? I, who never speak to that ox if I can help it, I would run and tell her of your delightful idea?"

Blossom smiled and, holding the gown in front of her, spun around. For once she would be dressed comfortably, too.

There was a knock on the door, one all too recognizable as Mrs. Ditchett's. Hurriedly but carefully, Ah Tup and Blossom returned everything to the trunk.

"My dear, it's time to be receiving!"

Blossom frowned, sighed, rolled her eyes and prepared for another afternoon drinking endless cups of tea, smiling endless meaningless smiles and listening to the stupid utterances of Lord Northrup.

One afternoon two days later, Emmaline watched Dulcibella Ditchett as she leaned forward for another pastry. "You're certain that he's going to ask for her hand?"

Mrs. Ditchett gained her objective but held the tart in the air as she spoke. "Absolutely positive, my dear. Neville Northrup is *completely* smitten."

"Do you think her guardian approves? I mean, Neville's a sweet boy, but hopelessly stupid."

"Mr. Fitzroy? It's up to Miss Flowers's father to approve, not him. And really, my dear Emmaline, what man who's made his money in trade is going to object to his daughter marrying into the nobility?''

"What of Miss Flowers? Does she seem agreeable?''

"I'm sure the girl will not refuse. She's always most courteous to Lord Northrup.''

Emmaline nodded. If the girl had any intelligence at all—and those blue eyes glowed with superior shrewdness—she would latch onto Neville as quickly as possible.

Emmaline suppressed a sigh. Miss Flowers's situation was very like her own when she had been a young girl entering society.

Lord Whitmore was not unlike Neville Northrup, too, although her husband was at least a handsome man. That made the inevitable nuptial duties more bearable. Indeed, Emmaline had tried for five years to give her husband an heir. It had seemed the least she could do to repay his kindness and indulgence, especially when he let her take control of the family purse strings.

Emmaline felt the old pang. After five years it had become all too obvious that she was barren.

Desperate, she had taken her first lover partly to discover if the fault was hers or her husband's. Now, after several lovers, she was still childless. Her husband, on the other hand, had three children by the mistress he kept in the country.

Whitmore said nothing to her about not providing a legal heir. He never complained or chastised. He turned a gentlemanly eye away from her lovers and let her run his finances, just as she ignored his mistress and made sure he had plenty of ready money. But not a day went by when she didn't feel the aching emptiness in her life.

Emmaline took a sip of tea and considered the situation. Darcy's little friend, whose presence in his home was the subject of much speculation, had managed to snare Lord

Neville Northrup and his two hundred thousand pounds. It was clear Neville didn't think there was anything unusual in Darcy's relationship with Miss Flowers and an announcement of their engagement would end the rumors.

Emmaline had known from that first meeting that Darcy wasn't engaged in an illicit affair with the beautiful Miss Flowers. His social ambitions were well-known to her, and if he had been carrying on a liaison with his ward, she would have sensed it. Still, there was something unusual in their relationship, and despite her efforts, she hadn't managed to figure out precisely what.

"How are the preparations for your ball proceeding, my dear?" Mrs. Ditchett asked as she put down her teacup.

"Wonderfully well," Emmaline said, coming out of her reverie. "I believe it will be one of the highlights of the season."

Mrs. Ditchett patted her hand companionably. "I'm sure it will be, my dear. What costume are you wearing?"

Emmaline smiled secretively. "You won't tell anyone?"

Mrs. Ditchett nodded and leaned forward.

"An Oriental slave girl!"

Mrs. Ditchett sat back, astounded. "A . . . a what?"

"A Chinese slave. I found the dress at the Crystal Palace."

"My dear, it's simply too scandalous!"

Emmaline laughed softly. "I get so tired of the same old knights and medieval ladies and former kings and queens. At least this will be different."

And I might actually get Darcy's attention, she finished in her thoughts.

"But it sounds so much like that terrible servant of Miss Flowers!"

"Oh?" Emmaline raised one delicate eyebrow.

"La, yes. She's an awful creature! Never does a thing one says, always chattering away in that absurd language!"

"Miss Flowers understands her?"

"I suppose so. She talks to her in it, too, try as I might to get her to stop."

"She must have spent a very long time in the Orient."

"Most of her life, I think. And the things she says! Really, you'd think she was one of those barbarians herself!"

"Really?" Emmaline leaned forward. "You must tell me more."

Blossom sat in the morning room, her chin on her hand as she gazed out the window. The garden was wreathed in mist, the air like smoke.

Her thoughts whirled around the strangeness of her life here, and the problems that seemed to be growing larger and larger with each passing day.

Things had appeared so simple in China. All that mattered was to help Honorable Wu, for he had helped her with his generous kindness. That had propelled her to offer herself to pay the debt—simplicity itself.

Only, not knowing how very strange this England would be, she had found herself in more trouble, like an ox caught in a mud hole.

Mr. Fitzroy had not wanted her. Or had he? He was trying to find a suitable husband. A great honor. Or was it?

He had told her many times that she was free to make choices, but in her heart she knew she wanted to stay with him. But that was not to be, and she was foolish to even imagine otherwise. Why then could she think of nothing but staying with him? Why did she keep dreaming of him in her arms, whispering endearments, dancing?

He had threatened to send Ah Tup away. She could prevent it by marrying Lord Northrup, but in doing so she would perhaps become another Precious Jade, bitter and angry, poisoning the life of all around her.

The Chief Eunuch interrupted her gyrating thoughts. He came forward with a calling card on a small silver tray.

Blossom glanced at the card. Mrs. Ditchett had taught her to read and write a little, and by now she was all too familiar with Lord Northrup's calling cards.

Mrs. Ditchett had always been present to greet callers, but this afternoon she had said she was going to visit friends and that Blossom should tell anyone who arrived that she was not at home unless the visitor was Lord Northrup.

"Show his lordship into the drawing room, please," she said wearily.

Powlett nodded and walked out of the room. Blossom watched him go and wondered if she had been too fanciful in thinking that the dignified, solemn man cared anything for Ah Tup. Perhaps it was time she found out. First, though, she would have to see Lord Northrup.

He was standing in the drawing room, biting his fingernails. "Oh, I say, how do you, Miss Flowers?" he said as he always did.

"I am very well, thank you."

He looked around, as if searching for something. "Beg pardon, but where's the charming Mrs. Ditchett?"

"She visits friends this afternoon."

"You mean we'll have some time alone?"

Blossom reflected that if almost any other man had said those words, she might have had cause for concern. Fortunately she could imagine no one more harmless than Lord Northrup. "She should return shortly."

To Blossom's shock and amazement, Lord Northrup suddenly threw himself down on his knees in front of her, grabbing her hands with his fleshy ones. "Oh, Miss Flowers, dear Miss Flowers," he said, his words coming out in a torrential rush that Blossom could barely understand, "I simply must tell you that I adore you. I love the very air you breathe, the floors you walk, the dresses you wear, the hair upon your head, your tiny exquisite feet. I must ask, no, dear Miss Flowers, beg that you will do me the honor to become my wife."

She was too dumbfounded to speak.

"Dear, darling Miss Flowers, everything I have shall be yours—at least as soon as it's finally mine. I love you—" his chubby lips smacked on her hand "—I love you—" smack "—I love you!"

"What the hell's going on here? And where's Mrs. Ditchett?"

Both Blossom and Lord Northrup turned to see Mr. Fitzroy standing in the doorway, his face bearing such a cold, angry expression that Blossom could easily believe he would indeed send Ah Tup away from her.

Lord Northrup stumbled hurriedly to his feet. "I...I..."

"You what?" Mr. Fitzroy's voice was low and full of menace.

"I..." Lord Northrup took a deep breath, his fleshy jowls quivering. "I was asking Miss Flowers to do me the honor of becoming my wife."

Blossom held her breath as Mr. Fitzroy's gaze swept over her, fear and uncertainty filling her.

"And?"

Lord Northrup gulped. "And that's as far as we'd got, Mr. Fitzroy."

He sauntered into the room, all the while looking at Blossom. "Well, Miss Flowers, how do you reply?"

Only a person of Lord Northrup's insensibility would have failed to notice the tension in the room, or not have realized that compared to Darcy Fitzroy, he was about as attractive as a slug. However, Neville Northrup was insensible and he was vain. He assumed that Miss Flowers was hesitating because she had been unprepared for the violence and passion of his declaration.

"How do you reply?"

Blossom couldn't speak, not with Mr. Fitzroy staring at her like that. It was very possible that she would have fled from the room without uttering a word, except that something unexpected happened.

Maybe it was the centuries of noble breeding. Maybe it was the expensive public school education. Maybe it was the romantic novels he read in secret. Or maybe it was basic human kindness. Whatever it was, it made Neville Northrup step directly in front of Darcy Fitzroy. "I say, sir, leave her alone," he said firmly. "She need not answer me today."

He is young and foolish, but his heart is kind, Blossom thought as she watched Lord Northrup glare at Mr. Fitzroy. Lord Northrup would do anything to please her. Ah Tup would be safe. "I will answer," she said.

The two men turned toward Blossom.

"I accept Lord Northrup."

"Oh, I say, really? I mean, you do? By heaven, that's incredible!"

"I am only her guardian. Her father must give his permission." Mr. Fitzroy's voice, hard and deliberate, filled the room.

"Well, sir, if you will tell me how I may contact him, I would be delighted to ask him." Empowered by Blossom's acceptance, Lord Northrup seemed quite another person.

"I am certain he will not refuse," Blossom said, looking at Darcy with an unreadable expression.

Darcy cleared his throat. He was caught now. "If you wish to write to Mr. Flowers, I will see that the letter is sent to him with the rest of his London correspondence." He was amazed that he could sound so calm when inside he felt as if a squall raged. He kept looking at Blossom, trying to see past her inscrutable face. Did she really want to shackle herself to this fat fool—or at least his money belt?

If she did, he would lose her forever. All at once it seemed he had never really known loneliness until this moment.

The next morning Darcy strode into his office, tossed his hat onto the nearest hook and sat down in his chair, scowling blackly all the while. Damn Northrup and damn the whole institution of marriage!

He still wasn't any closer to deciding what to do. He didn't want to say that Blossom's father consented, but he couldn't be sure whether it was for his own selfish reasons or because he really believed Blossom would be unhappy married to Neville Northrup.

After a brief rap on the door, Charles entered the room, his usual charming smile on his face. "I say, Fitzroy, what brings you here so early? Trouble at home?"

"That impudent pup Northrup."

Charles sat down. "Making a nuisance of himself? He seems quite taken with your lovely house guest."

"So taken he's asked to marry her."

Charles smiled blandly. "Well, well, well. How does the delightful Miss Flowers feel about it?"

"She accepted."

Charles, vastly more perceptive than Northrup, realized that Darcy Fitzroy was anything but pleased by this turn of events. "Do you think her father will agree?" he asked nonchalantly with his hawklike gaze on Darcy's face.

"Probably," Darcy lied.

Charles couldn't resist twisting the shaft rankling Darcy's bosom. "It would be a triumphant match. Her father shouldn't hesitate to approve."

Darcy merely nodded as Charles got up to leave.

Things were getting better and better. Imagine it. Lord Neville Northrup hearing that Darcy Fitzroy was an embezzler and the girl was nothing more than a whore just before the wedding. Or, even more delicious, perhaps just after.

Charles, a sadder but a wiser man, would go to Madeira to get his uncle's money with the beautiful Blossom. She would have no place else to go and no way to earn a living unless she plied her old trade. Surely accepting his protection would seem a better alternative.

Of course, once he was tired of her, she would fetch a high price at any brothel.

Chapter Fifteen

For weeks Lady Emmaline Whitmore's costume ball had been a subject of gossip and speculation, planning and subterfuge.

The first great concern was who would be invited. It was sure to be one of the high points of the season, and no one of any note or any hope of being of any note wanted to be excluded. For a time even the titillating speculation about Darcy Fitzroy and his beautiful ward ceased.

Then, for those select enough to receive invitations, the costume became a matter of almost cosmic importance. Who was going as what? Or whom? What fabrics? How ornate? How revealing? Ladies' maids were bribed, shopkeepers accosted, seamstresses pledged to secrecy.

Darcy, taking refuge in his club whenever possible, couldn't even escape the ball there, as the after-dinner talk inevitably turned to the expense of costume gowns and finery.

He was keeping as far away from Blossom and her lovesick suitor as possible. If she wished to make a good marriage, he would not stand in her way. As for the ruse of Blossom's father, well, perhaps the fictitious man could meet with a fictitious accident. That would be the simplest way out of that morass. Most of the time, though, Darcy tried not to think about her. Tried.

At last the night of the ball arrived. Darcy had remained adamant about not wearing some foolish costume, reflecting that he would let the other men look like imbeciles if they wished. He paced the floor of the study, wondering how much longer he would have to wait for Blossom and Mrs. Ditchett.

Finally he heard them descending the stairs and came out.

Both women were wearing voluminous cloaks. Mrs. Ditchett seemed smug, but Blossom... there was something of an air of subdued excitement that made her cheeks flush prettily, although he could see little of her face beneath the hood of the cloak. Darcy told himself to ignore her as he took Mrs. Ditchett's arm to lead them to the carriage.

"I think you'll find Miss Flowers's costume most lovely, Mr. Fitzroy," Mrs. Ditchett gushed. "And certainly worth every penny."

"I hope so."

"No one else has such an ornate garment. Madame Stitsokova assures me of it, and she has spies at all the other dressmakers, so we can be certain. The only person who stands any chance of outshining Miss Flowers is Emmaline herself but that's as it should be, since she is the hostess."

The rest of the way, Mrs. Ditchett proceeded to detail what she had learned about everyone else's costume choice, and how it was going to be overshadowed by Blossom's.

Blossom paid little attention, for she was trying to keep her red silk gown from showing beneath her cloak. She also wore a petticoat tied loosely over the gown, for without it her cloak would hang in such a way that Mrs. Ditchett would realize she wasn't wearing the ugly costume. Once at the ball, she would take off the cloak, untie the petticoat and be ready.

Charles, dressed as the knave of hearts, looked around the Whitmore's ballroom. Most people seemed to have arrived, including the nervous Lord Northrup dressed as a Crusader. Lady Gloriana Shrewtonbury, in something that was meant to be Grecian, hovered near Northrup's elbow.

Charles's gaze rested on the daring Lady Whitmore, who wore an Oriental costume that fit rather close to her shapely body. Other men were glancing at her, too, especially those whose wives indulged in the delights of the table overmuch.

He heard Darcy's familiar voice and saw Miss Flowers and Mrs. Ditchett disappear up the stairs to remove their cloaks. Darcy tossed his cloak to a footman and made for the nearest drink as Lord Northrup made a dash to the door. He was too late, for the ladies had already gone up.

Well, perhaps it was time to put a little flea in Northrup's ear about the state of Darcy's business. With that in mind, Charles wandered over toward his prey, neatly intercepting Northrup as the young man headed purposefully toward Darcy.

"Good evening, Lord Northrup."

"Oh, Horton-Smythe! Good evening. I was going to greet Mr. Fitzroy. Wish I'd never worn this demmed thing—Fitzroy looks the only sane man in the place."

"Ah, going to ask about all these rumors, eh? Don't be concerned, old man. Just a lot of flap over nothing."

Northrup stopped staring at Darcy and looked at Charles. "What's happened?"

"Nothing that won't be set right soon. Don't give it another thought, my lord," Charles said with a worried smile.

"I say, is this serious?"

"Not at all, my lord. Not at all. Shouldn't have mentioned it." Charles smiled again and moved off.

Northrup resumed his course but glanced over his shoulder at Charles, who grinned reassuringly and went to a spot near the door that afforded him a good view of the room. As Northrup reached Darcy, Darcy suddenly stared at the entrance to the ballroom.

Northrup did likewise, followed by every other person in the room, including Charles.

Blossom, in a silken Chinese gown of brilliant red and gold, ornately embroidered, entered the room. The garment showed every aspect of her slender figure to perfection. Her hair was done up in an elaborate style with ornaments that danced with each graceful step. She kept her eyes downcast, her dusky black lashes making little fans upon her pink cheeks above her ruby lips.

Lady Whitmore stepped forward, breaking the spell of silence that had pervaded the room. Instantly the narrow blue gown she wore seemed tawdry and poor compared to the richness of Blossom's garment.

No one knew it better than Emmaline, just as she knew the battle was over and she had lost.

Darcy handed his drink to the gaping Lord Northrup, then he crossed the room swiftly as the orchestra began to play the first dance.

Northrup quickly put the drinks on the first available flat surface and followed him.

Before Darcy could say anything to Blossom, Mrs. Ditchett erupted into the room, grabbing him by the arm and pulling him into a corner. "I'm so sorry, Mr. Fitzroy. I had no idea. It must have been some kind of conspiracy between her and that maid. I told you that maid had better go."

Darcy wrenched his arm away. "Never mind," he said quickly. He turned in time to see Northrup leading Blossom onto the dance floor. "Obviously it's not worth being overly concerned, considering Lady Whitmore is similarly attired."

"No, no, I suppose not..."

Darcy didn't stay to hear any more of Mrs. Ditchett's rambling, but went back into the ballroom. The moment the first dance finished, he strode across the floor to Blossom.

"May I have the honor of the next dance?" he asked, looking into her blue, blue eyes.

"Yes," she whispered, suddenly oblivious to Neville Northrup and everything else in the room except Mr. Fitzroy and the music. At once he put his arms around her and began to waltz.

The sensation of being in his arms as the music played was like one of her dreams become reality. She looked up into his face, at once excited and curious and not a little afraid at the determination she saw there. The music went on, weaving a subtle, charming spell all of its own, the room becoming a dizzying array of lights and colors and scarcely seen faces.

Until it stopped.

"Blossom." She held her breath, her heart leaping at the look in his eyes.

"Oh, Miss Flowers, may I have the next dance?"

Blossom turned to find Lord Northrup at her elbow. When she turned back, Darcy was at the other side of the room. She couldn't see his face, so she sighed and accepted.

But Charles saw everything.

"Darcy?"

"Yes?" He turned toward Emmaline, who had come up beside him.

"Is everything all right?" She looked up at him archly.

All right? He had never felt more wretched in his life.

For the first time he truly knew that he wanted Blossom, wanted her in his life and not just his bed. Wanted to see her face and hear her voice every day for the rest of his life. Wanted to make her happy, to share her smile. Wanted to see that stubborn gleam in her eye and the determined way she lifted her chin when she disagreed with him.

While they danced he had begun to hope that she felt something of the same way about him, until Northrup had appeared, reminding him that Blossom had chosen. Once again he was the poor boy at the banquet, desperately seeking only to be denied.

Nevertheless, when he replied, he looked steadily at Emmaline and managed to keep his voice calm. "What do you mean?"

"I've been hearing some rumors about your business."

"Oh." He shrugged his shoulder. "We've had a little bad luck lately, but it seems to be changing. That's to be expected in the shipping business."

Emmaline didn't look reassured, although she said, "Yes, I suppose you're right." She smiled. "How soon do you suppose it will be before poor Neville gets an answer from Miss Flowers's father?"

Darcy stared at the floor. "You know that he's asked for her hand?"

"My dear, I know everything about everybody."

He looked at her. "Do you?"

She smiled coolly. "Everything worth knowing, I meant. I must say I didn't know you could dance, Darcy. You seemed to be enjoying it, too."

"Would you care to dance with me?"

"Oh, I'm so sorry, my dear. My card is full." With that, Emmaline went over to her husband and began to dance, leaving Darcy standing alone.

"You seem to have made a complete conquest."

Blossom started. She had walked out onto the terrace for some fresh air and to think. Charles Horton-Smythe had come up silently behind her.

"Have I?" she asked, wondering what he meant.

"Yes, young Lord Northrup seems most anxious."

She nodded and looked away.

"With good reason, if I may say so."

He was too uncomfortably close. She moved away.

"That's a lovely gown, my dear. From China of course."

"Of course."

"Ah. You must miss it sometimes."

She glanced at him.

"You're forgetting I know all about you. I daresay young Northrup doesn't, eh?"

"I should return inside."

"So of course I understand why Darcy's so keen to see you wed to that young ass."

Blossom flushed hotly. She could barely stand to dance with Lord Northrup now, let alone marry him.

"What's this? Changing your mind, my dear?"

She turned away, wishing he would leave her. He seemed all too aware of what she was thinking. "Where is Mr. Fitzroy?"

"Getting drunk, I believe. Perhaps there is someone else you wish to marry?"

"No," she said quickly, moving away a little more.

"Darcy will never marry you."

She said nothing, but inched away a little more.

"He wants to marry a wealthy, titled woman, to increase his...what's the word? Ah yes, face."

Blossom bit her lip. "He danced with me," she said, trying to sound sure of herself.

"But you're prepared to do a little more than dance, I think." The cool, calculating tone of his voice frightened her.

"If I understand the transaction, you are the payment of Wu's debt, are you not?"

There was no point in lying; he knew the arrangement. She nodded, hoping Mr. Fitzroy or even Lord Northrup would come out.

"I don't think Darcy has made it quite clear enough that I'm his partner. His business partner." He came closer, his eyes gleaming in the moonlight above his thin smile. "We share the same debts, so we should share in the same payment."

Horrified, she fled into the ballroom as Charles chuckled silently on the terrace.

"Well, my dear, I must say it's a great pity you're not feeling well," Mrs. Ditchett said as they entered the carriage. "I suppose all the excitement is too much." The woman laughed slyly. "I thought Gloriana Shrewtonbury was going to burst her corset when you came into the ballroom!"

Blossom felt indescribably weary and looked out the window as Mr. Fitzroy climbed into the carriage beside her. She could still feel his strong arms about her, and hear the music of the dance. But she must not. She must not.

"Although you shouldn't have surprised me with your costume. I see now, of course, that it's even lovelier than the gown I selected. I was quite terrified that dear Emmaline would think I had something to do with your choice, since she had confided her costume to me, but I hastened to assure her that *I* had absolutely nothing to do with it. I thought Lady Whitmore looked stunning, as always, don't you agree, Mr. Fitzroy?''

Mr. Fitzroy merely nodded.

''My, my, we all seem to be fatigued this evening! Well, I suppose it's not to be wondered at.''

Miraculously Mrs. Ditchett managed to stay quiet for the rest of the journey home.

Ah Tup, waiting in the lower hall, looked carefully at Blossom when they returned.

''Oh, are you still waiting?'' Mrs. Ditchett asked petulantly.

Ah Tup nodded, or rather gave an impertinent shake of her head and followed Blossom up the stairs.

''*Ayee-ah!*'' she exclaimed when they were alone. ''Why do you look so sad?''

''I am not sure about marrying Lord Northrup.''

''He is rich,'' Ah Tup reminded her.

Blossom tried to force a smile. There were many things that she and Ah Tup agreed on and understood, but this, Blossom knew, would not be one of them. Ah Tup would consider Blossom's marriage a stroke of unbelievable good fortune. One man was as good—or bad—as another in Ah Tup's opinion, and the fact that Northrup was rich made up for any other shortcomings he might have.

How could Blossom explain that the idea of spending the rest of her life as Neville Northrup's wife, with all that that implied, filled her with sorrow?

So, while Ah Tup helped her undress and wash, Blossom made the pretense of being satisfied, if not delighted. Ah Tup may have suspected something was amiss, but she wisely kept her own counsel.

At last the house was quiet, and all Blossom could hear were the soft sounds of Ah Tup sleeping. Sleep would not come to her, only overwhelming sadness. Fearful of crying and waking Ah Tup, she climbed slowly out of the bed, crept to the other room and out the door.

Mr. Fitzroy's bedroom door was closed, and all was in darkness. Blossom went down the stairs, the tears beginning to fall on her cheeks.

A deep, ragged sob broke from her lips, and she hurried to the study, certain the heavy door would muffle the sobs she could no longer restrain. Once inside, she pushed the door closed and ran to the sofa, hiding her face in her hands as she sank down upon it.

Then she began to cry as if the sobs were being torn from her soul. She was trapped now, just as surely as she had been trapped on the ship long ago.

The tears she should have cried then, came now. The tears she should have cried at every beating Precious Jade gave her, came now. The tears she should have shed when she left Honorable Wu, came now. All the tears she had kept bottled inside, of sorrow and loneliness and heartache, came now.

Darcy listened for a moment, thinking he'd heard something outside his bedroom door. Deciding it was nothing, he pulled back the curtain and looked out into the dark, damp street. The fog seemed to have a life of its own, swirling malevolent fingers around the nearby buildings.

He dropped the curtain and turned back into the room, pulling off his necktie. He stared at it, not seeing the tie but a vision of Blossom as she stood at the entrance of Emmaline's ballroom, radiant and beautiful. She had looked as beautiful as the first moment he had set eyes on her. As desirable as that first night when she had been waiting for him in this very room.

Suppressing a groan, he began to pace. God, he mustn't think of her, especially not now, when he—*he*—had given Northrup permission to take her out of this house and out of his life.

Northrup had cornered him by the refreshments after Darcy had successfully avoided him most of the evening. He couldn't think up any more excuses, so he'd told Northrup he didn't see any cause for Mr. Flowers to refuse his permission. He had asked Northrup to keep the engagement quiet until they could receive official approval, however. The idiot had been pathetically grateful. Shortly after, Blossom had come into the room. She said she wasn't feeling well and wanted to go home. They had left before Northrup could say anything to her.

Darcy went back to the window. Maybe this would be a good time to go to Manchester. Or Liverpool again. Anywhere, as long as he wasn't near her.

He needed a cheroot and a drink.

Quietly he opened the door and walked softly along the hall. He went swiftly down the stairs and to the study. When he pushed open the door, he saw Blossom huddled on the sofa, sobbing.

He hesitated, afraid to stay but not willing to leave. Then Blossom lifted her tear-streaked face and looked at him.

He came inside and closed the door. "What is it?" he whispered.

She stood quickly. "I will go now. I should not be here."

He shook his head and came a few steps closer, thinking he knew what was troubling her. "I told Northrup he could marry you," he said, the words painful to say.

To his surprise, more tears welled up in her sorrowful eyes. She brushed her hand across her face but didn't stop crying.

"Isn't that what you wanted?"

He held his breath, scarcely daring to let himself hope otherwise. He forced himself to ask another question.

"Blossom, would you rather go home to China than marry Neville Northrup?"

"I cannot go back to China."

"Why?"

"There is no one there for me."

"What about Wu?"

"I would only bring trouble to him if I go back."

"Is there no one else, no other place you can go?"

She shook her head slowly, a vast loneliness filling her.

He looked out of the window. "Then I suppose a husband and a home here is a good thing."

He spoke so quietly, so gently, so sadly, that her tears began anew. "Yes," she whispered, knowing that there was only one husband, one home that she truly wanted.

"Are you sure, though, that it should be Northrup?"

His voice, the sorrow and sadness, the longing and the loneliness, surprised her. Now he was not the powerful lord. He was simply a man, a man perhaps as lonely as she was.

She told him the truth. "I marry Lord Northrup to keep Ah Tup with me."

He wheeled around. "What?"

"You said you would send Ah Tup from me. If I marry Lord Northrup, he will let me keep her near."

He came to her in two long strides and took hold of her shoulders, looking intently into her face. "Do you mean to tell me that you'd marry that fool because of a servant?"

Blossom nodded, watching him, afraid to let herself hope too much. "She is more than a servant to me. She is my *friend.*"

Mr. Fitzroy let go. "By God, that's an idiotic reason to marry a man."

"It was the reason *you* gave me."

He looked surprised.

"If Ah Tup returns to Honorable Wu's house, one day Precious Jade will beat her to death. For every lash I have had, Ah Tup has taken ten. Do not think that because she smiles, she has no fear, no pain. Her spirit is stronger than anyone's, but even she will eventually succumb."

"Her spirit's not stronger than yours."

Blossom shook her head. His intense gaze made her only too aware of her weakness.

"Blossom, I promise I won't send Ah Tup back to China."

Suddenly she felt like dancing again, twirling around the room safe in his arms. She brushed the tears from her face. "Thank you, Mr. Fitzroy."

"Do you still want to marry Northrup?"

"Yes."

He frowned, and she spoke quickly. "I am too much expense for you. If I marry, I am responsibility of my new husband, and you will be free. Also, the marriage settlement will end the debt of Honorable Wu."

"I don't want you to throw yourself away just because of money."

"You do not?"

"No, I do not."

She could scarcely breathe. "You mean I can say I no longer wish to marry Lord Northrup?"

He nodded slowly.

"But you will not be free of me."

He reached out and pulled her to him. "I don't want to let you go," he whispered as his lips found hers.

Her arms reached around him, feeling the desire and uninhibited yearning in his kiss. Before, she had known he was trying not to feel, but not now.

His lips propelled her into a realm of emotion and need and desire. His tongue boldly sought hers in her warm, moist mouth as his strong, sure hands traveled slowly over her, igniting a liquid flame of passion in every part of her body.

Then he lifted her into his arms and carried her toward the door, never breaking the contact of his searing kiss as they went upstairs to his bedroom. Once there, he set her down and closed the door, pausing for a moment to look at her.

"My God, you're beautiful," he whispered huskily.

She smiled tremulously. Slowly he unfastened her gown and let it slip unheeded to the floor.

He said nothing, but took her into his arms, pressing heated kisses on her throat, moving downward toward her breasts. She moaned softly, almost unbelieving at the response of her own body to his caresses.

He laid her on his bed, and she watched as he tore off his shirt. His eyes were hot and hungry, but she knew hers were, too, as she feasted on the sight of him. She reached up and pulled him downward, arching for him in her own need.

Every movement of his lips, his hands, his glorious body brought forth passion and fire in her limbs.

He lifted his face and spoke softly. "Blossom, if you like, I'll stop."

She looked at him confusedly. "Why? Are you not liking . . . ?"

His smile told her much, but his eyes told her everything.

"Take me," she whispered, knowing that she wanted to make love with him, and that they would be united in a way much more important than any mere satisfying of the desires of the flesh.

He stood up to remove the rest of his clothes. Watching her, he saw with delight the craving on her face, the yearning that, for the first time in his life, filled him not with a sense of power but tenderness and compassion. She needed him in ways no woman ever had.

And he needed her, too.

That made him more gentle than he would have supposed he could ever be when he lay down beside her. At first he simply looked at her, exquisite and perfect in her nakedness, the white of her skin seeming to glow in the pale illumination of the candlelight. He touched her long, dark hair.

His soft touch made her tremble, as if each part of her body wanted to touch a part of his. Undulating, stretching, she let herself enjoy the sensation of his caresses.

He was strong, powerful, masterful—and gentle, tender, soft. Lifting her face, she kissed his neck, running her tongue along the throbbing pulse point as he gasped. Then her mouth trailed down his chest. Her hands wandered over his hard, firm muscles as both their actions gathered speed.

He rolled on top of her, covering her flesh with his, his weight on his elbows as each hand framed her face. ''This might hurt a little,'' he cautioned, pressing a kiss on her lips.

''I know,'' she whispered, not afraid.

Wrapped in each other's arms, entwined in each other's bliss, they reached the zenith. They were together in a world of their own, no longer alone.

Chapter Sixteen

Blossom opened her eyes and watched Darcy in his sleep. His chest rose and fell with his soft breathing and his face was almost boyish. As if aware of her scrutiny, he turned toward her, reaching and pulling her close.

She smiled in the safe circle of his arms, happier than she had ever been before. She kissed his cheek lightly and then wiggled out of his embrace.

"Where're you going?" Darcy asked sleepily.

She picked up her robe and slipped it on before going to the commode. "I am going to wash," she said, pouring water into a basin. It was cool, but it would have to do. She dipped the cloth in it and returned to the bed.

When she touched the damp cloth to Darcy's chest, he sat up with a squelched yelp. "What the devil . . . !"

"I am going to wash you," Blossom said, continuing to wipe his chest with the cloth. "It is my duty . . . and my pleasure."

"I'll be damned," Darcy said, enjoying her ministrations now that the cloth wasn't quite so cold.

The cloth traveled lower and he sucked in his breath when she lifted the sheet.

"Ah, the one-eyed monk still sleeps," Blossom said, glancing at him with a mischievous grin.

"The who?" Darcy said, his voice a little strained.

"The one-eyed monk. Your helmeted warrior. This."

He gasped at her touch. "Oh, that."

She finished and deftly tossed the cloth into the basin.

"Am I supposed to do the same for you?" Darcy asked, smiling devilishly.

"No."

"Oh." He lay back down and pulled her to him. "I'll have to think of something else. My helmeted warrior is waking up."

"So I see."

He kissed her deeply, and she nestled close, running her hands along his arms. "What other names do you have?" he muttered as he nuzzled her neck.

"I have only one name."

He moved away a little. "No, I meant like one-eyed monk. I'm fascinated."

"Ah." She sat up and curled her legs under her. "For men?"

He shook his head, then moved back so that he was half sitting. "How about for this?" He indicated a part of her body.

"Ah. You mean the jade gate or the pearl on the step?"

"I like that, jade gate."

"Most men enjoy a jade gate."

Darcy chuckled. "I suppose that's true. And the pearl. That's a very wonderful thing...." Slowly his hand moved toward her body, his fingers teasing the nub until she squirmed with desire and moaned softly.

"I think the helmeted warrior should make another assault on the gate," he said, his voice deep with desire.

"Please, Dar-cee."

"That's the first time you've used my first name."

"You are offended?"

He chuckled quietly. "Not at all. I quite like it."

Suddenly there was the sound of Ah Tup's voice, subdued but angry, followed by Mrs. Ditchett's, equally angry and subdued.

"Damn!" Darcy jumped out of the bed, reaching for his pants.

Blossom frowned. "Ah Tup will see that Mrs. Ditchett doesn't enter, if that's what you fear."

Unfortunately Blossom had underestimated Dulcibella Ditchett when riled. The door burst open just as Darcy got his pants done up. The older woman barged into the room, followed by Ah Tup. "Merciful heavens!" she cried, "I don't believe it!"

Blossom pulled the covers up a little more. "In English society," she said coolly, "it is considered polite to knock."

Mrs. Ditchett caught sight of Darcy and reddened when she saw his naked chest. "Mr. Fitzroy! I'm shocked!"

To Blossom's dismay, Darcy didn't berate Mrs. Ditchett for entering his bedroom without permission. He merely scowled.

"This is disastrous! No one will ever marry her now!"

Blossom waited for Darcy to say that she wouldn't have to marry anyone, now that she was his.

Instead, he glared at Mrs. Ditchett. "Are you planning on telling anyone?"

"Well, I . . ."

"Then no one need know what has happened."

"This is certainly not the behavior of a gentleman!"

He took a step toward the woman. "I am not a gentleman, Mrs. Ditchett."

Blossom got out of bed and wrapped the sheet around her like an imperial robe. "Good morning, Mrs. Ditchett," she said regally. She turned to Darcy and bowed icily. "I am sorry you are ashamed of making love with me.'' Then she swept out of the room, Ah Tup going with her.

Darcy felt like throwing something, preferably at the interfering Mrs. Ditchett's head. The woman didn't even have the sense to leave the room.

''Perhaps, Mr. Fitzroy, we may yet salvage the situation,'' she said hurriedly. ''Miss Flowers wouldn't be the first bride to come to the altar in a, shall we say, less than pure state. I assure you I won't say anything.'' Then she finally went out.

Darcy didn't doubt that he could count on Mrs. Ditchett's discretion. After all, she was supposed to be chaperoning the girl. If it got about that Mrs. Ditchett had failed, it wouldn't help her position in society, either.

As he began to dress, he was filled with anger and loathing of the woman and the whole upper class. He could see all their reactions in that one fat female, hear their gossiping voices, see their pointing fingers, know how they would cut both himself and Blossom from their society.

They were all snobs and hypocrites. Not one in a thousand would come right out and say what they thought or felt, not like Blossom. She was wonderfully uninhibited. Making love with her had been the most delightful experience of his life.

Right now he wanted nothing more than to go to Blossom and ask her to be his wife, but he was too angry at Mrs. Ditchett and everything that she represented to act the romantic lover. He would calm down first.

He decided that it would be best to keep the true nature of their relationship quiet for the time being. English society was all too quick to condemn and there was still the uncomfortable matter of Neville Northrup. Of course the tentative engagement would have to be broken, but it was only decent to speak to Northrup first.

Then he would be with Blossom for the rest of his life. Darcy began to smile to himself as he picked up his watch and started to wind it, glancing at it. "Oh, blast," he muttered when he actually took note of the time. He'd have to leave for the office at once. Charles wanted him to sign an important contract this morning, and the other party was coming to the office right at the start of business hours. Well, he would simply have to wait a little longer before he talked to Blossom.

Ah Tup watched Blossom as she paced the floor. Ah Tup didn't say anything, because she knew it was always better to wait until Blossom spoke first.

When Ah Tup had awakened in the night and seen the honored lord carrying Blossom into his bedchamber, she had wanted to crow with delight. Instead she had gone to sleep outside the door so that no one would interrupt what was without doubt a marvelous thing.

She had heard enough to know that both the master and Blossom had experienced highest bliss in the huge bed. Ah Tup had even wondered whether sometimes, marriage might be worthwhile.

She was sure that now things would take their proper course. Blossom would become the master's concubine and have a place of honor in his house. Soon she might even bear him a son and so maintain that place, even if the honored lord was to take a wife.

If only the horrible Dish had not woken earlier than usual! She had expected the woman to sleep late after the ball. And then the Dish had actually gone into the master's room unannounced! Surely she was a barbarian among barbarians. Who would have thought she would talk to the master in the tone she used, and that he would not shout or curse at her? Who could understand these foreign devils?

"I do not understand these people," Blossom said, as if she had just read Ah Tup's very thoughts. "I thought all was going to be well. He was so kind, so filled with passion . . ."

Ah Tup tried not to look worried. "He was angry at the impertinence of the Dish, no doubt," she said soothingly.

"I thought he would tell Mrs. Ditchett that . . ."

"That what?"

"That he would marry me."

"You are his concubine. That is enough."

"Not here, Ah Tup. To be a concubine is to be like a street sweeper or dung collector."

"They are all stupid."

"No!"

Ah Tup stared at Blossom, who flushed bright red.

"I want to be Mr. Fitzroy's wife!" She paced back and forth. "If I understand things, he only has to ask *me*. Here there are no parents who must give permission."

"He did not ask you?"

Blossom shook her head slowly.

"Perhaps he will, *heya?*"

They heard Powlett's voice downstairs and Mr. Fitzroy's brief reply, then the opening and closing of the front door.

"I think he's gone out," Ah Tup said. "When he returns, he will ask."

"I wish I had someone I could talk to about these things."

"What about Mrs. Ditchett?"

"I don't want to ask her such questions. She thinks of men as if they were fish in the marketplace. Besides, I do not trust her."

"The Crow Woman?"

"No. Mrs. MacTavish gets angry when I speak of these matters."

"It is a pity we know no young female barbarian. Surely they would be able to help."

"Wait, Ah Tup! There is one! Younger Brother's future wife!"

"She does not come here."

"I will write a letter thing, as Mrs. Ditchett has taught me. I will ask her to come to visit me and drink tea."

"Will she?"

"Is she not to be married into the family? I am a guest of Mr. Fitzroy. She will come."

Ah Tup frowned. "Who can say if these foreign devils will do the correct thing or not?"

Blossom also frowned, then her eyes lit up. "I will tell her it is an urgent family matter concerning Mr. Fitzroy! She is a good woman. She will come."

Sally hummed a few bars from the song she had heard at the music hall as she entered Mr. Fitzroy's bedroom. She should have been tired after her late night. Instead she was anything but. She felt as if she could dance all day.

Mr. Horton-Smythe was so nice and handsome and generous. Taking her out for such a lovely dinner—and buying that nice bit of cake for Mother, too.

She paused as she wrung out the towel that was in the basin and closed her eyes, remembering how she'd let him kiss her in the carriage on the way home. Well, and why not? He was a gentleman, asking her if she'd mind and all. And not pawing at her like some of those other louts who'd taken her out for a bit of supper.

No, he was a fine gentleman. He gave her that bracelet, too. She sighed happily.

Of course, Mother had been a little worried when they got back so late, but Mr. Horton-Smythe had walked her in, which showed there was no harm in it.

She hummed again as she walked over to the windows and opened the curtains. He'd even asked her about her work, saying he wanted to make sure they were treating her right at Mr. Fitzroy's house. To be sure, he was maybe a little too curious about Miss Flowers, asking if she seemed overfond of Mr. Fitzroy or he of her. He was worried, he said, about Mr. Fitzroy taking advantage of Miss Flowers—and her, too. She'd set him straight on that. Mr. Fitzroy and Miss Flowers didn't hardly see each other most days, and Mr. Fitzroy never so much as looked in Sally's direction, which was a good thing. He terrified her. If he ever laid a hand on her, she'd scream so loud they'd hear her all the way to Piccadilly.

Now, if Mr. Horton-Smythe was to lay a hand on her, he'd no doubt be as gentle as a lamb. Not that he would, without her leave. Anybody could see he was too fine a gentleman to take advantage of a poor girl.

What would she wear tonight? It wasn't every day she got asked to a gentleman's house for dinner. She frowned a little. She didn't like lying to Mother, but she'd never understand. She'd say it wasn't decent. But anybody could see Mr. Horton-Smythe was a decent gentleman, and he'd have a maid or someone there. It wouldn't be as if she'd be all alone with him.

She didn't want him to think she didn't trust him. He'd never ask her out again, no doubt, if he thought that.

If he didn't ask her out again, he'd never fall in love with her and ask her to marry him. Looking out the window, she watched a fine carriage go past. There was a lady inside wearing a beautiful hat and gown. Someday maybe she'd be a lady like that.

"And why not?" she whispered to herself. "It might happen. Who's to say it won't?"

She heard Mrs. MacTavish in the hall outside and quickly went to make the bed before she was accused of being too slow about her business. Picking up the pillow, she began to punch it up.

There was a long, long dark hair on the pillow slip. Sally stopped and stared at it, her mouth falling open.

There was only one person in the house with hair like that.

My, but she'd have something to tell Mr. Horton-Smythe.

Blossom looked out the front window for the tenth time in as many minutes. She brushed another imaginary speck of dust from her gown and sat down on the sofa, only to get up again at the rumble of carriage wheels.

She heard a knock at the front door and in a few minutes Powlett escorted Elizabeth Hazelmore into the drawing room.

"Please, come in and sit down," Blossom said, her nervousness making her sound stiff and precise.

The ease with which Elizabeth maneuvered her skirt filled Blossom with momentary envy. Blossom also noticed her fine, clear skin, frank brown eyes and soft smile. Here was the epitome of English womanhood sitting before her.

This was what she could never, ever be. Maybe this was why Darcy had not asked her to be his wife.

"I was rather surprised to get your note," Elizabeth said softly, her brows wrinkled. "Jeremy's told me that things seem to be going wrong with the business, but I don't understand how I can be of help."

"There are business troubles?"

"Yes, I believe so. Isn't that why you wanted to talk to me?"

"No, but, please, tell me of these troubles."

Elizabeth knotted her slim hands together on her lap. "Apparently there are rumors going about the city that Mr. Fitzroy's having financial difficulties. Jeremy was rather upset by it all."

"Who says these rumors?"

"That's just it. Nobody really knows who starts these things, but Jeremy heard it from somebody who spoke with..."

"Yes?"

"Lord Northrup."

"Lord Northrup? What does he know of business?"

Elizabeth frowned and hesitated before replying. "I understand he gets very good advice."

"I shall find out about these rumors."

"If I can help in any way, please ask. Jeremy's really very concerned about his brother."

Sally came in bearing the tea tray and set it down before leaving the room. Or rather, going out into the hall and lingering near the open door, ostensibly dusting.

"Why did you ask to see me?" Elizabeth asked when Miss Flowers handed her the teacup. Indeed, it was obvious that something was bothering her hostess very much, judging by the trembling of the bone china cup, and since it wasn't the rumors, Elizabeth's curiosity was piqued.

"I wish to ask..."

"Yes?" she prompted gently.

"I wish to ask, if men and women enjoy..." Miss Flowers took a deep breath and began again. "Mr. Fitzroy took me in his bed last night and of course that was why I was sent to him, but now I wish to know if he will make me his wife."

Elizabeth tried not to look completely horrified as she set down her rattling teacup. She knew little of what Miss Flowers was trying to describe, but she had overheard her mother and her friends whispering a few times over scandalous goings-on. Apart from the fact that such a thing indicated a woman of very loose morals, which was bad enough, she knew no unmarried couple should share the same bed because doing so in some way led to the woman getting with child. "Did he . . . did he *force* you?"

"Oh, no."

"He took advantage of you?"

"Is that another way to say he made love with me?"

"Not precisely." Elizabeth realized that somehow Miss Flowers didn't seem to appreciate the magnitude of what she and Mr. Fitzroy had done. She knew Miss Flowers had not been raised in England, but still she shouldn't seem quite so...pleased about it. "Did you...did you *want* to go to his bed?"

"Yes. Of course I was sent for that, but he pleased me very much."

"Your father sent you to Mr. Fitzroy so that he could take advantage of you?"

"My father is dead."

Now Elizabeth was completely confused. "I don't understand."

"I was sent from China to pay a debt, but Mr. Fitzroy said that was not the custom here. Then he wished me to marry, so I said yes to Lord Northrup, although I would rather make love to a fish. Last night, Mr. Fitzroy and I made love and now I need to know if I will be his wife."

Elizabeth decided Miss Flowers was trying to describe an arranged marriage. Apparently Miss Flowers was supposed to marry Darcy Fitzroy, he decided against it and wanted her to marry someone else. Lord Northrup proposed and Miss Flowers had agreed, although she had fallen into sin with Mr. Fitzroy.

For herself, she knew that she loved Jeremy so much that it would be easy to do whatever he asked. Indeed, sometimes, when he kissed her, she found herself wishing he wouldn't stop.

"What should I do?"

Elizabeth focused on the immediate problem. "Did Mr. Fitzroy say that he loves you?"

"No."

"Did he ask you to be his wife?"

"No."

"I'm sorry, Miss Flowers, truly. I can't speak for Mr. Fitzroy, but I do know that he has acted like a dishonorable man. He sinned greatly, taking advantage of a woman who was living under his roof."

Sin. Blossom's heart began to pound and dread knotted her stomach. Sin. She knew that word. It was to do something wrong, very wrong. Terrible.

"I have sinned, too?" she asked weakly.

There was sorrow and pity in Elizabeth's eyes. "I'm sure you didn't understand the implications. *He* should have known how to behave."

Blossom understood from Elizabeth's tone and her pitying look that she *had* sinned. By sinning she had lost face. A shame flooded through her.

"What should I do now?" she asked in a small voice, as if she were once again a lost child.

"You must leave here immediately. Please, come stay with us. We'll be delighted to have you."

"That is the thing to do? To leave?"

Elizabeth, showing an aggression few would have guessed she possessed, stood up. "Yes, at once."

"What of Ah Tup? She will come, too?"

"Who is she?"

"My servant."

"Of course, certainly. I'll go home now, and tell Mama. Where is Mr. Fitzroy?"

"I believe he is at his business."

"Good. Hurry now, and collect your things. You shouldn't stay in this house a moment longer than necessary."

Chapter Seventeen

Charles could not figure out what was going on.

He had just spent the better part of half an hour telling Darcy that several of the creditors were worried about the business, but the man seemed not to hear a word of it. For all the attention Darcy was paying, Charles could have been describing a new carriage.

The man kept grinning like an idiot, too.

"We'd better do something before everybody jumps ship," Charles said.

"Oh, it's probably just some flotsam from *China Lady*'s late arrival. It'll blow over soon."

"It might, but it might not. I tell you, it's exceedingly troubling."

"Well, don't worry too much. I'm sure everything will turn out all right."

"If it doesn't, don't say I didn't try to warn you."

"Very well, I won't."

"I say, Fitzroy, what's going on?" Charles demanded, not keeping his exasperation from his voice.

Darcy smiled, the expression lighting up his handsome face. "Oh, nothing in particular," he said.

Charles wanted to strangle him. How stupid did Darcy think he was?

"How is Miss Flowers these days?"

"Wonderfully well. Is there anything else you needed to talk to me about?"

"I thought you might want to check the repairs to *China Lady*. They seem to be taking rather longer than usual."

"Fine. Anything else?"

"No. I think that's everything."

"Good." Darcy stood up. "Then if you'll excuse me, Charles, I'll go see *China Lady*." With that, Darcy walked out of the room, whistling.

Whistling! The man had never whistled in all the time Charles had known him.

Charles stared after him. He didn't like surprises, and Darcy's behavior was definitely surprising.

A few hours later, but still much earlier than usual, Darcy strode into the foyer of his house. Powlett was waiting, as usual, but most unusually, the man actually had an expression on his face.

The butler was perturbed.

"What's happened?" Darcy asked.

"Miss Flowers has left, sir."

"Gone shopping?"

"No, sir. She has packed and left the house."

Darcy stared at Powlett in disbelief. "Where's she gone?"

"I believe she is temporarily visiting Miss Hazelmore."

Darcy became aware that Sally was dusting in the drawing room, and nodded toward his study. "In there."

Powlett went where he was bidden.

"Now," Darcy demanded. "Tell me what happened."

"Miss Hazelmore was invited by Miss Flowers to tea. They had some conversation and then Miss Flowers packed her things and left."

"Ah Tup?"

To Darcy's surprise, Powlett looked down at the floor and blushed. "She, too, has gone."

"With Miss Flowers?"

"Yes, sir. Miss Flowers left this note."

Powlett held out a small piece of paper. In Blossom's round, uncertain hand, it said, "Mr. Fitzroy, We have done a great wrong. I do not wish to see you now. Blossom."

"Get me Mrs. Ditchett."

"She left this morning."

"*What?*"

"She gave me to understand she would send for her things at a later date."

Darcy frowned. "Did she say why?"

"No, sir."

Thank heaven for small mercies, Darcy thought. "Get my carriage ready. I'll go and get Miss Flowers. Tell Mrs. MacTavish to wait dinner for us."

"I'm sorry to inform you, sir, that Mrs. MacTavish is no longer here, either."

"What the devil's going on, Powlett?" Darcy demanded.

Powlett held out another note, this time from Mrs. MacTavish. Part of the ink was ruined and blotched, but he could make out "...terrible thing and I must go at once. Mrs. MacTavish."

Darcy sat down in the nearest chair. It seemed that somehow or other Mrs. MacTavish had found out about last night. It didn't surprise him that she would leave at once.

Mrs. Ditchett had obviously deserted like a rat from a sinking ship.

But why had Blossom gone? What had Jeremy's intended said to her?

No, what had Blossom said to *her?* If Blossom had told Elizabeth what had happened last night, it was no wonder the daughter of a minister would convince Blossom to leave the house. No doubt she'd made *him* sound like a fiend in human form, if she was as pious as she looked.

"Sir?" Powlett said softly.

"What?"

"What are you going to do?"

"Damn good question."

He could go to see the Hazelmores and try to talk to Blossom, but he didn't doubt they'd keep her as far away from him as a cloistered nun. How could he even begin to explain his feelings to Blossom, let alone Elizabeth and her father? His experience with women had been woefully lacking. Before, all he'd been concerned about was getting them into bed, not talking to them about their feelings, or apologizing for behaving like a libertine.

He needed to talk to Jeremy. Better yet, he needed Jeremy to come to the Hazelmores with him and explain. They'd listen to Jeremy, if not him.

He got up. "I'm going to Oxford."

Powlett's eyes widened for an instant. "Would you like me to prepare a bag, sir?"

"There's no time for that." He hurried to the door, but paused and clapped his hand on Powlett's shoulder. "Don't worry. I'll get them back," he said.

He thought Powlett almost smiled with relief.

Mrs. Ditchett sobbed loudly, holding a small piece of lace that was supposed to be a handkerchief up to her nose. "Who ever would have guessed he was a *cad! A rake!* An *unprincipled libertine!* To think—in his own house!"

Emmaline handed her guest another cup of strong tea.

"I mean, she's ruined, absolutely ruined! And how does it look—*I* was her chaperon! Oh, this is *terrible!*"

"You're sure then, that he . . ."

"There's no doubt of it, my dear. I mean, she was in his bed, completely *naked* and so was he! She didn't even bother to deny it—*that's* how unprincipled she is!"

Emmaline stared down at her teacup. She should have known this would happen. She couldn't blame the girl, not if her assumptions about Miss Flowers's past were correct. And Darcy was simply much too tempting. "Have you told anyone else this?"

"I came right here the first thing. I've left his house. I gave orders to the maid to pack my things."

"Where's Mr. Fitzroy now?"

"He's at his office, I suppose. The bold rascal—as if nothing's happened!"

"Has he proposed to Miss Flowers?"

"Not that I know of—and I'm sure I would have heard of that. After all, she left the room before I did and then I heard him leave the house shortly afterward...."

"Miss Flowers was not upset?"

"The shameless trollop! She didn't even have the decency to pretend! Really, she was more annoyed at being *discovered, I* think. Such goings-on! A decent woman couldn't stay a moment in such a place." Mrs. Ditchett took a gulp of tea. "I don't suppose you have any spirits? I'm really so put out."

"Certainly." Emmaline rang a bell and asked the maid to bring some sherry. "This all happened this morning?"

"Yes, at the crack of dawn. My nerves may never recover, waking from a sound sleep to discover all this! And that awful Chinese servant actually had the gall to raise her voice to me! It took me most of the morning to get dressed, I was so upset."

Emmaline kept the skepticism off her face, but if she knew Mrs. Ditchett—and she knew her well—the woman had more likely been waiting to see what was going to hap-

pen than lying around in a state of shocked sensibilities.
Clearly, she had decided the best thing to do was c̓ camp.
This did not bode well for Darcy's reputation. His social
standing would be destroyed when news of his liaison with
Miss Flowers became public knowledge, as it surely would.

At that moment James appeared in the doorway bearing
a silver tray with a card on it. Emmaline took it.

"It's Lord Northrup."

"Oh, my dear! I can't see *him!* Oh, the humiliation. After all I did to promote that match! I couldn't bear to face
him."

"He knows nothing of this?"

"I shouldn't think so. *I* certainly haven't told anyone."

"Go up to one of the bedrooms and lie down for a little
while. You'll feel better. Leave Lord Northrup to me."

Mrs. Ditchett got to her feet with surprising alacrity. "I
really think that's a good idea. I am feeling quite faint."

As Mrs. Ditchett hurried out, Emmaline turned to James.
"Show Lord Northrup in."

"You haven't told anyone else this, have you, Sally?"
Charles asked, handing her a small glass of sherry as she sat
down on the red velvet sofa.

Sally looked up at him, taking her gaze from the beautiful, delicate crystal. "No, sir, not a soul. But it ain't…isn't
proper carryings-on, I must say. Mrs. Ditchett leaving and
Mrs. MacTavish and then Miss Flowers and her maid packing up."

"Nobody told you what happened? I think we can guess,
though, eh, my dear?"

"I didn't tell nobody else about that there hair."

"Ah." He smiled and looked at her companionably before sighing softly. "My word! I must say it's a distressing
thing to find out that your partner is a man like that." He

shook his head sorrowfully. "Of course, having a pretty girl so close by does tempt a man." He looked at her intently.

Sally took a sip of the sherry. She'd never had it before, but it sounded so fancy. Just like this house, with its fine furniture and curtains and rugs.

Unfortunately, the sherry tasted terrible. She tried not to make a face.

Charles went around behind her. "Here, my dear, let me take your wrap." He lifted it from her shoulders, his hands resting there a bit longer than strictly necessary.

"Thank you," she said softly, taking another small sip.

He sat beside her on the sofa, his body close to hers. "Dinner won't be ready for some time yet."

"Oh." She stifled a small twinge of discomfort. He was a gentleman, after all. He'd been to Eton and Oxford. She could trust a man like that.

He smiled at her, but instead of warming her as his smiles had done before, she suddenly felt a chill as cold as snow down her back.

"You know, Sally, you're a very fine young lady. I'm sure you've had plenty of young men vying for your attentions." He moved a little closer and reached out to run his finger along her cheek.

She flushed and took another sip. "Oh, not so very many, sir."

Charles smiled again as his arm snaked around the back of the sofa behind her. "Is that so? I'm surprised to hear it. Tell me, Sally, do you like men?"

"Well, yes, I suppose so. . . ." She paused awkwardly.

One hand was on her shoulder now and he reached out to take the sherry—the drugged sherry—from her hand. "I'd like to kiss you again, Sally."

She tried to move away, but her head seemed all fuzzy. "What about the servants?" she whispered.

"All out for the evening. I so much wanted to be alone with you."

She knew she should stand up and leave, but her legs felt like a load of wash. She was frightened of him, of the look in his eyes, of the way he moved closer and closer, his arms trapping her like a fly in a web.

"You don't mind, do you, Sally?" His face looked evil, like those gargoyles on churches, as he bent down and kissed her.

"I...I..." She wanted him to stop and tried to push him away. But she couldn't. Her arms were too weak. Useless.

"I didn't think you would. You should be honored, my dear, to think that a man like me finds you worthy of notice." His hand on her shoulder gripped tighter as he began to undo the buttons on her bodice.

"I...I..." *I must go,* she wanted to say, but she couldn't seem to make her mouth move properly.

He pushed her back onto the sofa. "Don't be afraid, Sally. You'll enjoy this, I promise you. And afterward, I'll give you another lovely bracelet...."

A short time later Charles adjusted his clothing as he looked at the girl softly sobbing. He frowned. "Come, come, my dear. Nothing to get so worked up about."

He tossed a cheap bangle bracelet at her as she feebly tried to button her bodice. "There. I told you I'd give you something."

The girl looked up at him, her cheeks streaked with tears, her eyes puffy and red from crying. Charles wondered how he'd ever thought her pretty.

"You're no gentleman!" she accused.

Suddenly he grabbed her wrist, his grip tight and hurting. "I am! I am the Honorable Charles Horton-Smythe, you little guttersnipe, and don't you ever forget it!" He let go and took a deep breath, transforming from a vicious brute to the urbane gentleman before her very eyes. "But, my dear, you're no lady. Besides, Sally, what's a man to think of a girl who willingly comes alone to his house?"

By now the girl had gotten to her feet. "You're no—" She stopped when she saw the look in his eyes.

He smiled coldly. "Your opinion is of no consequence to me, or anybody else."

"I'll tell Mr. Fitzroy."

Charles slapped her across the face. "Do you think he'll listen to you, you little whore? And if he listens, who do you think he'll believe? Now get out of here. I never want to see your face again, not even at Fitzroy's."

The girl collapsed in a sobbing, hiccuping heap at his feet. "Oh, what am I to do?" she wailed, over and over again.

Charles looked at her dispassionately. Perhaps he shouldn't be so quick to get rid of her. She was still employed in Darcy's house. She might yet provide some information.

He reached down and pulled her up. "Now, look, my dear, there's no need for all these tears." He pulled out his silk handkerchief and wiped her face as she stared at him. "After all, you're quite a pretty little thing. You could become very wealthy, if you met the right sort of gentlemen."

She was too upset to say anything, so he continued uninterrupted. "Many rich women got their start just like you, you know. I'd be more than willing to introduce you to some of my friends. You'd like that, now, wouldn't you? A fine house and a carriage and beautiful clothes?"

Sally, ashamed, half-drugged, degraded, thought that she had no other choice. Not now.

Slowly she nodded her head.

Chapter Eighteen

Blossom sat in the large window seat of the Hazelmores' parlor and watched the various members of the family as they employed themselves after dinner.

Mrs. Hazelmore, a plump, pleasant woman who had made Blossom and Ah Tup feel welcome despite their unexpected arrival, sat knitting a sock. Miss Elizabeth Hazelmore played a light air on the piano, her two sisters sat on either side of their mother, reading, and on the hearth rug a kitten worried an old ball of yarn.

It was a very tranquil scene, Blossom realized, distinctly at odds with her tumultuous feelings.

In the time since her hurried rush to leave Darcy's house, she'd had opportunity to think. She simply couldn't believe that the barbarian notion of sin could be so distinctly at odds with what, in China, would be considered only natural.

She remembered Miss Hazelmore's questions, about force and "taking advantage." If the woman was not willing, she could see the sin in that.

She couldn't help wondering if she had been too hasty, listening to Elizabeth when she should have trusted Darcy. Perhaps that was why he had not come for her.

Tomorrow she would tell them that she wanted to go home.

"Come, my dears, it's time for bed," Mrs. Hazelmore said, putting down her knitting. "Elizabeth, you and Miss Flowers may remain for a little while, if you like."

Elizabeth smiled and nodded as her mother hustled out the younger children. Blossom sighed, wondering briefly what it would have been like to grow up in England with such a family.

Then she realized Elizabeth was looking at her. "Yes?"

Elizabeth flushed. "I'm sorry, I was just thinking that this must be very difficult for you."

Blossom nodded and said softly. "Yes, I miss him very much."

"Do you love him?" Elizabeth asked quietly.

"I think I do. If only I knew what you mean by love. Can you explain it?"

Elizabeth looked startled. "Why, love is . . . caring about a person, even more than your own self. Love is wanting to be near someone, to keep him safe, to make him happy."

Blossom nodded. "Yes, I love him."

She stood up and paced the floor. "I should have waited for him. I trust him. Now he is probably angry with me."

Elizabeth frowned. "No, you did the right thing. If he's an honorable man, he'll come here."

"I want to go home."

Elizabeth stood and went to her, looking intently into her face. "No. That is precisely what you must *not* do. If Mr. Fitzroy intends to marry you, he will come here. If he does not, you are much better away from his influence."

Blossom wasn't convinced, but she realized that Elizabeth's knowledge of the proper conduct was what had prompted her to contact Younger Brother's intended wife in the first place. She sat on the sofa.

Elizabeth joined her, and as she did, Blossom saw that the girl was giving her a sidelong glance.

"What is it?" Blossom asked.

"Well, it's not any of my business and I know it's not something that should be discussed, but I can't help thinking that—" she colored even more "—it must not be so terrible, being in bed with a man."

"To share the zenith?"

"To... what?"

"To share the supreme moment, when a man and a woman..."

"I... that's what I was thinking. Pardon me, it's very unladylike to talk about things like that."

"Sharing the zenith is the greatest pleasure a man and a woman can share."

Elizabeth whispered, "I don't know anything at all about men and their... needs."

"Why not?" Blossom demanded. "You are to be married, are you not?"

"We simply don't talk about such matters." Elizabeth looked around furtively. "But, please, I'd like to know something about what happens on the wedding night." She bit her lip nervously. "Does it hurt?"

Blossom saw that Elizabeth was truly afraid, and her heart went out to her. "Only a little the first time. But you will soon forget. The pleasure quickly takes away the pain. I am sure Mr. Jeremy will be most gentle."

"Thank you." She looked around again. "I hope I'm not upsetting you, but what *exactly* happens?"

As Blossom proceeded to tell her, including describing the male anatomy, Elizabeth grew paler and paler and Blossom grew more and more disgusted by the barbarian custom of keeping what was perfectly natural a great secret. They treated the relationship between men and women as if they were divulging the answers to the Imperial examinations.

When Blossom finished, she smiled. "It is not a torture, Miss Hazelmore. Believe me, it is the most wonderful pleasure." She had a sudden moment of illumination. "Especially, I think, if you love the man."

"Thank you, Miss Flowers. I'm glad that I won't be completely taken aback on my wedding night."

"I think it would be wise, Miss Hazelmore, if you would not let Mr. Jeremy know that you are enlightened. If it is the custom here that such things be kept a great secret, he might not understand."

Elizabeth smiled and nodded. "I agree. He would probably consider my curiosity rather bold," she said. She patted Blossom's hand. "Don't worry, Miss Flowers. I'm sure everything will be all right. I've sent for Jeremy. Tomorrow Papa will be back from visiting Grandmother, too. He's sure to be able to have some good advice."

In the past, Darcy had never ridden through the town of Oxford without noticing the calm, cathedral beauty of the place, and without becoming jealous of every person in a scholar's gown. It wasn't their education he envied—such matters as Latin and Greek would have done him little good in making his fortune—but that they had the means to simply enjoy the best years of their youth.

This time, however, Darcy only noted the familiar landmarks as they pertained to his progress toward Jeremy, and hopefully some way out of the morass of his personal life.

His carriage rattled into the courtyard of Christ Church College. A few minutes later Darcy strode into Jeremy's room without bothering to knock.

"Who's—" Jeremy began, then turned around. He held what appeared to be a letter in his hand, and when he saw who stood in his room, his eyes widened. Then, to Darcy's surprise, they narrowed. "What are you doing here?"

"I had to talk to you."

"Oh?"

"I have a problem."

Jeremy waved the letter in his hand and then pointed to another handwritten page on his desk. "I've just heard that from two different people. It would seem that you have more than one problem."

Darcy threw himself into the nearest chair. "What are you talking about?"

"I got two letters in today's post. One from Charles Horton-Smythe and one from Elizabeth. I must say, Darcy, I never took you for a hypocrite."

Jeremy's tone and expression made it very clear that he was speaking in earnest.

"I can guess what they're about."

"Elizabeth has taken poor Miss Flowers to her house after your despicable treatment of her, and Charles says there seems to be some more disturbing rumors about your business that he's not able to quash. Not only that, but you apparently don't care at all. I must say if you do business in the same way you 'protect' young ladies entrusted to your care, I'm not surprised."

Darcy jumped to his feet. "If your charming Elizabeth had not interfered, I would be engaged to Blossom right now. Instead, your future bride has absconded with her and now I'm a despicable cad."

"Did you make love to Miss Flowers, Darcy?" Jeremy demanded.

"Who are you to sit there and ask questions like that?"

Jeremy would not be dissuaded. "Did you make love to her?"

"Only once, if it's any of your damned business," Darcy said sullenly.

Jeremy looked as if he'd scratched a golden idol and discovered clay instead. "Only once? Is that supposed to make your action less offensive? That you only took advantage of the poor girl *once?*"

Darcy strode across the room and grabbed Jeremy's shirt, hauling him up. "Listen, you insolent pup. That 'poor girl' was *brought up to be some man's mistress.*"

Jeremy stared, openmouthed.

"She's not some old friend's daughter I'm chaperoning. She *belongs* to me, a gift from a Chinese merchant. He owed me a lot of money, but instead he sent *her.* She's been trying to get into my bed ever since she got here." He let go and Jeremy stumbled back.

"That's..."

"The truth. I tried to get rid of her, to get her married to somebody. Anybody."

He turned away, but not before Jeremy saw his eyes. "Only you hadn't counted on falling in love with her yourself."

Darcy strode to the large window in the spacious room that *he* paid for. He spoke without turning around. "I think so, but how can a man tell?"

Jeremy went toward his brother. "Darcy, Elizabeth didn't understand. When she got Miss Flowers's letter asking her to come to tea, she went because she was concerned about you. Miss Flowers said you were in trouble. So she went thinking it might have something to do with all these rumors about your business."

"How did Elizabeth know about the rumors?"

Jeremy smiled. "She's quite fascinated by business. I don't always understand where she comes by her knowledge myself, but some of her friends are married to city men.

"At any rate, she went to tea. Miss Flowers wanted to discuss something personal and finally told Elizabeth about...you know. I'm afraid she thought the worst."

"You weren't so quick to trust me, either."

"Well, I'm a man and I've seen Miss Flowers. I could understand how you might be tempted."

"Tempted? Good God, Jeremy, you don't know how I've been tempted!"

"Elizabeth thought she was helping Miss Flowers. I'm sorry, Darcy. We didn't understand, although I must say I still don't think you should have..."

"Well, it just happened."

"There's something else troubling you, isn't there?"

Darcy sat down heavily. "I still don't understand why she left. She must have been angry or upset."

Jeremy looked contrite. "You don't know Elizabeth, Darcy. I daresay she didn't give Miss Flowers much of a chance to think. Elizabeth can be quite compelling if she thinks she's in the right."

Darcy felt a little better. "I suppose I'd better get to know my future sister-in-law better, in that case. To protect myself, if nothing else."

"Is that why you came to see me?" Jeremy asked softly.

"Yes. I want you to go to the Hazelmores' with me and help me get Blossom back."

"I'd be happy to and I think the first thing you should do is tell Miss Flowers how you feel."

"I can't do that. I don't know how."

"There's no mystery to it. Just tell her. If she cares for you at all, she'll understand the meaning. Then ask her to marry you. Oh, and you'll have to let poor ol' Northrup know he's been jilted." Jeremy went over and put his hand on Darcy's shoulder. "Darcy, I saw the way she looked at you. I don't think you have to worry about her caring for you. Stay the night here and in the morning, we'll go and see her."

Darcy nodded and put his hand over his brother's in a rare gesture of love.

"Help yourself to one of my dressing gowns, Darcy. You look exhausted."

Darcy grinned. "I am." He went into the next room.

Jeremy picked up the letter from Charles Horton-Smythe and read the worrying words once again.

Perhaps they were only rumors, after all. Once Darcy got formally engaged to Miss Flowers, they could sort everything else out.

"Papa came home late last night. I hope you weren't disturbed," Elizabeth said over breakfast the next morning.

Blossom had heard the sound of a carriage and a man's hearty voice, but not wishing to cause them any discomfort, she shook her head.

"I'm glad," Elizabeth said. "He said we could meet him after matins."

Although Blossom had no idea what matins were, she nodded in agreement.

A short time later, dressed in a walking dress of brown and cream, she joined Elizabeth at the front door of their cottage. The Hazelmores lived outside London in an area that was still more country than suburb. The area was green and lovely, and the Hazelmores' garden bloomed delightfully. Blossom would have liked to linger for a while, but Elizabeth was clearly impatient to begin.

Over in the distance Blossom saw a huge stone building, and they began to walk toward it. They approached what Blossom assumed was the back of the building, where there was a small, heavy wooden door. Elizabeth pushed it open and went inside. Blossom followed.

The air...there was something about the musty air of the place that she recognized, but how she couldn't say.

"Papa must still be in the nave," Elizabeth said, leading the way farther inside the dark, damp place.

They turned a corner and came to another door, which Elizabeth opened only wide enough to peek through. "Oh, there he is. Mrs. Vye's talking to him. Come on, he won't mind if we interrupt."

Elizabeth opened the door and led the way inside.

Blossom halted and stared about her. This place, this big place with the benches, the cross thing on the wall above the table, the vessels on the table, the books...everything was familiar, yet different.

Then the man at the end of the aisle turned, his white surplice moving like a ghost, the two ends of his stole like animal tails.

"Father!" Blossom whispered.

Chapter Nineteen

Darcy stared at Elizabeth, his heart pounding with dread. "Fainted? Is she ill? Can I see her?"

Elizabeth had never seen a man so upset, and she wouldn't have believed it possible of Darcy Fitzroy if she wasn't seeing it with her own two eyes. "I don't know. The doctor's with her now."

"I'm going up," he said, pushing Jeremy aside and bounding up the stairs. He burst into the little bedroom to see Blossom lying on a small bed, her eyes closed and her skin white as snow. He knelt beside her, ignoring the man who must be the doctor and another other man wearing a clerical collar, and took her hand. "Blossom, Blossom!" he called softly.

Her eyelids fluttered and she opened her eyes. For a moment he was afraid she wouldn't want to see him, but she smiled and his heart leapt with joy.

"Dar-cee," she whispered. "You come for me?"

He kissed her hand, then looked into her face. "Yes, my darling. And then I never want you to go away from me again," he said, his voice filled with love.

"I don't think the young lady should be disturbed," the doctor said sternly.

"What happened?" Darcy asked, looking at them but keeping a firm grip on Blossom's hand.

The man in the clerical collar, whom Darcy realized must be the Reverend Hazelmore, said, "She came into the church with my daughter and suddenly fainted."

"You got her inside a church? She told me she wouldn't go in one."

"Why is no one speaking to me?" Blossom demanded, her voice weak but imperious. "I tell you."

Darcy turned to her with a smile on his face, but his eyes were serious.

"I did not know what the building was. I did not know it was a temple."

"My dear young lady, it's a *church,*" the doctor said.

Darcy gave the doctor such a black look that the man shut his mouth with a snap.

Blossom's brow wrinkled. "When I was inside, I think, 'I know this place,' or one much like it, long, long ago. Even the smell is familiar to me, Dar-cee. Then I saw this man—" she pointed at Reverend Hazelmore "—dressed in the white gown with the cloth around his neck. Like my father."

"Like your father? I thought he was killed."

"Yes, I saw him dead with my own eyes. Ever since, until today, that was my memory of him. But then, when I saw the gown..."

"I think the young lady should be allowed to rest, gentlemen," the doctor said, with a glance at Darcy.

He nodded and stood up. Blossom didn't let go of his hand. "Everything's going to be all right now," he whispered tenderly. "I'll be downstairs."

"I want to go home," she said.

"You will," he promised.

The doctor preceded Darcy and the minister down the stairs and into the drawing room. There was no sign of Jeremy or Elizabeth or any of the other members of the Hazelmore family.

"She's not seriously ill, is she?" Darcy asked, his voice low and fervent.

"No, I don't believe so. She's had a shock and that made her faint. She should be fine after a good night's rest."

Darcy nodded and the doctor seemed poised to leave, but Reverend Hazelmore laid a detaining hand on his arm. "I must ask this, Doctor. Could she be with child?"

Darcy suddenly felt as if a load of ballast had fallen onto his chest.

"No, I don't think so," the doctor said, obviously trying to mask his surprise at the question, "although I must say I didn't consider that possibility."

Both of the men glanced at Darcy, who spoke quickly. "I don't see how she could be."

Reverend Hazelmore frowned.

Darcy began to blush. "I mean, I suppose there's a very remote chance."

"I don't believe this matter requires *my* attention, Reverend," the doctor said. "If the young lady is with child, it is in its very early days yet. Still, that might account for the fainting spell. If she faints again, or feels sick to her stomach, send for me." Before heading for the door, he gave Darcy a look that made it clear that he now considered him a rogue and a scoundrel.

Darcy's hatred for medical men boiled up, but he fought to get it under control. The doctor didn't know how things really were between Blossom and himself, and he shouldn't blame the man for thinking the way most of society would. He took a deep breath and prepared to meet more of the same attitude from Reverend Hazelmore, but first the minister saw the doctor to the door.

As he waited for the man's return, Darcy stared at the empty grate. Pregnant! Blossom pregnant with his child! The thought had never occurred to him. Indeed, he hadn't had time to think about such things. Of course, it *was* possible, even though they'd only been together once.

"Mr. Fitzroy, I realize you may consider my intrusion into your personal affairs unwarranted."

Darcy turned toward the door as Reverend Hazelmore returned.

"However, I must say that I hope, for the young lady's sake, you'll allow me to intercede."

"I'm going to marry her."

The minister indicated a chair and Darcy sat down. His host, with a sad and serious face, followed suit.

"I had planned on asking her to marry me anyway, before I got here."

"Because she might bear your child?"

"Because I love her." Darcy cleared his throat, feeling impossibly young, although he wasn't much more than ten years younger than the man sitting across from him. "If she's pregnant, the baby has to be mine."

"You are certain?"

"Of course," Darcy said, getting rather annoyed. He wanted to go home with Blossom. "She was a virgin." He stopped when he saw the look on Reverend Hazelmore's face.

"I'm sorry to hear that, my son. She's young and she was entrusted to your care by, I take it, a man who is dead. I should have hoped that would have rendered his trust in you a sacred one."

"Look, Reverend, you don't understand." He'd had enough of being considered an unprincipled villain. "In a manner of speaking, Miss Flowers seduced *me.*"

This time there was no slight disgust on the clergyman's face, but outright revulsion.

"It's a long story. Her father didn't send her to me before he died, or anything like that."

"I think it would be best if you explained everything, Mr. Fitzroy. My time is at your disposal."

Darcy sighed. He was very tempted to tell the man to mind his own business, but since Blossom was in his house, perhaps it was. He shrugged his shoulders and told the minister the whole story, beginning with the debt.

When Darcy finished, Reverend Hazelmore leaned back in his chair, his expression thoughtful. "Well, I must say that was quite different from the story I expected to hear, although I should have been forewarned. Elizabeth did mention that Miss Flowers's case was rather unusual, but she had no time to go into details. China, you say?"

Darcy nodded.

"I knew a young man who went to China. I went to Oxford with him, in fact. He was from Yorkshire, and his name was Cooper."

"Cooper!" Darcy's mind flew back to the day at the Crystal Palace when the young daughter of Sam Cooper caught his attention because she looked so much like Blossom.

"Yes. He was quite evangelical. Rather much for the Church of England, if truth be told. However, he always wanted to go to China and last I heard he had succeeded. Miss Flowers reminds me of him, now that you tell me her history. But it could be merely fancy, and an odd connection to my own past."

"That's more of a clue to her true name and family than anything we've found out. As a matter of fact I met a man named Cooper from Yorkshire not too long ago. I thought I saw a family resemblance."

"Is that so? Well, I could provide you with an address, although it's been years since I had any contact with him."

"I would appreciate that."

The minister frowned. "However, Mr. Fitzroy, we mustn't forget the reason Miss Flowers is now a guest in my home."

"I want her to come home with me today. I'll arrange for a wedding as soon as possible."

Darcy was taken aback by the hard look that came into the pastor's eyes. "Hadn't you better ask Miss Flowers if she wishes to be your wife?"

Before Darcy could respond, Reverend Hazelmore continued. "As far as I can understand all this, the poor girl is rather confused and uncertain. I think a rest and some time away from society would do her good."

"You don't mean away from me?" Darcy felt a cold finger of fear along his spine, a fear that this man would somehow prevent Blossom from coming home with him. "I love her."

"I beg your pardon?"

"I love her," he said firmly.

"I'm very happy to hear it, my son. Your feelings do you credit. However, I feel it would not be wise for you to cohabit."

"I'll get a chaperon."

"You had one before."

"What if she's pregnant? Shouldn't we marry at once?"

"I am not one of those who believes that marriage is the perfect answer in such a circumstance, especially if entered into hastily," came the minister's surprising reply. "I was going to propose that Miss Flowers remain here, as our guest.''

Darcy stared at the floor. His heart protested the plan, but his mind told him that Reverend Hazelmore was trying to do what was best. It *would* look rather shocking if Blossom was living in his house when they announced their engagement. Despite his disdain for the dictates of society, Darcy knew that he couldn't step outside the boundaries *that* much.

There was still Northrup to consider, too. The young fellow was a fool, but he had feelings, too. Darcy actually felt sorry for him, sorry enough to want to break the engagement as gently as possible. That would not be easy if Blossom was living with him.

A visit to Yorkshire, to try to solve the mystery of Blossom's identity, might be in order, too.

Darcy sighed heavily. ''I will abide by your wishes,'' he said.

''I'm glad you agree. Naturally you may visit her as often as you like, and her servant is welcome to stay as well.''

''Thank you.''

''Now, sir, I think you should go upstairs and tell the young lady what you have so feelingly revealed to me.''

Darcy stood up and smiled. Before he left, he hesitated for a moment. ''Perhaps, Reverend, it would be best not to say anything about the Coopers. Nothing may come of it, after all.''

''As you wish.''

Darcy went upstairs once again, this time feeling abashed and—damn it—shy as a boy. He knocked on the door and opened it slowly.

Blossom was sitting up in the bed, the satin coverlet pulled up to her chin so that only a tiny ruffle of lace showed around her neck. She looked better, the pink returning to her soft cheeks.

Ah Tup, reacting to a subtle nod from Blossom, sidled past him and out of the room.

"How are you feeling now?" he asked.

"Wonderful," Blossom replied, thinking that word didn't begin to convey the extent of her emotions. She watched Darcy as he came inside the room.

Then he smiled. Such a smile! Her heart began beating rapidly. Excitement coursed through her body. She wanted to get up and run to him.

He came to the bed and took her hand in his, looking down into her eyes. At that instant she knew, without doubt, without question, that she loved him and he loved her.

"Blossom," he said, kneeling beside the bed. "Blossom, will you marry me?"

She answered him quickly and decisively with a deep, lingering kiss. Slowly she drew back. "I would be honored," she said, smiling.

Darcy smiled back, then frowned a little. "I want you to come home with me—"

"I want to go home, too," she interrupted.

"Please, let me finish," he said, but not harshly. "Reverend Hazelmore thinks you should stay here for a few days."

The regret in his voice touched her. "I don't want to. I want to go with you. I *choose* to go home with you."

Darcy laughed softly. "I'm glad to hear you understand something of your rights. However, I need to get some business cleared up, and I can't think clearly with you near me."

"Why not?"

"Because—" his hands cupped her face "—because all I can think about is *you*."

She moved his hands away and tried to look stern. "Does this mean I am going to be the wife of a poor man whose business has become a ruin?"

"What it means is, I'd better take care of some business so that I have some time to devote solely to you, my love."

"Ah, I understand. Then, when you tire of me in a day or so, you will be able to return to your business and never think of me at all."

He leaned closer until his lips were close to hers. "I don't think I'll ever be tired of you."

She kissed him quickly, then moved away mischievously. "I will see to that, Dar-cee. We have not even begun Water Lily's teachings."

When Darcy got home later that day, he was surprised to find Powlett prowling the stables. "Ah, Mr. Fitzroy!" the butler said, his icy demeanor defrosting a little. "Lord Neville Northrup is awaiting you in the drawing room. He's been there all afternoon, sir."

Darcy walked quickly toward the house, Powlett following behind, and wondered if Northrup had somehow discovered what had happened the other night. "What does he want?"

"He declined to say, sir, but he seems most anxious. Most anxious indeed."

"I see."

Powlett suddenly halted and, in a gesture of familiarity totally at odds with Darcy's experience of the faithful retainer, put his hand on his employer's arm. "If you please, sir, I must know about Ah Tup—and Miss Flowers. Are they returning?"

Darcy glanced at Powlett's face. Then grinned. "Why, Powlett, what makes you ask?"

Powlett actually blushed. "I am merely concerned for their welfare, Mr. Fitzroy."

Darcy, a man in love himself, took pity on his butler and refrained from making a comment along the lines of "in a pig's eye." Instead he said, "I'm going to marry Miss Flowers, so I think we can safely assume that Ah Tup will become a permanent resident of our household."

Powlett smiled so broadly that Darcy had the impression the man was making up for years of stony facial expressions in one moment.

"Keep this between us for now," Darcy cautioned, certain that if he didn't say something, Powlett's face would cause instant speculation among the rest of the staff.

"As you wish, sir."

Powlett's face immediately returned to its usual blank, causing Darcy to wonder just where Powlett had learned to keep his emotions, which were obviously in existence, under such strict control.

Powlett seemed to guess the meaning of his employer's look. "Army."

Darcy grinned and went inside to see Neville Northrup.

Neville nervously crossed his legs, then uncrossed them, fearing creases in his trousers—or, more precisely, fearing his valet's reaction to creases. For the fiftieth time that afternoon, he got up and walked to the window, then back to the chair where he sat, crossed his legs, feared creases and stood up.

At the sound of the heavy footsteps coming down the hall, Neville tugged at his fine chesterfield coat, resisted the urge to touch the cravat Chambers had spent forty minutes arranging and prepared to meet Darcy Fitzroy.

Fitzroy strode into the room like a knight in one of the King Arthur stories, or a general. Neville's legs turned to jelly and his palms began to sweat. Still, he knew what he had to do. He thought about the previous night, took a deep breath and cleared his throat.

"Good afternoon, Lord Northrup."

"Good afternoon, Mr. Fitzroy."

"To what do I owe the honor of this visit?"

Neville tried to remember that he was a lord while the man before him was simply a merchant, but that didn't work. He felt like an errant child.

Clearing his throat again, he took a halting step forward. "I came, Mr. Fitzroy, that is, I wanted to talk to you about..."

"Yes, my lord?"

For a brief instant Neville thought Mr. Fitzroy seemed different, a little more kindly disposed toward him perhaps. But that might be his mind playing tricks. Nevertheless, it gave him the slight boost he needed to speak. "I want, that is, I have come to say that I've been thinking about my engagement to Miss Flowers. I fear that perhaps I have been rather overbearing in my attentions and premature in my proposal, leading her to make a decision in haste. Since this decision will influence the rest of our lives, I think perhaps I should withdraw my offer for the present time."

"Am I to understand you wish Miss Flowers to release you from your engagement?"

"Yes."

Fitzroy walked over to the window and Neville began to fear that the man was going to hold him to the engagement, or demand some sort of recompense. But when Fitzroy turned around, he didn't look angry.

"I see. Well, Lord Northrup, since you feel that way and since no formal announcement has been made, I think it would be best to acquiesce to your wishes."

Neville's knees went weak with relief. "Thank you, Mr. Fitzroy. Is Miss Flowers at home?"

"As a matter of fact she isn't, but I don't think you need to see her. I'll tell her our decision."

"Oh, I say, would you? That's awfully kind and decent. I always knew you were a decent fellow, despite the rumors to the contrary. Please extend my regrets to the charming Miss Flowers. Good day!"

Lord Northrup bustled out of the room and hurried straight to the mansion of Lady Emmaline Whitmore.

"Lord Northrup did what?" Charles stared at Darcy, who was sitting smugly behind his desk in his office.

"He broke off their engagement."

"Whatever for?"

"He *said* he feared they had made a hasty decision."

"Will he still marry her, do you think?"

Darcy's smile made Charles dread what was coming next, and when his partner spoke, it was as bad as he'd feared. "I'm going to marry her myself."

Charles managed to recover quickly, despite the wreck of part of his schemes. "Well, congratulations, old man!" he said, his lips twisting into a smile. "When's the wedding?"

Darcy leaned back in his chair and grinned. "As soon as possible, I hope. Reverend Hazelmore will perform the ceremony, I'm sure. First, though, I need to go to Yorkshire."

"Yorkshire?" Charles said casually, but his mind was racing. Mitchell's letter had mentioned a Yorkshireman.

"Yes. I shouldn't be gone too long."

Charles wondered if Mitchell had written another letter to Darcy that he hadn't intercepted, but he doubted that Darcy would sit there discussing this business so matter-of-factly if he had.

"I think we can handle things for a few days, old man, but I have to remind you that the creditors seem to be getting nervous."

"Again? What about this time?"

"I'm not sure."

"Well, try to find out. We can't fight what we don't know."

"Of course. Congratulations again, eh, what?"

"Thanks."

Charles walked out of Darcy's office and into his own. Once inside he picked up his newspaper and began tearing it into little pieces as he stared at it unseeing.

So, Darcy was marrying her himself! He had hoped to use Sally's interesting information against Darcy, but now Miss Flowers was safely lodged with a clergyman. That talkative Ditchett woman probably wouldn't say a word about what had happened since it would do little to credit her ability to chaperon. Sally's word wouldn't hold up against a man like Darcy, and Mrs. MacTavish had apparently disappeared into the Scottish mist.

Well, he would simply have to use his original plan and expose Darcy as an embezzler. The only question now was the best way to proceed.

Chapter Twenty

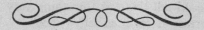

Two days later, Blossom and Elizabeth strolled arm in arm through the Hazelmores' fragrant garden. In the late afternoon, it was a paradise of lovely scents and quiet warmth, surrounding the girls like the embodiment of youthful dreams and hopes.

"I cannot wear a white wedding dress," Blossom said firmly. "It is the color of purity."

Elizabeth nodded, frowning a little. "Perhaps under these circumstances, white would not be an appropriate color."

"It would be a bad omen to wear the color of mourning."

"Here, we wear black for mourning."

"That is the color of wealth and prosperity," Blossom said, beginning to wonder how many other things she would discover about English customs.

Suddenly Jeremy Fitzroy came running into the garden. One look at his face, and both girls felt as if a storm cloud had appeared on the horizon.

Blossom's first thought was of Darcy. "What is it?" she asked quickly, running forward. "Has something happened?"

"Darcy's all right. At least, he's not hurt." Jeremy reached her and stopped, holding out his hand to Elizabeth, who seemed to be rooted to the ground as firmly as the rosebushes. "But something terrible has happened!"

"What?" Blossom demanded.

"It's the business. Apparently Darcy's been *embezzling.*"

Blossom could tell this was something very bad by the horrified expression on Elizabeth's face. "What is this, embezzling?"

"Charles Horton-Smythe says that Darcy's been stealing money from the company for his own personal use. He has the ledgers to prove it, ledgers that he found in Darcy's safe. It amounts to thousands of pounds! He says that unless we pay back the money Darcy stole, he'll be forced to go to the police."

"Dar-cee owns the company. How can he steal his own money?"

"It's not his money, Blossom. It belongs to the stockholders. If they find out, the company will be ruined, and so will my brother."

"Dar-cee is not a thief."

Jeremy looked at her. "I know that. At least, I can't believe this myself. But Charles is one of his oldest, most trusted friends, as well as his business partner. He looked absolutely sick when he told me about it."

"These ledgers, what are they?"

"The account books of the company, where they keep a record of the money."

"Did you see them?"

"Yes."

"And they looked true?"

"Yes."

"You believe this man before you trust your own brother?"

"How can I not, when I saw the books myself?"

"Who keeps the books?"

"The clerks. Every night they're locked in a safe."

"Safe? What is this safe?"

"It's a heavy metal container, with a very special lock. Nobody could get in it except Darcy and Charles."

"Then Charles is lying."

Elizabeth and Jeremy gave Blossom a look that was openly incredulous. "But the books..." Jeremy began.

"Charles Horton-Smythe could change them."

"I suppose, but why should he? If the business is ruined, so is he."

"If Dar-cee did not take the money, and I do not for a moment think he has, who else? Perhaps this man hopes to accuse Dar-cee to take suspicion away from himself."

For the first time since he'd seen the books, Jeremy began to hope. "That might be true. But Darcy's paid Horton-Smythe well. Why would he steal from the company?"

Blossom stamped her foot in exasperation. "I say this one more time. Dar-cee would not steal. I believe this with all my heart. I have never trusted that Horton-Smythe, who has the eyes of a snake."

With that, she turned and hurried from the garden, going straight upstairs. She found Ah Tup putting away some clean clothing. "Ah Tup, I need your darkest trousers and blouse. I am going to Mr. Fitzroy's business tonight, when it is dark."

"Alone?"

Blossom thought for a moment. "No. You can keep watch for me."

Ah Tup nodded.

* * *

Sam Cooper smiled when he saw who stood at the door of his house. "Come in, come in, Mr. Fitzroy. Glad to see you. What brings you to Yorkshire?"

"Good evening. I'm sorry to disturb you so late," Darcy said, coming into the comfortable, if small, parlor.

"Think nothin' of it. Mary, my dear, here's Mr. Fitzroy, that I met at the exhibition."

Mr. Cooper's pleasant-faced wife came bustling into the room. "Very happy, I'm sure. I'll just call Sarah to put on the kettle for a nice cup of tea."

"I don't mean to trouble you."

"Oh, tsh! It's no trouble. Sarah!"

The young girl that so looked like Blossom came shyly into the room. "Yes, Ma?"

"Be a love and put on the kettle. Oh, and take Mr. Fitzroy's cloak."

Darcy divested himself of his cloak and gave it to her. Sarah smiled and left. Mrs. Cooper, picking up a basket of knitting, sat down beside the hearth. "Have a seat, Mr. Fitzroy."

Darcy complied.

"Now, then, what can I do for you?" Mr. Cooper said, lighting his pipe.

"I came to see if you knew a man named Saul Cooper."

"Aye, I certainly did. That's my brother."

"Does he live near here?"

Mr. Cooper shook his head sadly. "No. I don't know that's he's *living* anywhere."

"He's dead?"

"Missin', more like. He went out to China sixteen years ago. We got some letters for a while, but then they stopped."

"Was he a missionary by any chance?"

"What's all this about?"

"I might have some information about his fate."

Mr. Cooper's eyes widened. "Aye, well, Saul was a missionary, all right."

That would explain the admonition not to go into their temples, Darcy thought.

A puff of smoke from the pipe hovered around Mr. Cooper's head. "He truly thought the heathen were all doomed unless they converted to Christianity. He could get pretty worked up talking about it. Even after his wife died out there, he wouldn't come back." Mr. Cooper blew out another ring of smoke. "I reckon the Chinese killed him. We heard he shipped for home, then . . . nothing."

"Did he have children?"

"He had one, a little girl. Saul could be a hard man where he thought the proper Christian road lay, but he doted on her."

"Do you have any idea what happened to her?"

"Dead, we supposed, if the ship went down. Flora was a sweet little thing, with her big blue eyes."

Mrs. Cooper put down her knitting. "Where's Sarah with that tea? You look like you need a drop, Mr. Fitzroy."

Darcy shook his head. "It's all right. Mr. Cooper, I believe I know what happened to them."

Mr. Cooper's pipe almost landed on the floor. "What? How?"

"I do a lot of business in Canton. One of the Chinese merchants there found a young girl, who was not Oriental, and took her into his household. He recently sent her to me.

"She has little idea of her family, although I must tell you her father was killed by pirates."

Mrs. Cooper's knitting and Mr. Cooper's pipe sat untouched.

"She looks very much like Sarah, has blue eyes and dark hair and says her name is Blossom."

"Here's the tea," Sarah said softly.

"Blow the tea!" Sam Cooper leapt out of his chair. "Ma, I'm getting Mam and goin' to London."

Darcy stood up.

"My mother looked after Flora many a time when she was little. If anybody'll know her for sure, it'll be Mam. And if Flora remembers any of us, it'll be her, too."

"It's a long ride to London," Darcy said, desperately hoping that the woman would come, but afraid she would be too old and frail for such a journey.

"Not to worry. Mam'd walk if she thought she'd see Flora again. She'll do, never fear."

For the first time since she had arrived in London, Blossom blessed the thick, yellow fog. It provided an additional covering as she and Ah Tup, muffled in dark cloaks, quietly left the house. They hurried down the street, turned a corner and got a cab. Blossom asked to be taken to one of the streets near Fitzroy Shipping.

When they arrived, they hurried away into the fog, leaving the cabdriver to stare after them.

Lady Whitmore gazed thoughtfully at Charles Horton-Smythe as he stood in her magnificent drawing room.

"I thought your husband, as one of the principal stockholders, should know this, before it becomes public knowledge."

"I see." Lady Whitmore gracefully gestured to a nearby seat. "You have no alternative to going to the police with this information?"

Charles kept his voice carefully concerned. "Well, I had hopes that Darcy might be compelled to repay the money, but I don't think he has sufficient funds."

Lady Whitmore smiled enigmatically. "How much money has he stolen?"

Blossom expelled her breath as she helped Ah Tup move the last of the wooden boxes beneath a window. She looked up at the grimy window, one of several on the main floor of Fitzroy Shipping. Without saying anything, she began climbing up, her hands holding on to the slippery, slimy walls.

It was only when she was high enough that she saw the iron bars. With a curse, she climbed back down and looked at Ah Tup in dismay. "I cannot get in that way. It is barred."

Ah Tup glanced around nervously. "Then we should leave. I do not like this place."

Blossom shook her head. "Not yet. We must first find a way inside."

With that thought in mind, she surveyed the back wall. There was a wooden door, but they had already tried it and found it bolted.

She spotted a very small window at the bottom of the wall where the wooden boxes had been stacked. Moving them had exposed the window. She signed for Ah Tup to come closer. "Look. I can enter here."

Ah Tup frowned skeptically. "It is a very small window."

"Am I fat?" Blossom whispered indignantly, kneeling down on the ground. She pushed at the frame, but the window wouldn't budge. She picked up a piece of wood nearby and carefully hit the window so that it cracked. Then she took off the dark shawl she had wrapped around her head, tied it around her hand and pushed in the glass. Carefully she pulled out the rest of the pieces attached to the frame.

"Stay here and watch. If anyone comes, crawl in after me and wait."

"But..."

"Do as I say." Blossom sat down and put her feet through the narrow opening. Slowly she thrust her legs in, then lowered her hips. To her great relief she felt her feet touch something solid. Bending her knees, she moved into the dark, dark cellar.

Her eyes, already used to the dim light in the alley, adjusted quickly. Rats rustled in the darkness, running over the floor. Trying not to feel squeamish, Blossom climbed down carefully from the packing crate and searched for a door.

She spied stairs and made her way to them. Once on the stairs, she tiptoed up quickly and held her breath as she tried the door.

It moved. Cautiously she opened it.

The lamps in the street provided some illumination. Still cautious, Blossom went down a small corridor that opened out into the main office. She cursed herself for not finding a way to visit in the daytime, when someone could point out which one of the offices was Darcy's and which was Charles Horton-Smythe's. As it was, she would have to guess.

That proved surprisingly easy. She found the largest one and recognized the scent of Darcy's tobacco. Proceeding to the next one, she recognized the smell of Horton-Smythe's cologne, curling her lips with distasteful remembrance. In the corner was a large iron box with a strange front.

Only a fool would hide false account books in the safe thing and she didn't believe Horton-Smythe was a fool, not if he had convinced Jeremy of his own brother's guilt.

She went straight to the huge mahogany desk.

Blossom had seen many secret hiding places. Honorable Wu had several in his house, always fearing the day the peasants might revolt, or the government decide he was an enemy. Precious Jade had a few where she secreted her choicest jewels, believing the places unknown. Ah Tup had laughingly told Blossom of the lengths Precious Jade had gone to keep the knowledge secret, including going to the hiding places in the middle of the night. Little did Precious Jade know that a servant, beaten and reviled, had made it her business to find out such things.

As Blossom gazed at the desk, she almost laughed out loud. Really, the English were truly barbarians if they couldn't disguise a hiding place any better than the one in his desk. It took her only a moment to find the spring that made the hidden drawer pop open.

Inside the drawer, there were some large books filled with writing and numbers. She picked them up.

Moving quickly, she pushed the drawer back and hurried to the corridor, down the steps and into the dark cellar. She stumbled in the darkness, knocking over another box and dropping one of the heavy books. Scrambling around, fearful of the rats but desperate not to lose the book, she finally found it.

Ah Tup called softly, "Is it you?"

"Yes!" Blossom called back. "Come, take these!"

Ah Tup's face appeared in the small aperture. Blossom shoved the books up and began to climb onto the box.

"What's going on here?"

She glanced over her shoulder. Charles Horton-Smythe stood on the top of the steps, his eyes gleaming like those of the rats in the darkness.

"Go!" she cried to Ah Tup.

"But mistress, I..."

"Go! Take them to Younger Brother!" She heard Ah Tup's feet run down the alley. Then she got down and faced the man moving slowly toward her.

Chapter Twenty-One

"This is a most unexpected pleasure."

Blossom ignored Horton-Smythe until she was certain Ah Tup was out of the alley, then she looked at him squarely. "I came to find the books that lie."

"Books that lie? What is that, some quaint Oriental notion?" He came a little closer. She smelled wine and realized his eyes were bloodshot.

"No. They are books that you have changed to make it appear that Dar-cee is a thief."

"Oh, you think that, do you?"

"I know that."

He came even closer, his mouth turned up in an evil grin and his eyes suspicious. "How do you know?"

"I know Dar-cee would not lie and he would not steal. You, however, I believe would do both."

"Indeed?"

Suddenly his hand clasped hers tightly. "What else do you believe me capable of, my dear?"

"Anything," she said. She tried to stay calm, to think clearly. She had known fear many times, and although she was afraid now, she was far from terrified. Horton-Smythe had had much wine, and that would cloud his judgment.

He pulled her toward the stairs, but Blossom yanked her hand from his. "Why have you done this? He was good to you."

Horton-Smythe's eyes grew hard, his mouth tight. "*He* was *good* to me? A merchant was *good* to a nobleman? He didn't give me anything I didn't deserve.

"He was the one who should have been thankful for having a man of my rank willing to be his *lackey*. Where would he have been, without me?"

"He would not be accused of a crime."

Horton-Smythe scowled. "So what? What is a merchant to me?"

"I thought he was your friend," she said softly, inching backward.

"I hate him. A man of his birth thinking he could worm his way into society with money. If my father weren't a drunken sot, I'd be able to show Darcy Fitzroy just how lowly he was."

She moved back a little more. "You have done all this because your father lost face?"

He glared at her. "Yes, and I'd do it all again." Suddenly he reached out and grabbed her arm so tightly that she cried out. "Oh, no. You're coming with me."

"Where are you taking me?"

"To a safe place, very secluded and quiet. No one will bother us there."

"You would not dare to harm me. Dar-cee would kill you."

"He'll have to find me first."

"He will."

"I don't think so. I've planned all this very carefully."

"Ah Tup has taken the books. She will go to his house right away. If you let me go, I will tell him that you didn't hurt me."

His other hand took hold of her other arm. "But Darcy isn't there, is he? Only his brother—the fool he was going to put in *my place*—who wouldn't know how to button his shirts without Darcy!" He took a deep breath. "Be that as it may, my dear, I simply can't have you talking to people. I have other plans."

She began to struggle, calling him all manner of foul things in Cantonese.

His grip remained as firm as iron. "I assume you're not flattering me, but no matter—for now."

She lifted her arm and bit his hand as hard as she could.

He pushed her back, knocking her to the ground. She struck her head, and for a moment the room seemed to spin around, only to stop on him looking down at her. She put her hand to her head and felt the warm moistness of blood.

"That was singularly stupid, Miss Flowers, and utterly useless."

With a cry of fear, rage and hatred, Blossom leapt to her feet. One of Water Lily's last lessons had dealt with unwanted advances by men who might try to woo her attention away from her master. Surely there could be no advance more unwanted than this.

Without hesitation Blossom did what Water Lily had said while Horton-Smythe was too surprised to respond. She used her knee, her fists, her fingernails and her feet until he lay moaning on the floor. She didn't wait to see if he was capable of following, but ran shakily to the box and climbed up and out the window. Then she ran through the alley and down the next one, her only thought to get away from Horton-Smythe. She kept on running, not even pausing to glance behind her.

Until she realized she didn't know where she was. Out of breath and dizzy, she stopped, leaning against a stone wall.

A new fear crept over her. She had never been outside alone. In China, she had not been allowed beyond the walls of Honorable Wu's house. On the journey to England she had had Ah Tup with her at all times, and afterward, she had always been with Darcy, Mrs. Ditchett or Elizabeth.

Gasping for air, she tried not to panic. It seemed a long time since she had escaped Horton-Smythe, but he might be trying to find her. She must get home.

Home. Where a man who loved her lived, a man she loved with all her heart.

Somehow, someway, she would make her way through the alleys and streets. She felt the wound on her head and the blood trickling down her neck, then glanced down at her trousers and blouse. The night air was damp and chilly, and already she was beginning to shiver with the cold.

Nevertheless, she raised her head and slowly, cautiously, began to walk away.

Powlett stared at Ah Tup in dismay. He was very glad to see her, but it was evident that something was extremely wrong. He could understand nothing from her frantically garbled language as she stood in front of him, her clothes filthy and tears streaming down her face.

She had arrived only minutes ago, pounding on the door, babbling incoherently and carrying what appeared to be ledgers. A cabdriver had followed her, demanding to be paid. That at least the butler could understand, so he paid the fare.

Now he gently grasped Ah Tup by her slender shoulders. "Please, speak slowly. I can't understand."

"It is my mistress. He has her!" There followed more frenzied Chinese.

Powlett led the girl into the drawing room and tried not to let a sense of fear pervade him. "Who has her? Where? Explain yourself." He made Ah Tup sit on the sofa, regardless of the dirty state of her clothing.

"*He* does! The evil one, the Horton-Smythe!"

Powlett's eyes widened for an instant, then he ran into the hall and bellowed, "Mr. Jeremy!"

Moments later, Jeremy rushed into the drawing room, hastily doing up his shirt. "What is it? What's going on?"

Ah Tup jumped up and held out the ledgers she had been clutching to her chest. "Here. We went to get, but he came! Hurry to the place! My mistress . . . !"

Jeremy looked at Powlett. "These are account books." He turned to Ah Tup. "You went to the office? You took these?"

"My mistress found them. Now she is in danger!"

Jeremy nodded once and ran to the door. "I'll get my horse."

Ah Tup began to weep silently, moaning as if in great pain. Powlett sat beside her. Very tenderly and as awkwardly as a lad, he put his arms around her.

Charles stood in the alley, the fog swirling about him like the embodiment of his dishonest plans.

Ruined now. His wonderful plans, ruined. By her.

And she was nowhere in sight.

She couldn't have gone far. He felt the pistol tucked inside his coat and went down the alley. It led into another, narrower one and he took it. Then another.

He would find her and shoot her. Like a dog.

All the time he'd spent creating the false books. Creating the false uncle. And now, just when it was all to come to fruition, that whore had to destroy everything.

Well, perhaps not everything. Most of the money was safely in Madeira. He knew there was a ship leaving tonight bound for Portugal. He could be on it and out of the country before anyone realized it. He would withdraw the money from the bank and take the first vessel leaving, no matter its destination. Then he would like to see somebody track him down.

He stopped and pulled out his watch. The hour was growing late. It might be better to get to the ship now and escape before daylight. He turned and began to walk back to the office.

A figure stepped in front of him so that he had to stop. "Sally!" he said when he recognized her. "What are you doing here? Shouldn't you be...busy?"

The girl glared at him, her eyes full of hatred. "Busy entertainin' more of your friends, you mean?"

"Busy earning money."

"Bein' a whore."

"If that's the way you choose to look at it, but at least you're no streetwalker."

"No thanks to you."

"As you wish. Now, if you'll excuse me..."

"I'm havin' a baby."

He paused. "A risk of the job. I can tell you who to see to get rid of it."

"It might be yours."

"Or it might not."

He made to walk past her, but she moved quickly, grappling with him in her effort to make him stay. "You can't just leave me standin' here in the street! Oh, what have you done to me, you monster!''

Exasperated, Charles pushed her away with considerable force, so that she fell in the gutter. He didn't say a word, but began walking away.

Suddenly a shot rang out. Turning, Charles stared at Sally's terrified face and the smoking gun in her hand.

Then he slowly sank down upon the pavement where he lay motionless, shot in the chest.

Darcy had doubted Sam Cooper's insistence that his mother could make the journey without discomfort, but he had to admit that her son had been right. They had been on the road for several hours—all night, in fact—but she seemed as if she'd just stepped into the carriage.

As the sun rose and they drew nearer to the city, Darcy felt for the first time in many days that everything was going to be fine. No, better than fine. Wonderful. He began to imagine how it would be. Blossom, a delightful, charming, never-boring wife. Jeremy and Elizabeth married. Jeremy coming into the business. He even went so far as to envision visits with the Coopers, with his wife and—he almost gasped with sudden sheer happiness—children of his own.

It was more than he had ever dared to dream before.

Soon the carriage was driving through familiar streets. As they got closer, it would have been difficult to tell who was more excited, Darcy or Mrs. Cooper. At last they arrived. Before the carriage had even come to a halt, Mrs. Cooper was reaching for the door.

"Now then, where is she? Where's my girl?"

"Patience, Mam. Only a little more time."

Darcy opened the carriage door, got down and prepared to help Mrs. Cooper, who gave him a terrible glare as she jumped nimbly down. "Young man, don't try to pamper me! I don't like it and I won't abide it!"

Darcy could well believe this was Blossom's relative. He smiled and said, "I'll go to Reverend Hazelmore's now and bring her for a visit."

"No, no. Let's all go!"

"I think it would be better if I could prepare Blossom a little," Darcy said, which was partly true. It was also partly true that he wanted to have her to himself for a little while. If the Coopers were her relatives, they might want to take her back to Yorkshire. He'd have a lot of long, lonely journeys to Yorkshire and back in his future, until they were married.

Mrs. Cooper looked about to protest, but Sam spoke first. "I agree. Come on in, Mam, and calm yourself a little."

"Oh, very well."

Just then the door to Darcy's house opened and out stepped Mrs. MacTavish. "Mr. Fitzroy!"

Darcy bounded up the steps. "You're back!" he exclaimed.

"Yes." His housekeeper wrung her hands nervously. "It appears there's been some misunderstanding. I had to go to my sister's. She was suddenly taken sick."

"Well, glad to have you home," he replied with a broad smile. Home. With Blossom for his wife, he would truly have a home. "We've got some guests. This is Mrs. Cooper and her son."

Mrs. MacTavish nodded a greeting.

"I'm going to the Hazelmores'..."

"Sir!" Mrs. MacTavish's tone and the look on her face got his attention at once. "Sir," she repeated, her tone softened. "Please, come inside. Something's happened."

Darcy frowned but obeyed, going into the drawing room. Mrs. Cooper, her son and Mrs. MacTavish followed him.

Ah Tup, her face tear streaked, Jeremy and Powlett were already in the room.

"What's going on?" Darcy demanded.

Ah Tup began to cry and a shaft of fear lodged in Darcy's heart.

Jeremy stepped forward, his eyes tired and sorrowful. "It's Blossom—she's missing."

"*Missing?* What do you mean?"

"My girl isn't here?"

"Now, Mam, keep quiet a minute."

Darcy strode up to Jeremy, ignoring the others in the room. "What happened?"

"She went to your office last night."

"What for?"

"To get your account books." Jeremy rubbed his forehead. "While you were gone, all kinds of rumors about your business started flying about. Charles was quite upset and he showed me what he said were the accounts. They revealed that there had been certain...irregularities. You'd taken money with no explanation...."

"That's a damn lie."

"I know that. Now." Jeremy looked completely wretched. "At first, when I saw the books, I confess I doubted you."

Darcy's voice was hard, his gaze boring into his brother's. "Go on."

"Blossom said right away that she didn't believe it. I tried to explain about the books, and she was certain they'd been altered." Jeremy put his hand on Darcy's arm. "You have to believe me, Darcy. I had no idea she'd go to the office herself to look for the real books."

"Did she go alone?"

"Ah Tup went with her."

"Books? Who cares about books? Where's my granddaughter?"

Jeremy looked over at the indomitable matron. "We don't know. Charles came upon them as they were leaving. Ah Tup got away and brought the books, but Blossom . . ."

Darcy felt as if every drop of blood had drained from his body.

"I rushed over to the office as soon as we heard, but there was no one there."

Darcy didn't hesitate. "I'm going to Charles's house."

"He's not there. We've already checked."

"Oh, my baby! To think I've come so close!"

"Now, Mam, we'll find her."

There was a loud knock at the front door. As everyone stared at each other, afraid to think what it might herald, Darcy strode out into the hall and opened the door.

To his surprise, Emmaline stood on the threshold. "Have you heard?" she asked at once.

Fear, as cold and merciless as the freezing waters of a river, struck at his heart. "What?"

"Charles Horton-Smythe. He's dead."

Emmaline would not have believed Darcy Fitzroy could look so shattered and . . . and *afraid*.

"Where? How?" he blurted out.

A gray-haired head appeared in a nearby doorway, a woman Emmaline had never seen before.

"Have they found my baby?"

"No, not yet."

At his words, the old woman retreated.

Emmaline glanced at Darcy, who said, "Come to my study."

Emmaline followed him and pulled the door shut behind her.

"What happened to Charles?" he demanded at once.

"They found his body in an alley, not far from your offices. He'd been shot."

"Do they have any idea who did it?"

"No. He was in a rather unsavory part of the city. The police think someone tried to rob him, then ran away once they'd shot him."

"His wallet and watch?"

"Still in his coat."

Darcy didn't say a word.

"I also came to tell you that you needn't fear for your business. I can assure you that several investors are quite convinced of your honesty."

Darcy didn't reply, and she realized her last words had been unimportant to him. "Darcy, what is it? What's happened?"

"It's Blossom. She's missing."

Blossom. Not Miss Flowers. So it was true. Darcy's relationship with his ward was definitely intimate. "Charles is involved, isn't he? Did she find out about his embezzling?"

Darcy nodded. "How did you know?"

"He came to me and tried to tell me *you* had done it. He may have had some foolish idea that I would be only too happy to find a way to discredit you. I knew that man should be watched, but I didn't think he'd stoop to anything like this."

"Blossom went to the office to look for evidence that I wasn't the one stealing from the company. He found her there and no one has seen her or heard from her since."

"You don't think *she* killed him?"

"If she had, she would have come home."

Tears sprang into Emmaline's eyes at the anguish in Darcy's voice. "Don't worry, Darcy. We shall find her." She didn't want to tell him that it was more likely Charles had taken her somewhere. He wouldn't kill her right away, not a man with such a bestial nature. He would want to do other things first.

When she spoke, she tried to sound hopeful. "It could be that she got away from him and he simply went down the wrong alley."

"Then she could be anywhere, lost and maybe hurt."

Perhaps it would be better to prepare him for what they might find. She took a deep breath. "Or she could be hidden in one of Charles's houses."

Darcy stared at her.

"Oh, my dear. You didn't even know that about him? That he owns property in the city of a most disgusting sort?"

"I'm beginning to realize I didn't know him at all."

Emmaline smiled sadly. "You always were much too trusting, my dear. Come, I'll take you there."

"How do you know where to go?"

"I make it my business to find out these things."

Darcy went to tell the others that he was going to look for Blossom and that he didn't know when he might return. When he came outside, Emmaline gave her driver a few brief instructions. As they entered the carriage, she sat opposite him.

Darcy gazed at her steadily. "Emmaline, I can't tell you what your help may mean to me."

Emmaline, who had considerable fortitude, didn't have the courage to look into Darcy's face. No one would ever feel for her the way he felt about Miss Flowers and it was a torture to realize that now. "You love her very much, don't you?"

He didn't answer. She reached out to put her hand on his cheek and gently turned his face so that he looked at her. For once, Darcy wasn't trying to hide his anguish, and the sheer magnitude of his fearful torment moved her deeply. "Oh, my poor dear! We will find her. We must!"

"Emmaline, why...?" he began brokenly, but she put her finger to his lips.

"Because I care about you."

He looked even more upset, and she hurriedly began to tell him the truth. "Darcy, I could never love you, or any other man, try as I might to believe otherwise. That capacity has, for good or ill, been driven out of me. But I want you to be happy. Miss Flowers loves you very much, as much as you love her."

"Emmaline, oh, God, Emmaline. I don't think I can live without her," he whispered.

"Then we'll find her," she said briskly, wiping her eyes and determined to distract him, at least a little. "My husband has considerable influence with the authorities."

"Thank you, Emmaline." He took a deep breath. "But I think you're wrong about yourself."

"Oh, don't worry about me, Darcy." She tried to sound nonchalant. "I'm quite content to have control of my husband's purse—and some others besides."

He raised his eyebrows.

"Didn't you wonder why Neville Northrup was so easily persuaded to break the engagement with Miss Flowers?"

"You don't mean..."

"He's quite like having a puppy, and for now he amuses me greatly. He lets me invest his money for him, too."

Darcy wasn't fooled by her tone for an instant. "I'm sorry."

She looked away. "Don't be. Please. I couldn't bear to think of you, or anyone, pitying me." Her head came up, her poise returned, and so did her cool manner. She glanced out the window as the carriage began to slow. "We're here."

Darcy stared in disbelief at the filthy tenement. He knew such places existed in London, as did everyone, but he had never been near such a squalid, fetid building. "Charles owns this?"

"He owns three more just like it in other parts of the city."

"I would never have guessed."

"No, *you* wouldn't. His methods and motives are totally foreign to a man of your character. However, they are not so foreign to me."

Darcy turned to the beautiful, perfectly groomed woman sitting across from him. "You don't own places like this, do you?"

"No." She looked at him. "I'm not that greedy."

Darcy nodded and got out. "Wait here."

Emmaline didn't have to be told to comply. The street below the carriage wheels was slimy with dirt and other things that his nostrils identified.

Darcy pushed open the door and almost immediately collided with a huge, stinking man. The man, his face covered in grime and a drunken look in his eyes, pushed Darcy into the wall. Immediately Darcy felt for his wallet—and immediately realized it was no longer in his coat. "Stop!" he called out.

The man turned to him and Darcy saw that he wasn't really drunk at all. "I want my property," Darcy said, his voice low and distinct.

"What?"

"I want my wallet."

"Do you? Come and fetch it then."

Darcy saw the gleam of a knife and dodged just in time. The man lunged for him again, but he had underestimated his well-dressed opponent. Instead of attacking a city-bred gentleman, he found himself grappling with a man desperately seeking a woman he loved, a veteran of street fights and brawls, a man who knew how to protect himself with his fists and his feet, and a man who, when he got the knife in his hands, knew precisely how to use it.

The thief backed into a corner of the narrow hallway. He reached into his dirty coat and tossed the wallet at Darcy. "Here, take it!"

Darcy picked it up without taking his eyes from his attacker. "I want information."

The thief grinned nervously, but his glance kept flicking from Darcy's face to the knife in his hand. "Anything you likes, gov."

"Have you seen the man who owns this building?"

"Who's that?"

Darcy had the knife to the man's throat in an instant, his hand gripping the other man's shirt. "I said, have you seen the man who owns this building?"

"I can't rightly say, gov. Don't know who owns it."

"Then have you seen a gentleman and a lady?"

"No, sir."

Darcy pressed the knife into the man's throat, just enough to dent the skin. "Are you certain?"

"Certain sure, gov!"

"Is there anybody here who might know the landlord?"

"None that I knows of."

Darcy believed him. It would be prudent for Charles to use an intermediary for collecting rent in a place like this. And whatever else Charles was proving to be, he was prudent.

Darcy let go. The man rubbed his hand against his throat. "Get out of here," Darcy muttered. Then he proceeded to search the rest of the stinking place, to no avail. There was no sign of Blossom, and nobody knew anything of Charles and a lady.

It was the same at the other properties Emmaline took him to. As they drove from tenement to tenement, Darcy demanded that Emmaline tell him all she knew about Charles. He realized she was reluctant, but he wanted to know. He needed to know.

He learned the full extent of Charles's villainy, the amount of money he'd stolen, the incredible rents that he charged on buildings that should have been torn down, the brothels he'd patronized and the prostitutes he'd abused. These last reports made it quite clear that Charles enjoyed hurting women, which almost drove Darcy mad with panic. He could easily envision Charles taking Blossom somewhere, hurting her, even killing her and dumping her body somewhere like so much refuse.

The last part of their journey brought them close to the offices of Fitzroy Shipping. Darcy scanned the street on one side, while Emmaline surveyed the other. She sighed softly and he realized they had been searching all day.

"You should go home, Emmaline. Order your coachman to take us there."

She turned to him. "You're exhausted, too. I'll have the driver take you home first. Rest a while and eat something. Your brother will have the police searching."

Darcy shook his head. "I can't rest until I find Blossom." He went back to staring out the window.

"Stop!" he called out almost immediately. Emmaline moved to look out his window. They were now close to the banks of the Thames and she could see a group of people huddled below on the reeking shore, looking at something that had washed up from the river.

The carriage halted and Darcy moved to open the door. Emmaline reached out and grabbed his arm. "We can send the driver," she said quickly.

Darcy turned to her, his face full of both an awesome strength and a terrible fear. She knew it was useless to try to detain or spare him. Without a word Darcy stepped down and walked toward the little crowd, his back rigidly straight, his hands clenched into fists at his side.

Chapter Twenty-Two

As Darcy drew closer, he realized most of the people muttering about the thing laying on the ground were mudlarks, the poorest of the poor, mainly children and elderly woman who made their living scavenging in the mud. When they saw that he was coming toward them, they turned their dirty faces and stared at him. In the waning light of evening, they looked like grotesque inhabitants of another world.

Finally, he was close enough to tell what had caught their attention. A body. His throat tightened and breathing became even more difficult. It was a human body. A woman's body, in a soaking, muddy dress. He forced himself to go closer, bend down and gently turn the body over.

Not Blossom! Oh, thank God! Not Blossom!

But he knew her nonetheless, he realized with a gasp of shock. It was Sally, the housemaid. He looked at the tallest person standing nearby. "When did you find her?"

"A little while back." The person who spoke was only a boy.

"Did you find anything else?" Darcy asked. "I'll pay."

One of the old women, a toothless hag, stepped forward and drew out a relatively clean reticule from somewhere within her garments. "This. I found it on the steps yonder."

Darcy took the purse and opened it. Inside he found a paper, a note from Sally. He read it slowly, then handed the old woman a sovereign. Her eyes widened and she clutched it hungrily, scurrying away.

A policeman joined them, explaining that the fine lady in the carriage had alerted him to the "trouble." Darcy told briefly how he had come to know the drowned girl and gave the note to the officer. He read it and shrugged his shoulders, by his expression clearly used to the corpses that washed up on the shore of the river. "Suicide, eh? Lord, I've seen this too many times. What's all this about some fellow named Smythe?"

"She shot the bastard, I gather."

The policeman looked shocked.

"The man was my partner. He was also a thief, a scoundrel who abused women and was quite capable of ruining an innocent young girl. You need have no pity for the likes of him."

"Oh. But surely you don't think she..."

"Yes, I believe what she says—that she shot him, then threw the gun in the river and herself after it. I only wish someone had stopped her."

"Well, she put an address on the note. That'll make things easier."

"I suppose someone will have to inform her mother?"

"Yes."

"I'll do it."

"You don't have to, sir."

"I think it's the least I can do."

"We're supposed to be keeping a look out for a young woman, but I don't think her name was Sally. Blossom something, I think."

"This is a different young lady. I know Miss Blossom Flowers."

"Do you, now?"

But Darcy had already turned and started to walk away.

Darcy persuaded Emmaline to go home. From her mansion he took a cab and went on his horrendous errand to tell Sally's mother what had happened to her daughter, all the while fearing more and more that Blossom, too, would be found dead, if she was ever found at all.

As a little crowd of the sympathetic and curious gathered outside the doorway to the humble dwelling, Darcy told Sally's mother as gently and compassionately as he could about her daughter. The woman sat in stony silence for a long moment. Darcy, not sure what to do, sent one of the children hovering nearby for the apothecary. Then the woman gave one long, low moan and began to cry. A matronly neighbor hurried into the room, taking the bereaved mother into her arms as tenderly as one would an injured child. The apothecary, a careworn, soft-spoken man, listened as Darcy explained the circumstances, then began to make a mixture to quiet the sobbing woman.

No longer needed, Darcy went out to his waiting cab and only then realized he was crying, too.

Blossom clutched the shawl more tightly around her face, using her other hand to try to keep the long skirt from dragging in the dirt.

During the early morning, she had seen a woman hanging some wash on a rope in a narrow back garden behind a gloomy-looking row house. Hoping the woman might understand, and being as quiet as possible, Blossom had climbed over the fence and taken a skirt and a large cloth to use as a shawl. Unfortunately, the skirt was made for a woman much taller, and the shawl, she soon realized, had been used as some kind of a mop. It smelled terrible.

As the day progressed, she felt less fearful about being alone. Since she had to ask for directions several times, she had to make her way through busy streets. But most people ignored her, and she began to think that if Horton-Smythe was trying to find her, he would have less chance if she was in a crowded place.

She knew Darcy's house was on a street near Mayfair, and thought that if she could get there, she would be able to find her way. A few people she asked were clearly mystified as to what a person was doing asking the way to such a place, but they didn't question her.

By now she was very hungry, but she had gone without food many times before, thanks to Precious Jade. More troublesome were her aching feet, and, with darkness falling once again, the chill night air. She knew she would soon be too sore and weak to walk much farther.

Then she saw it, shining in the sunset just over some trees. The Palace. The Crystal Palace. With renewed strength she hurried toward the park, pulling the shawl from her head for a moment. Hyde Park. Yes, she could hide there, at least until morning. Perhaps all she needed was rest. She knew now she wasn't so very far from Darcy's house. Tomorrow she could find it, and she would be home.

She waited until a cab passed, and then began to cross the road. All at once the horse neighed loudly and halted, making the cab jerk to a stop.

Blossom gasped with fear, but it wasn't Charles Horton-Smythe who jumped down from the carriage.

It was Darcy!

"Blossom!" he cried, running toward her. In an instant, she was also running. She leapt into his eager embrace.

"Oh, my darling, my darling," he whispered, clutching her to his chest.

"My love!" she answered.

"Are you all right? Where have you been?"

"I am very well, thank you, sir," she said, smiling up into his beaming face.

"Where have you been?"

"Hey, get out of the middle o' the road!" another cab-driver yelled.

Darcy picked Blossom up and deposited her inside the cab. "Did he hurt you?" he asked as he joined her.

"No. Oh, Darcy! I was so frightened, but now I am so happy!"

He kissed her tenderly, taking her hand in his as if he'd never let it go. "We're going home."

As they sat together in the carriage, she told him what had happened and how she had made her way to Hyde Park.

He, in turn, told her about Charles Horton-Smythe, and, with some reluctance, about the fate of Sally. By the time they reached his house, their joy had become quiet, subdued by what had happened and what might have been.

Nevertheless, Blossom felt great happiness as she entered the house with Darcy. He pointed to the drawing room, and she went in. And halted. And stared.

"Grandma Nanna!" she whispered as Mrs. Cooper rose shakily to her feet.

"Oh, my baby! Flora! Flora!" the woman cried.

Blossom ran into the elderly woman's arms and buried her face against her grandmother's shoulder.

Darcy blinked his suspiciously moist eyes and glanced at Sam, who beamed broadly. "Aye, it's her, sir. No doubt of it. We didn't even tell *you* what Flora called Mam, just so we could be certain. Aye, it's her. My own lost niece, come home at last!"

Blossom lifted her face and looked at her grandmother's eyes that she remembered from so long ago.

"I'll leave you alone for a while."

Blossom whirled around. "No!" she cried, making Darcy pause in the doorway. "You think to leave me again? Never, never!" She went to him and pulled him into the room, looking up into his face. "Where you are is my home and there I will stay," she whispered. She turned around. "Grandma Nanna, this is the man I will marry."

"Maybe you'll come back for a visit before the wedding at least," Sam said with a wink.

Darcy tried not to betray his feelings, but he would rather have faced a hurricane in midocean than be without Blossom again.

Blossom shook her head. "I'm sorry, but no. I will not leave Dar-cee again."

"Why don't you all stay here until the ceremony?" Darcy suggested.

"Yes, oh, yes!" Blossom cried happily.

And so it was decided that Blossom's family would remain in London as Darcy's guests until the wedding. Since they could act as chaperons, Blossom, too, could remain in his house until the ceremony, which took place as soon as it could be arranged.

Other guests on that festive occasion presided over by the Reverend Hazelmore included the groom's brother and his future bride, Mrs. MacTavish in a new black silk dress, Lord and Lady Whitmore, Lord Neville Northrup escorting Lady Gloriana Shrewtonbury, Mrs. Dulcibella Ditchett, who claimed she had known this would happen all along, several prominent investors in Fitzroy Shipping, and, nestled together in a pew toward the back of the church, Mr. Percy Powlett and Ah Tup.

That night, alone in their bed, Blossom kissed Darcy gently. "Now I am yours," she said, "according to the customs of your country and you, dear husband, are mine."

"Command me then. I hear and obey," he replied with a smile, running his hands over her smooth skin.

She laughed softly, leaned forward and whispered in his ear.

"Good God! I thought I'd heard of everything!" he exclaimed.

Blossom smiled seductively. "Am I not trained by the most famous concubine in all of Canton?"

Darcy grinned slyly, then to her surprise and delight, he said in Cantonese, "Am I not the most fortunate of men, having such a supreme lady?"

"Dar-cee!" she cried, vastly pleased.

"I got Ah Tup to teach me," he said, chuckling softly.

"I am the most fortunate of *women*. And now—" she kissed him slowly, deeply, leisurely "—and now I will make sure you never wish to leave this bed."

"I think you might succeed, my darling."

* * * * *

HISTORY IN THE MAKING!

Join Harlequin Historicals as we celebrate our 5th anniversary of exciting historical romance stories! Watch for our 5th anniversary promotion in July. And in addition, to mark this special occasion, we have another year full of great reading.

- A 1993 March Madness promotion with titles by promising newcomers Laurel Ames, Mary McBride, Susan Amarillas and Claire Delacroix.

- The July release of UNTAMED!—a Western Historical short story collection by award-winning authors Heather Graham Pozzessere, Joan Johnston and Patricia Potter.

- In-book series by Maura Seger, Julie Tetel, Margaret Moore and Suzanne Barclay.

- And in November, keep an eye out for next year's *Harlequin Historical Christmas Stories* collection, featuring Marianne Willman, Curtiss Ann Matlock and Victoria Pade.

Watch for details on our Anniversary events wherever Harlequin Historicals are sold.

HARLEQUIN HISTORICALS . . .
A touch of magic!

HARLEQUIN®

Temptation

Rebels & Rogues

Jared: He'd had the courage to fight in Vietnam. But did he have the courage to fight for the woman he loved?

THE SOLDIER OF FORTUNE
By Kelly Street
Temptation #421, December

All men are not created equal. Some are rough around the edges. Tough-minded but tenderhearted. Incredibly sexy. The tempting fulfillment of every woman's fantasy.

When it's time to fight for what they believe in, to win that special woman, our Rebels and Rogues are heroes at heart. Twelve Rebels and Rogues, one each month in 1992, only from Harlequin Temptation.

HARLEQUIN®

Temptation

the **Fortune Boys**

A funny, sexy miniseries from bestselling
author Elise Title!

**LOSING THEIR HEARTS MEANT
LOSING THEIR FORTUNES....**

If any of the four Fortune brothers were unfortunate enough to
wed, they'd be permanently divorced from the Fortune
millions—thanks to their father's last will and testament.

BUT CUPID HAD OTHER PLANS!
Meet Adam in #412 **ADAM & EVE** (Sept. 1992)
Meet Peter #416 **FOR THE LOVE OF PETE**
(Oct. 1992)
Meet Truman in #420 **TRUE LOVE** (Nov. 1992)
Meet Taylor in #424 **TAYLOR MADE** (Dec. 1992)

**WATCH THESE FOUR MEN TRY TO WIN
AT LOVE AND NOT FORFEIT $$$**

If you missed #412 *Adam & Eve* or #416 *For the Love of Pete* and would like to order them,
send your name, address, zip or postal code, along with a check or money order for $2.99
for each book ordered (please do not send cash), plus 75¢ postage and handling ($1.00 in
Canada), payable to Harlequin Reader Service, to:

In the U.S.
3010 Walden Avenue
P.O. Box 1325
Buffalo, NY 14269-1325

In Canada
P.O. Box 609
Fort Erie, Ontario
L2A 5X3

Please specify book title(s) with your order.
Canadian residents add applicable federal and provincial taxes.

FBOY2

HE CROSSED TIME FOR HER

Captain Richard Colter rode the high seas, brandished a sword and pillaged treasure ships. A swashbuckling privateer, he was a man with voracious appetites and a lust for living. And in the eighteenth century, any woman swooned at his feet for the favor of his wild passion. History had it that Captain Richard Colter went down with his ship, the *Black Cutter,* in a dazzling sea battle off the Florida coast in 1792.

Then what was he doing washed ashore on a Key West beach in 1992—alive?

MARGARET ST. GEORGE brings you an extraspecial love story this month, about an extraordinary man who would do anything for the woman he loved:

#462 THE PIRATE AND HIS LADY
by Margaret St. George

When love is meant to be, nothing can stand in its way ... not even time.

Don't miss American Romance
#462 THE PIRATE AND HIS LADY.
It's a love story you'll never forget.

PAL-A

HARLEQUIN SUPERROMANCE®

A PLACE IN HER HEART...

Somewhere deep in the heart of every grown woman is the little girl she used to be....

In September, October and November 1992, the world of childhood and the world of love collide in six very special romance titles. Follow these six special heroines as they discover the sometimes heart-wrenching, always heartwarming joy of being a Big Sister.

Written by six of your favorite Superromance authors, these compelling and emotionally satisfying romantic stories will earn a place in your heart!

SEPTEMBER 1992

#514 **NOTHING BUT TROUBLE—Sandra James**
#515 **ONE TO ONE—Marisa Carroll**

OCTOBER 1992

#518 **OUT ON A LIMB—Sally Bradford**
#519 **STAR SONG—Sandra Canfield**

NOVEMBER 1992

#522 **JUST BETWEEN US—Debbi Bedford**
#523 **MAKE-BELIEVE—Emma Merritt**

AVAILABLE WHEREVER
HARLEQUIN SUPERROMANCE
BOOKS ARE SOLD

HARLEQUIN PRESENTS®

A Year Down Under

Beginning in January 1993, some of Harlequin Presents's most exciting authors will join us as we celebrate the land down under by featuring one title per month set in Australia or New Zealand.

Intense, passionate romances, these stories will take you from the heart of the Australian outback to the wilds of New Zealand, from the sprawling cattle and sheep stations to the sophistication of cities like Sydney and Auckland.

Share the adventure—and the romance— of A Year Down Under!

Don't miss our first visit in HEART OF THE OUTBACK by Emma Darcy, Harlequin Presents #1519, available in January wherever Harlequin Books are sold.   YDU-G